OBJECTS OF DESIRE

A RITA MARS THRILLER

VALERIE WEBSTER

Objects of Desire: A Rita Mars Thriller
Valerie Webster

Published 2023 by Valerie Webster
with Ignited Ink Writing, LLC
2076 Skylark Court
Longmont, CO 80503
www.valeriewebster.com

Cover design by Lucy Holtsnider
Editing and Interior Design by Ignited Ink Writing, LLC

Library of Congress Number: 2023916370

ISBN: 978-1-952347-08-5

First print edition published in 2023
Printed in the United States of America

OBJECTS OF DESIRE
A Rita Mars Thriller

By Valerie Webster

Acknowledgements

No, I was not creating my version of Oppenheimer for the last two years. Yes, I did spend a lot of time in the basement. But that's where the writing happens! So, first thanks is to Dotty Friedrick, my partner, who often wondered if I was working or sneaking downstairs to watch *Law and Order* on my PC and consume mass quantities of Oreos.

I am one of the luckiest writers ever as I have such insightful beta readers. I want to especially thank my sister, Sharon Kriegisch, who gave me such terrific feedback. I want to thank Rick Green, whose writing skill, articulation and sense of literate aesthetics I've always admired.

I've also had astute editors on *Objects of Desire*. I want to thank Rae Haller, who troopered through several unplanned hospital stays to help me. And I also want to thank Geoff Lapin, my fave downhome guy and fabulous musician, who happily combed my work for those elusive Oxford commas and fat-fingered misspellings. Most of all I send my deep appreciation to Caitlin

Berve who formally edited and formatted my first book, *Driven*, for publication. She has been the foundation of *Objects* editing as well.

As for cover design, Bill Holtsnider created a "first impression" design that sparked inspiration. Designer Lucy Holtsnider crafted the final design to catch the thriller reader's eye with her mastery of image and color. That cover invites exploration of the book.

I built my character, Patrick Dwyer, based on Ed Chambers. He is not only a gifted photographer, but he has joked me out of slumps, praised me where deserved and been a perpetual fountain of idea and emotion.

Mary Walewski I save for last. She was my anchor when, in a freak accident, I suffered an injury that left me unable to use my right hand. Mary took up the slack, kept my presence on social media and cheered me up and onward. I owe you, Mary.

I feel myself fortunate to have these people in my life and in my work.

Prolog

"I ain't here to clean the house." The person on the porch blocked the usually sunny, open doorway.

"I'm sorry?" The woman inside the house stood waiting for an answer. She was a tiny person, slim, and noticeably agitated by the unexpected break in her routine.

"I brought you something."

"I have a meeting this morning. I'm afraid I have to get ready. Maybe later." The woman inside started to close the door, but a booted foot wedged in the frame to stop its progress.

A broad hand with thick stubby fingers rested against the door. "Just take a minute."

The woman inside hesitated, irritated, undecided.

"Promise. A minute." The boot in the door stayed in place.

"Uh, ok." The woman ran a hand through her hair. "But I really need to finish dressing for my meeting."

"No problem." The beefy palm touched the door but did not push. The woman inside opened her house. The figure stepped in, overshadowing the home owner by almost a foot. "Nice house. I always wondered what it was like in here."

"You have something for me?" asked the woman.

"I do." The visitor took time surveying the foyer and living room as the two stood by the still open door.

"Can we hurry this up? I need to leave." A trickle of sweat beaded at her temple. She glanced toward the kitchen where her cell phone lay on the counter.

"Ok, so let's get you ready to go." The figure snagged the woman's arm and clutched it so that the woman's sleeve crushed with the pressure.

"Hey, let go." The woman pulled against the grip but she was no match. "Stop." She dug her nails into the grasping arm.

"Let's go upstairs." The woman was half-dragged, half-lifted toward her stairwell.

"What is the matter with you? I'm going to call the police." The woman threw all her weight away from her trapped arm trying to loosen it. "Stop," she cried. She began to flail with every ounce of her strength.

The intruder shook her head. "Now you know you don't want to do that. We need to get you packed up and ready."

The woman now grabbed the banister as the intruder strong-armed her up the steps. She could not hold against the brute strength of her attacker who easily drew her upward.

"Gotta suitcase?" The attacker maintained the commanding grip and held fast while going through the woman's chest of drawers, her closet and bathroom, throwing clothes and toiletries into a small roll-aboard that had been in the bedroom closet. All the while, the impinged victim wrestled, clawed and dug her teeth into the arm that tightened around hers.

The woman screamed again, but the free meaty hand covered her mouth. The attacker drew out a roll of duct tape and secured the woman to a vanity chair. She then took a pillow case and made a gag.

"Get you all set up here," said the attacker. "You'll need stuff. Now I know this is a little bit of a surprise for you. But don't worry, I will take care of you."

The woman in the vanity chair bowed her head as tears streamed down her face.

"Ok, so we've got everything, I think." The attacker shut and snapped the suitcase. "I wanna take that pillow case off your mouth but you can't scream. You gonna be good?"

The woman nodded and her intruder unknotted the pillowcase.

"Uh, I think I should leave a note," said the woman.

"I don't think so." The intruder had removed the gag, but made no move to release the woman from the vanity chair.

The woman's eyes roved quickly back and forth as she scoured her brain for an escape plan. "People will wonder where I am and we don't want them to know, do we?"

"That's my girl," said the attacker. "Good idea."

$$\cdot\!\!-\!\!\bullet\!\!\Longleftrightarrow\!\!\bullet\!\!-\!\!\cdot$$

Chapter 1

"You never know when you've had your last chance." Rita ran her thumb over the worn inscription on her father's Vietnam Zippo, scarred, scratched, and savaged by time and war. Her father had told her often that this lighter had ignited flame thrower tanks in "Zippo raids", served as a shaving mirror, and roasted popcorn, and its fluid pinged on leeches to make them drop off.

Robert Lloyd Mars was not about bravado. Before her mind could examine that thought about her father, a man strode into her office. He had on an ancient Joe Banks navy blazer over a white polo and wrinkled grey slacks. It was the high shine duty oxfords that snared Rita's attention. Cop.

Even at a slice below six feet, the man stood almost a foot over the diminutive former investigative reporter. Rita had the body type of a long-distance runner, slight like a whippet. She wore a gold ankh that centered in the V of her unbuttoned Henley and had a face that resisted the wear and tear of long nights in smoky rooms and early mornings coursing miles on running trails.

Rita's assistant, Beverly Hills, was out of the office for a late lunch. Rita stepped from behind her desk and came into the waiting area.

"Can I help you?" she asked.

"Ms. Mars?" the cop said and flashed his shield. "Detective Billy Bolton. Baltimore City Police."

Rita nodded. "Is something wrong, detective?" He strode into her personal space. *He thinks I killed her* popped into Rita's head.

"Ms. Mars, I'd like to talk to you about Diane Winter." Diane was Rita's ex. Rita was betrayed with one casual fling after another, followed by angry words, tears and promises for change from Diane. Still after bitter separation, Rita kept her pain close and alive. She'd thrown off all her armor to trust in the sheer intensity of her feelings. It would take time for a scar to soothe the wound.

"Diane Winter? What's happened?" Rita tensed for a blow.

"That's what we're trying to find out," Bolton said. His long, spidery fingers pulled an electronic tablet out of a black shoulder bag. "Woman named Palomina filed a missing person on her two days ago. Hasn't shown up for work. Packed a bag, though, and left a note to somebody named 'Eddie'. When was the last time you saw her?"

"I haven't seen her since I unexpectedly ran into her around last Christmas at a grocery store." *Eddie? What the hell.*

"Weren't you once partners?" The nickname, "Eddie," was derived from a Martin Short character, Ed Grimley, years ago on *Saturday Night Live*. Diane used to call Rita by that name as a joke. How do you explain that to a cop?

"Partners?" Rita repeated. "Yes, we were. But we haven't been together now for almost two years. Do you happen to have that note with you—or a copy? Might jog my memory."

"Let me see." Bolton poked the screen of his tablet and read. "Eddie. Ha-ha. You win for voting me most likely. Going away for a while. Pay Misty for me. Diane." Bolton looked up. "Any thoughts?"

"Hmm. I'm sorry. I don't think I can help you." Cold—numbing, paralyzing cold—gripped Rita. *Pay Misty for me, for god's sake. Diane, what are you trying to tell me?*

•───❦❧───•

Chapter 2

Rita watched her mother steady herself on her sister's arm as she got out of the car. Like a sparrow in a headwind, she powered herself up the steps to Rita's front door. Sarah Mars, married name Townsend, guided her mother patiently; Sarah epitomized genetic whim with all her father's good looks and none of his dark disposition.

"Yo, Mama," Rita called. "Wuz up?"

"My baby girl." Annie Mars lifted both arms to her older child.

Rita stepped forward into the embrace. *I'm not a baby and I'm not a girl* popped into Rita's head. She stopped long ago giving voice to that futile objection.

"Come on in," Rita said instead. "Got your coffee already made."

Her sister guided their mother to the kitchen table where a plate of Oreos graced center table. Rita scooped up an empty mug and filled it from the coffee maker. She nudged the fridge door and grabbed the Half and Half. Annie was already diving into the cookies as she sat.

"Long ride," Annie said, brushing crumbs with the napkin. "Thank you, honey."

"Yes, it was a long ride." Sarah sat beside her mother and poured the Half and Half until the coffee was a creamy shade of caramel. "But I had lots of help."

"You know I hate those big trucks." Annie shoveled in two heaping spoonsful of sugar. "Scare me to death. I had to say something."

"I have permanent bruises on my arm attesting to that fact," Sarah said.

"You'll live," said Annie.

Rita watched her mother settle into the anticipated buzz of sucrose Nirvana. How did other daughters view their mother? In her head, her mother was Annie and not "Mom". She was not to be obeyed but to be helped, watched over. Certainly there were flares of heated disagreement, but never the kind of full body armor conflict she waged against her father.

"So where are you and Robert going?" Rita asked her sister.

"Outer Banks. I am going to sit in the sun by the water all day and hear nothing but waves and sea gulls." Sarah went over to the coffee pot and helped herself.

"How's she doing?" Rita nodded her head toward her mother as she sat at the table.

"Shockingly good." Involuntarily Sarah glanced at the woman focused on a last bite of Oreo. "I cannot believe her labs are so good. I mean, even with the meds she's taking, her diet of sugar, coffee and cigarettes would've killed a normal person years ago." She shook her head. "She forgets a lot. She'll seem 'with it' and then say something off the wall. She gets confused easily. Keep an eye on her."

"Honey, you know I'm sitting right here." Annie spoke on cue. "And there's not a darned thing wrong with me."

"Mom, you lie," said Rita.

"Do not."

"I recall the 'my blood pressure is fine' report after which we ended up calling 911 for the heart attack. I also remember the last visit we let you see the doctor alone and ..."

"So, honey, where do you want me to smoke here?" Annie picked up her purse and stood.

"Resting my case. Mom, I have a spot on the back porch for you." Rita jumped up to shepherd her mother. "Great view, nice chair—and an ash tray."

With Annie ensconced on the porch, Rita returned to the kitchen table. "I wanted to tell you. The police visited me the other day. Diane Winter has gone missing." Sarah knew her sister and Diane had parted in furious quarrels over Diane's cheating.

"Surely, they don't think it was you?" Sarah frowned.

"I don't think I'm on the suspect list, but they are going to check every possible association." Rita sipped the cold coffee she had left on the table.

"She was a strange woman," Sarah said.

"Damaged." Rita countered.

"Hmm."

"I recognize that 'hmm'. I won't pry."

"Yeah, well." They lapsed into silence. Sarah broke it first. "You're a lot more forgiving than I am."

"Not really. You and Mom would be the first to forgive. With Diane, while I might understand the cause, I sure as hell did not get over the effect. I still have the rage that you and Mom would have been done with." Two years after the breakup, the phantom pain of a severed relationship lingered fresh and as sharp as broken glass.

"Your father's daughter." Sarah said.

"Entirely."

The porch slider rolled back and Annie Mars picked her way cautiously over the threshold. "Gotta find the 'Ladies'."

"Mom, it hasn't moved since you were here a month ago."

Annie opened a door off the kitchen. It was the basement. Sarah and Rita exchanged glances.

"Not down there, is it?" Annie said. "I'm turned around in here."

Rita took her arm and steered her toward the powder room. As she came back to the table, Sarah spoke, "That's what I mean about Mom. One minute here, the next off the map."

"I get it. I'll keep an eye," Rita said as a shadow of worry crossed her face.

"She's failing, Ree."

"I'll be there. I promise," Rita said.

A silence of acknowledgement passed between the sisters.

At last, Sarah spoke, "I'm still surprised that you survived him."

"Dad?"

Sarah nodded. "He was a category 5. Mom and I battened down and waited out the storm. You, you always ran headfirst against the wind."

"Well, never mistake that for bravery. Fear is an amazing driver. I was afraid of being consumed."

"Hey," called a tiny voice from the hallway, "where did you hide the TP?"

"Coming, Mom." Rita called back.

Rita and Sarah spent the next half hour going over doctor appointments, meds and meal plans for Annie. Annie spent that half hour eating cookies, smoking and visiting Rita's powder room now that she had found it.

"Look," Sarah said as she was leaving, "don't lose Mom in the video arcade the way you lost Madison." Madison was her daughter and three at the time.

"I'm sure Mom will not crawl under a pinball machine." Rita sniffed. "And we found Madison."

"Arcade security found Madison." Sarah smiled. "Love you, Ree. Don't change." She slipped her arms around her in a reassuring hug.

"We are gonna have a great time," Annie said as she waved at Sarah's car disappearing down the long, sloping drive.

"Oh, Mom." Rita gave her mother a one arm squeeze. "I know we're going to have a good time."

♏

"Why are you whispering?" asked Captain Mary Margaret Smooth. Mary Margaret was Rita's childhood best bud who was now the head of Baltimore City's Vice Squad. "I cannot make out a word you're saying "

"Sorry," said Rita, tossing a glance over her shoulder to see if her mother might have gotten up from her nap. "I'm afraid my mom might hear me."

"You're mom's there? That is very sweet. We should all go out for dinner. Or I know she still likes to go to church. Want me to take her? You profess to be a heathen and I still like going to mass. We could all go to brunch after. I'm sure Bev would come too."

"Thank you, Mz Social Director. We'll get to that later," Rita hissed. "I need your help."

"I'm not going to like this, right?" Mary Margaret sighed.

"You shouldn't. I had a cop visit yesterday, and he questioned me about Diane's disappearance."

"You a suspect?" Mary Margaret responded.

"Very funny. The detective read me a note Diane left, and I swear, Smooth, that note was meant for me." Rita glanced again over her shoulder. "Can you check what's going on? The cop's name was Billy Bolton. Young guy."

"Charming Billy," Mary Margaret said with a sneer. "That guy is constantly in the cross-hairs of the headhunters in Internal Affairs. When he was a beat cop, he used to hassle the homeless, take their things, dump their booze. He'd roust prostitutes and give them a choice of jail or a blow job. And he was a regular Blue Falcon."

"Don't know that expression," said Rita.

"No matter the situation, Billy will portray himself as the smartest, doing things the way they should be done. He'll throw anybody but his partner under the bus. That's how he got the tag Charming Billy."

"Lovely."

"I am warning you, Rita. This guy is capable of anything," Mary Margaret said.

"Me too," Rita replied.

"I'm not fooling around," Smooth stated with her stern Mother Superior voice. Smooth had been a novitiate but was bounced for her "particular friendships."

"And I promise not to either," Rita reassured her. Rita heard the sound of a toilet flushing. "Gotta go, Smooth. I'll call when I can."

Chapter 3

She was cocooned in a profound silence where all earthly losses are melded into the recognition that we are alone in the universe. A butterfly in amber, forever perfect; forever *isolated*. Rita waved her arms and struggled to cry out against the pressure on her chest. Panic. The headlights of a passing car released her from the no man's land between sleep and waking.

Rita sat up and listened. Had she cried out? Did she wake her mother? Her big rangy tabby, The Great White Hunter, curled on the end of the bed, never raised his head. This was "just the usual" night stuff to him. No, Mom was still asleep; the house was still. There was that lingering drift from a lit unfiltered Camel and her father entered her head. He appeared every time with her sleep terror.

♏

Rita assured her mother that the lurching box of an elevator would carry them both safely to the third floor and Rita's office. While Annie was busy hyperventilating, Rita put an arm around her and guided her into the contraption that was narrow and wooden like a coffin on cables. Her mom was a white-knuckled mess at the landing.

"Mom," Rita said. "I have been up and down in that thing a million times."

"You never know when these things give out." Annie steadied herself as Rita held the door open to her office waiting room.

"MAMA!" A stunning black woman in a perfectly accessorized Blanc Noir work out ensemble shot up from her desk.

"Beverly Jean Hills." Annie threw out welcoming arms. Beverly Hills, nee Charles Tyrell Wheatly, wrapped strong, sculptured arms around the tiny white woman. She scooped her up like a favorite doll.

"I missed you, Mama." The three-tour Afghanistan vet deftly swung the old woman in her arms and gently lowered her to her feet. "And you know my name is not Beverly Jean." Bev laughed.

"No," said Mom.

"Yes, Mama." Bev put her hands on her hips. She glanced at Rita. "Stayin' awhile, are we?"

"Mmm," was all Rita uttered. "Mom, you go on in my office. I'll get you coffee."

"And I got some doughnuts." Bev accented the last syllable. "Fresh from that Krispy Kreme place you love," she called after Annie.

"You shoulda been her child," Rita said as she headed for the coffee.

"I'd have been all right with that. Not sure how your Daddy would have taken it." Bev went back to her desk for the bakery bag already sporting deep greasy spots on the outside.

"Can you watch her for a bit? I have a meeting." asked Rita.

"Of course. More doughnuts for us," said Bev. "Meeting?"

"Wench du jour," Rita replied. "The sweetheart of WJX News."

♏

The WJX TV studios occupied a one-level industrial, nondescript building on Baltimore's TV Hill in the Woodbury section of the city. Two mammoth broadcast masts with cross hatchings of transmission lines scored the skyline. The area assumed the name TV Hill with the residence of four of the city's television stations and two radio stations. The original housing in the area, built for early 19th century textile workers, reflected the blue-color identity of Baltimore City.

Rita shot up the Jones-Falls Expressway from her office. On her way to meet Diane Winter's latest conquest, Laura Palomina, she flipped through her opening gambits. One by one she tried them on, discarding this one as too aggressive, that one as too submissive. She sighed, turned on the radio and hoped for inspiration.

"Hi," Rita said to the receptionist, a substantial black woman with the face of an angel and polished red nails crafted by the devil. "Rita Mars to see Laura Palomina."

"Miz Palomina's in makeup right now."

"She's expecting me. Can you let her know I'm here?" Rita tapped her foot but kept the smooth even face of calm presented to the receptionist.

"Sure thing," said the receptionist as she dialed her phone to whisper something Rita could not hear. "She'll be right out," she said as she replaced the receiver.

Rita stood at the desk. Waited. Waited. Checked her watch after twenty minutes. Damn you, Rita said to herself. Her temp rose and she could feel the flush on her face. Take a deep breath, deep as that well I'd like to throw Palomina into.

A made-up for the morning news blonde stood in the doorway that led to studios, dressing rooms and offices. No TV smile. It was a sharp face, striking, with all the prettiness edged in contempt.

"You'll have to come to the dressing room." Palomina turned on her heel without concerning herself if Rita followed.

Just chill, girl, Rita told herself. I could not breathe if I was wearing that dress, she observed as she followed Palomina's undulating hips down a short corridor.

The dressing room was tiny. Commanding immediate attention was the makeup table and mirror, lights on and set to on-air intensity. Ghosts of anchors past in uniformly sized black frames adorned one wall. There was a dressing screen and a clothes rack with both dresses and suit coats. The room had once been a bright blue on two walls which had now aged to grey. Since there were no windows, it seemed like the one white wall was to simulate light.

"I need a touch-up, so you'll have to make this quick," said Palomina as she closed the door behind her. Rita noticed there was no name on the front of that door—the room was probably shared by several members of the news cast, maybe all.

Palomina whirled dramatically, bracing herself against the makeup table as she faced Rita. "What do you want?

"What do you know about Diane going missing?" Rita asked.

"What do you think I know?" said Palomina.

"If I had an opinion about that, I might not be here."

"Well, I've spoken to the police. I don't know anything. I spoke to her the night before she disappeared and then tried texting and calling most of the next day. That night after work, I went to her house. Nada. I called the police."

"You don't know who she saw or talked to last?"

"No." Palomina crossed her arms.

Liar! Rita said to herself. "Are you two even still together?"

"Think you can weasel your way back? I do know that'll never happen." There was a tap on the dressing room door. "Gimme five," Palomina called out.

Rita ignored the comment. "You know nothing about who she was talking to or people she was working with or anyone she might have been at odds with? Because, from her announcement about leaving, it seemed you were the next big thing in her life."

"I'm the *only* big thing in her life."

"Lucky you. But you either know her who, when and where or you're not really involved. She doesn't work that way."

"You don't know a damned thing about how her life works." Palomina was rattled even if it didn't show in her face or tone of voice.

"Look, I'm not here to argue. I want to try and find her. You seem to be a lot more interested in holding your place than actually finding your partner." Rita watched for the tell.

It was Palomina's right foot, tapping. "The police will find her—and they've got a pretty damned good idea of who to start with."

"Really?" said Rita. "And who is that?"

"You." At that Palomina strode to the door. Palomina and her hips exited.

"We haven't been together for two friggin' years!" Rita called after her.

"Close enough for police work," Palomina called back without turning around.

♏

"Hey, I can't come over tonight," Rita said into her cellphone while sitting in her home office. "With Mom here, I have to stick close."

"No sweat. I think I might offer to help at My Sister's Place then," Smooth said. My Sister's Place was a Catholic Charities domestic violence shelter for women. "I sometimes answer the help line for them."

"I'm sorry," Rita offered.

"It's all good," Smooth responded. "But tell me about that meeting with Laura Palomina."

"She is a piece of work. I stood around waiting for her. She acted like she couldn't be bothered and then accused me of having done something to Diane." There was a pause on Smooth's end of the conversation.

"I have to say that was not my experience with her when she came to do a story on Our Daily Bread at Christmas."

Our Daily Bread was another Catholic Charities program, a soup kitchen located in the city near the ramp onto I-83, the Jones Falls Expressway. Built in the early 80's it housed a soup kitchen, dining room, storage, classrooms, dormitories and a few residential apartments for homeless men. Mary Margaret spent her mornings assisting volunteers serving breakfast to some of the more than 1,000 homeless who came every day. For all her "particular friendships", Mary Margaret never surrendered her fidelity to serving.

"Tell me your experience," Rita said.

"She was doing the usual Christmas story about the needy, but she wasn't perfunctory about what she asked. She talked to the people who came in for food. She was good with them, warm, not condescending. I've seen a lot of Christmases there. Reporters get the assignment done and move out as quick as they can. She volunteered a crew for a non-holiday shift—the hardest times we have getting volunteers—and they showed up. Gotta say, I was impressed."

"A floozy with a heart of gold," Rita said.

"Maybe, but not like I saw it."

"Ok, I got it. Maybe I bumped into her armor." Rita sighed.

"And she into yours," Mary Margaret countered. "You don't have to play badass with me."

"You know me too well," Rita said.

"Indeed, I do, girlie," Smooth agreed. "By the way, have you talked to any people she worked with?"

"I have a list of people I knew when we were together. I intend to talk to them and also find out if there are any new 'friends'."

"Sounds like a plan," said Mary Margaret.

"I hope so," said Rita. "Anything you can tell me about this detective who's stalking me?"

"Some of his cases have been thrown out over questionable searches and inaccurate surveillance reports. He had a suspension about ten years ago for an edited suspect video."

"Lovely," Rita said.

"Be careful. This guy seems never to worry about the illegality of his methods. He's relentless. And I don't know who his rabbi is, who on the force has his back, but they've got to be pretty high up."

"Good to know. I've run into these types before. I'm ready."

Chapter 4

Constructed in 1975, 100 East Pratt Street was home to most of the financial services firms in Baltimore City. It had evolved to a 653,000-square-foot, 10-story office building with a 28-story tower situated on Baltimore's Inner Harbor. The tower was a testament to the tenets of modern architecture with over 110,000 square feet of aluminum, glass and steel. It gleamed in sunlight. By night, the roof's structural steel grillwork, reminiscent of ship's rigging, was a beacon of purple light visible across the entire city.

Rita stopped at the entry to the 100 East Pratt lobby. Two years ago, she had stopped coming to visit Diane, to stop by for lunch, to chat with her co-workers. The awkwardness enveloped her like a too-tight wool sweater. She looked back in hesitation. This was business and she refused to surrender to unease.

On the ninth floor, Rita emerged from the elevator and instinctively marched to the desk of Lakshmi Devi, Diane's admin. Lakshmi's office was beside Diane's, the same glass walls, transparent, bright and open, but smaller than her boss's. Rita focused on Lakshmi. She avoided glancing at Diane's empty office.

Every time Rita visited, she was mesmerized by Lakshmi's face with her smooth dusky skin, high delicate cheekbones and dark liquid eyes. So often in the past, she and Rita and Diane had lunched and laughed together. Rita brushed that memory aside as she approached.

"I am so happy to see you again." Lakshmi jumped from her office chair and hurried to hug Rita.

"And I'm happy to see you." Rita swallowed the lump in her throat and threw her arms around Lakshmi.

"How are you doing, my friend?" Lakshmi stepped back to look into Rita's eyes.

"Still standing," Rita answered without meeting Lakshmi's gaze.

"I was so sorry about the break-up. Please sit." The women took seats, Lakshmi behind her desk and Rita in the visitor chair.

"Tell me how you're doing. How is the new husband?" Rita asked.

"He is a good man. I think my father was happy to hand me over even though he does not accept the idea of *paraya dhan*. I chose my own husband."

"I don't know *paraya dhan*." Rita said.

"The short version is that women are not part of the family but property waiting to be handed over to a rightful owner."

"I had no idea," Rita said. "I'm glad your family doesn't think like that."

"So please tell me how I can help find Diane. This place doesn't work as well when she's not here." Lakshmi gave an involuntary glance toward the office of Diane's second in command. "I'm assuming you are already assisting the police."

"The police unfortunately think I did something to Diane." Rita's brow furrowed into a frown.

"No," said Lakshmi. "How can that be?"

"I suppose they have no other suspects." Rita watched a swirl of pigeons roll and dip across the Inner Harbor skyline. "But I would like to ask for your help, if you feel comfortable with that."

"Anything I can do. I can only tell you, though, what I told that Detective Bolton. I didn't see any suspicious people hanging around her and she never said anything about someone she was having trouble with."

"Any new people she's more friendly with after I departed the scene."

Lakshmi shook her head. "Not to my knowledge." She pursed her lips. "I'm sorry I'm no help."

"Will you take my card? If you think of anyone or anything . . . my cell number is on there. Call me. I don't care what time or what day."

"I promise." Lakshmi paused. "You were so good together. I never expected it to end."

Rita pretended to look out the window again. She stifled the lump in her throat. She couldn't speak for a moment.

Lakshmi opened her arms and the women hugged. "You and Diane seemed so perfect together. This other woman . . ."

Yes, Rita said to herself, this woman and the many before her.

♏

The Sip N Bite was alive with a noon hour feeding frenzy. Hardhats jostled women in heels. Waitresses elbowed through the incoming tide, hot plates and iced sodas secured above the fray. A dizzying aroma of disinfectant and coffee and frying burgers wafted in and around the crowd.

At the back in their usual booth, sat Mary Margaret Smooth. She waited, facing the door, eyes scanning the crowd, always watchful and never availing herself to surprise. Rita waved a hand above the shoulders of a threesome of construction workers.

"Are they giving away free food here today?" Rita plopped down in the worn red banquette opposite Mary Margaret.

"You say that every time you come in here." Mary Margaret took a swig of black coffee. She wore a Class B short-sleeved white shirt, collar starched to complete immobility, and regulation duty black trousers. No tie in the August heat. Twin silver bars pinned to the collar identified her as a captain. Gold wreaths indicated she was a twenty-year vet.

"Hey, I call 'em like I see 'em. You order yet?" Rita pushed the menu aside.

"I knew you'd be late so I ordered for you. Salad, extra feta, extra pita. Coke, no Pepsi."

"Damn, you're good. And you look good. With all that shiny gold and silver, I feel like I should be saluting you."

"Why am I thinking this is not a 'hi, haven't seen you in a while' kinda lunch?" said Mary Margaret.

A harried waitress with a wisp of sweaty hair dangling squarely between her eyes set food before the two women. Rita winked at her. "Thanks, hon." A ripple of acknowledgement crossed the waitress' lips and she was gone.

"Can we eat first? I hate it when you kill my appetite." Margaret picked up a quarter of her turkey club and held it like a talisman while she waited for Rita.

"Sure. No big deal." Rita plunged into her salad. "I told you Diane is missing. Well, I went to see Diane's admin, Lakshmi today and I paid Laura Palomina a visit."

"I asked you nicely," said Mary Margaret as she halted chewing.

Rita took a sip of Coke. "Palomina was her usual arrogant self."

"You should stay away from Palomina." Mary Margaret took a second but timid bite of her sandwich. "What do you need from me?"

"Easy peasy," Rita said. "See what's in Diane's missing person's file."

"I feel nauseous."

"Peek to see if I'm in the mix for person of interest."

"Mother of Pearl!" Mary Margaret put down her chunk of turkey club.

"It is not a thing."

"Right about that. Not 'a' thing. It's 'the' thing." Mary Margaret slurped her coffee. She motioned to their waitress, taking a breather near the cash register.

"Wrap this to go, please," said Mary Margaret when the waitresses arrived tableside. "Now you," she pointed at Rita, "start at the beginning of this fairy tale."

♏

Rita gunned up the driveway to her house. Late, per usual. Her assistant, Beverly Hills, had been with Annie for three hours. She slammed the Jeep door. Bev was going to have a fit.

"Yoo hoo!" Loretta Mondieu from next door waved a hanky from her front yard. Loretta had early Alzheimer's. In front of her house was a large stone goose she had named Scarsdale; Scarsdale had a wardrobe the breadth of which would rival any Kardashian. "My name is Loretta Mondieu. My husband is Vernon—though he's not here right now. And you are?"

"Hi, Loretta. I am happy to meet you, but I gotta get inside. My mom's visiting."

"Well, isn't that lovely, dear. We'll talk later. Give my love to Hodge." Hodge was Loretta's long dead uncle. Loretta's home and Rita's had belonged to Loretta's family farm since the world began in this part of Maryland horse country.

"Sure will. And Scarsdale looks lovely," Rita called. She noticed he was wearing denim overalls and a straw hat today.

"Honey, you're home from the wars." Annie Mars tottering over to Rita and threw her arms around her. "Want some cookies Beverly and I baked?"

"Did you fly to Europe for lunch?" Bev picked up a waiting gym bag. "I am late for my trainer appointment, and he ain't gonna be happy."

"I am so sorry, honey," said Rita putting a hand on Bev's lululemon Define jacket. "Nice." Rita ran her hand down the sleeve.

"Baby, your mama, was fine. I just gotta go." Bev swung the gym bag over her shoulder and headed out the back door.

"Is that cat dead?" Annie asked Rita, "He's not moved for hours."

"That's his schtick, Mom. He's going to want to go outside when the sun goes down and he'll prowl the night."

"Like my daughter." Annie shuffled toward the kitchen table where the cookies were still on cooling racks.

"You aren't gonna eat real food if you eat those."

"I'm eighty-five. Don't care." Annie reached for a cookie. "And what have you been doing all day?"

"Paperwork. Had lunch with Mary Margaret." Rita started the coffee machine.

"You seem troubled, honey. Everything ok?" Annie settled herself into a seat at the table. "And how is Mary Margaret. I often prayed she'd be a good influence on you."

"I'm not troubled." Rita poured coffee into Annie's cup.

"Let me try again. What's the matter?"

"Mom, nothing." Rita turned away.

"It's those deep plowed lines at your brows. That's always how I knew your father was in trouble."

"I'm not him." Rita sat with her own cup of coffee and reached for a cookie.

"Nope, not in the darkest ways," said Annie, "but you are the keeper of his better self."

Rita turned away and sighed. She harbored all his darkness but did her best to keep that side from her mother.

"Guess, we're both going to nutritional hell," Rita said, restoring her composure.

Annie handed Rita another cookie. "Always sit with the sinners, more interesting."

Rita sighed. She didn't want to be in the glare of the Diane case. The cops would be in her way of trying to find her. Damn.

♏

Rita plonked herself in front of her office. Where to start looking for Diane. Rita knew nothing and Diane's latest flame-out was zero help. She had to reach out to people who worked with Diane. She had to start with people who knew them both. In an hour, she had nothing. Some she contacted didn't even know Diane was missing. Days had passed since the cop visit and still no story in the *Baltimore Sun*.

Her cell phone blasted "La Marseillaise." A name popped up that she recognized.

"Hey, Bunny," Rita answered. "Bunny" was Andrea "Bunny" Blyth-Cramer, a friend of Diane and her family. Bunny was from an old Baltimore family whose members regularly graced the social news of every Baltimore-related publication. If there was even a remote chance of a society photo op, Bunny or her relatives were going to be there.

"Rita," said Bunny, "how lovely to speak with you."

Rita doubted that. "How are things?"

"I sent you an invite to the Gala that my boss is sponsoring at the Baltimore Art Museum in two weeks. We so hope you're able to attend this year." Bunny was a personal assistant to Marianne Whitlock, widow of deceased billionaire William Whitlock.

Whitlock was one of the founding members of the private equity Whitlock-Stern Group. Whitlock had ditched his wife of forty-five years and married Marianne who was twenty years his junior. After only two years of happily being hated by his ex and their children, William succumbed to a scuba accident off Puerta Vallarta when he took a stingray barb to the chest while too close for a photo.

"Bunny, you know I'm not good at these things." Rita tried not to sound whiny.

"Now I know that is so not the case. Bring your friend, Mary Margaret. It's going to be just a spectacular affair."

"I'm sure, Bunny."

"Then I'll take that as an RVSP." Bunny gushed. "You will be in such fantastic company."

"Of that I'm sure," said Rita. Damn, why did I agree? I am such a weenie. No, I'll grill people who know Diane. Rita straightened herself in her chair. "So be sure and include Mary Margaret Smooth on the guest list."

"Lovely."

Rita texted Smooth. "Get a dress. We're going to the Gala."

She received back an emoji that looked distinctly like a steaming pile.

Chapter 5

"Where are we?" Diane asked. It had only been hours since she'd been rushing to ready herself for a meeting. She was sweating and lost and scared out of her mind.

"A great place. I picked it 'cause I know how much you like the water." Two massive hands undid the blindfold.

"I can hardly see." Diane blinked into brilliant orange sunlight.

"Your eyes will work in a minute." A log-like arm wrapped around Diane and squeezed her snugly to a stolid body. "It's beautiful here. Like you. I spent a long time thinkin' about where we could go."

Diane breathed in a waft of salt marsh and could hear the cry of geese on the wind. No surf so not the ocean. She surveyed her surroundings. No sight of habitation. It was sunset. The burning sphere of the sun unrolled a golden path across the water toward her. Two barges dotted the fiery demarcation between sky and water. She saw the remnants of an abandoned duck hunting blind off to the north of where she stood.

"I want to go home," Diane said, already missing the bed she'd shared with Palomina the night before.

"We are home," responded her abductor. "Bought this camper just fer you."

Diane started to cry. Under her breath, she whispered, "Rita, come get me."

♏

"You drive like a crazy person!" Annie Mars threw her feet up against the glove box in her daughter's Jeep Wrangler.

"Mom, you're getting footprints on my dash." Rita shot forward into an opening in the torrential traffic on the Jones-Falls Expressway.

Annie clutched her seat belt. "You're gonna have pee stains on this seat if you don't slow down, girl."

"Mom, it's morning rush hour. It's always like this. If I don't keep up with traffic . . ."

"Look out, there's a Queen Victoria!" Annie pointed to the left lane.

"What?"

"A cop."

"Mom, that's a Crown Vic not a Queen." Rita snugged into the exit lane at 60 MPH with only a slice of space between her Jeep and the BMW 500. A woman in a Beemer laid on her horn.

"I may have to go back to the church." Annie squeezed her eyes tight and gripped either side of her seat.

"We're getting off at this exit, so chill, Mom."

Beverly Hills greeted them at the office door. "Good morning, beautiful ladies." Bev wrapped her arms around Annie.

"I thought I was gonna die." Annie leaned back from Bev's embrace. "Have you ridden with her driving?" Annie nodded her head in Rita's direction.

"Not unless it's life and death," Bev said. "Now you just sit right here, honey, and I'll get you some coffee. Got some special treats for breakfast. How you want your coffee, Miss Annie? Still cream and five sugars?"

"Do not put that much sugar in her coffee," Rita said. "Especially since I see you've been to the Otterbein Bakery this morning. Who's on first this morning?"

"Well, Miss TV Palomina called six times before you got here. Started at 5 AM. Probably doin' the 6 AM news by now."

Rita paused, coffee cup at her lips. "Odd. She sure wasn't talking to me when I went to visit."

"I'm sure you wowed her with your charming self." Bev handed Annie her coffee and winked. Annie smiled back in concurrence.

"Yeah, sure of that," said Rita. "Mom, you want to spend a few minutes out here with Bev; I need to make a call and I'll be right back." Rita headed into her office.

"I've heard that one before." Annie went to the coffee service cart and picked up the sugar shaker. "You just take your time, honey."

At her desk, Rita flicked on her computer and punched a number into her cell phone.

"My dear," said a smooth male voice, "I haven't heard from you in quite a while. I am hoping this is not a distress call."

"Patrick," Rita said, "I don't know yet, but I wanted to reach out to you in case the tide turns."

Patrick Dwyer was the last and unreproductive member of an infamous criminal attorney family. For years, the Dwyer family sons had managed to enrage every single community in Baltimore by mining the miniscule fine points of criminal law, blowing open legal loopholes and freeing the worst of the worst embezzlers, burglars and even a few murderers. If you were faced with an open and shut case in the Clarence M. Mitchell, Jr. courthouse, you would sell your soul to have Dwyer in first chair.

"Turning tides can go positive as well as negative. But please continue," said Dwyer.

"Remember my ex, Diane Winter?" Rita asked.

"I do." Dwyer had been married six times but no union had produced an heir. "As well as my first wife. Lovely woman, though her desire for . . . but I digress." Dwyer was said to have an eidetic memory.

"She's disappeared, Patrick. Gone." Rita leaned forward, voice grim, face rigid.

"And as a former partner, the police have gaffed you like a trophy tuna?"

"I don't know just yet. A cop was here at my office, asking questions. I visited Diane's current attraction the other day and she intimated I was the sole suspect. But I don't know that for sure. I asked Mary Margaret to look into it."

"I see, my dear." Dwyer went quiet.

Rita could hear the tapping of a keyboard on the other end of the call. "What do you think?"

"I think I will contact one of my sources. And of course, you'll notify me or my assistant, Rosalina, if Baltimore's finest invite you to Central Booking."

"Not a problem there, Patrick." Rita eased back in her chair and took a breath.

"And now my dear, I'm off to the Blue Moon for their exquisite 'Full Moon' French toast. Au revoir."

There was a sharp rap on Rita's closed door. "Miz Mars. You have a visitor." When Bev used that tone and title, Rita understood it was no joke.

In the middle of the office stood Billy Bolton. Annie had curled up on the waiting room sofa and now eyed the visitor. Bev had gone back behind her desk but, she too, kept wary watch.

"Sorry to bother you so early in the morning," said Bolton, "We'd like you to come downtown to talk about Diane Winter and anything you might know about her disappearance."

"Detective Bolton, I have an office to run here and appointments this morning. I'd like to make an appointment when I'm free."

Bolton did not immediately respond and appeared to be deciding how to handle this situation. He pursed his lips. Indecision. "Uh, two o'clock work?"

"I have an appointment." Rita consulted the calendar on her phone.

"Change it," Bolton said.

"Why can't we do this first thing tomorrow morning—or afternoon? I have all day free tomorrow."

Bolton shook his head.

"Am I under arrest?" Rita asked.

"Depends. This is your chance to clear things up."

Annie jumped in. "She hasn't done anything."

"Who's this?" Bolton nodded his head in Annie's direction.

"My mother," Rita said and added, "Mom, it's ok. I'm going to take care of this."

Bolton stood staring at Rita without speaking. Finally he said, "I'll be back."

"Like the Terminator."

"Don't get smart with me." Bolton's face reddened with anger.

"Wouldn't think of it," Rita said. She and Bolton locked eyes and she wasn't backing down. She'd met these "little" men before and would give him no quarter.

Bolton pivoted and left the office without closing the door.

"Honey, you got one pissed off cop there," Bev said.

"He can get glad or stay mad," Rita said. "Right, Mom?"

"Just like your father. Throwing gasoline on the fire."

♏

The Bishop L. Robinson, Jr. Police Administration Building, named for the City's first African American police commissioner, was a short walk from Rita's office. It was August, steamy in the hazy sunlight filtering down through the canyons of aging brick towers that had once been the domain of city movers and shakers. Now those monoliths were tired, sagging structures whose once crisp red exteriors succumbed to weather and wear. Many stood vacant with commercial availability signs.

The Robinson building, built in the early 90's, was bordered on one side by the Jones Falls Expressway and hemmed by East Fayette and East Baltimore Streets. Across Fayette was the Baltimore War Memorial and beside police headquarters was the District Court House. It dominated the landscape with its grandeur. The structure rose from the pavement like a majestic Rubik's Cube with its tight, towering exterior grid of gold colored glass; this building put its neighbors to shame.

"Damn." Rita yanked a tissue out of her pocket and blotted her forehead and temples. In only a few blocks, the August heat had her sweating like she'd run a mile. Inside HQ's lobby, she stood for a moment waiting for the air conditioning to restore her. She glanced around for Patrick Dwyer.

Through the wall of glass that protected the lobby oasis from the Fayette Street swelter, Rita saw a familiar Moroccan Blue Flying Spur glide to the curb. A six-foot blonde emerged from the driver's seat in the summer chauffer attire of a white polo with black slacks. The blonde opened the passenger back door on the curb side.

Patrick Dwyer emerged. The blonde towered over his 5'10" frame. Dwyer wore a slate grey double-breasted Armani suit with a Hermes mauve tie and matching pocket square. The cut of the suit smoothed Dwyer's bulging paunch. Under his arm was a slim leather folio.

"My dear." Dwyer extended a manicured hand.

"Patrick." Rita envied how soft and perfect those hands were. She was almost embarrassed to share a handshake with her own garden-bruised, do-it-yourself nail care fingers.

"Before we proceed. I need to ask just a few questions. You understand, from our past engagements, I must know the truth and any of the demons that inhabit it." Dwyer's face was going jowly, his lips narrowed, but his eyes were alive and clear and sharp.

"Do you mean, did I make off with Diane Winter? Definitely not. Other than what Detective Billy Bolton told me at the time, I don't even have a timeline of events."

"You're in the dark?"

"Completely." Rita waited for more questions but Dwyer turned toward the reception desk. One of the clerks signed them both in.

"No other questions?" Rita tagged after him as they went through the metal detectors and police exam of Dwyer's leather bag.

"You and I have been on this road before," Dwyer said. "If you say that's all you know, then my experience—and my gut—give you full credence. After you, my dear." Dwyer gestured entry into the elevator bay.

Detective Billy Bolton met Rita and Patrick at the elevator. "Thanks for coming today," he said to Rita as he eyed Dwyer.

Rita did not acknowledge the greeting but turned to introduce her attorney.

"I know Mr. Dwyer by reputation." Bolton hesitated but shook Dwyer's hand. He then led the two through the hive of a huge open room ablaze with daylight and ordered into tight rows of chunky L-shaped desks, each with a monitor and a phone and cluttered with personal effects and papers.

"We'll be in this room," said Bolton when he stopped in front of a door marked "Interview Three."

She and Dwyer stepped inside. Rita glanced at Patrick but he seemed oblivious. She recognized this set up as a custodial "interview" room, not the "soft interview" surroundings used for victims and witnesses. Time to take a deep breath. Rita decided not to comment.

The room was 8x10, no windows with soundproof panel walls, a heavy gypsum board ceiling. Inside was a tiny table with two chairs on either side. Two video recording cameras were mounted roughly at seven feet high in the middle of opposite walls to capture details of the interview participants from multiple angles. Below the recording camera was a pressure zone mic which would filter out extraneous environmental sound for optimum speech clarity. In opposite ceiling corners were two CCTV cameras which allowed protective surveillance outside of the room. The table was bolted to the floor; there was a cuff bar across it to secure unruly interviewees and a panic bar on the wall on the police side of the table.

Rita realized she was holding her breath.

"Did you feel you needed an attorney to be with you today?" Bolton asked.

"Did you feel you needed to speak to me in a custodial interview room?" Rita responded.

"Touché," said Bolton.

"Touché is a competitive expression." said Rita.

"So it is." Bolton's tone did not change. "Let's get started."

Patrick Dwyer did not blink or move during the exchange between his client and the detective.

"Miss Mars, just wanted to say that I have been a fan of the work you've done in investigative reporting. That dirt you dug up on the pedophile priests was one I liked specially," Bolton said.

"Thanks," said Rita. Here we go, she said to herself.

"People who hurt kids are the worst part of my job for sure." Rita nodded.

"Had a case like that about three years back. High school coach. Hated that guy," Bolton said.

"Interesting," said Rita. Wait for it . . .

"So, when was the last time you saw Diane Winter?" Bolton asked.

The slam dance commenced.

♏

"What's your assessment?" Rita asked when she and Patrick Dwyer had exited police headquarters in silence, waiting to be far from any chance of their discussion being overheard.

"You, my dear, are to be commended. Silence and non-elaborative responses are key when the adversary seeks to extract anything that can be twisted to your disadvantage."

"You mean I kept my mouth shut at the right times," said Rita. At that point, Dwyer's Bentley purred to the curb before them.

"'If you know the enemy and know yourself, you need not fear the result of a hundred battles.'" Patrick took Rita's hand and pressed it to his lips. His voice was soft, comforting.

"Sun Tzu, Art of War."

"A philosophy for all times," Patrick called over his shoulder as he walked to his car.

The blonde chauffeur held the passenger side door for Dwyer. Before he slid into the lush leather back seat, in a hard-edged tone, he stated, "Bolton has been investigated by Internal Affairs more than once for manipulating evidence and suspect statements. Be aware. There are no other persons of interest in this case at this moment." With that, Dwyer slid into the back seat.

"Got it." Rita touched the car's window and leaned in. "I'll be in touch."

Dwyer's driver eased into traffic. The swelter of the day returned to Rita's awareness as she watched heat waves ripple on the asphalt.

Time to bring in the cavalry.

Chapter 6

"You look divine," Rita said as Mary Margaret Smooth sidled into the passenger seat of Rita's freshly detailed black Jeep.

"Shut up. Climbing into this car is brutal in this sheath." Smooth slid her hand between herself and the seat's soft leather. "I hope I'm not going to feel like a mummy the whole night."

"It's for a good cause. Quit whinin'." Rita's back tires threw gravel as they took off.

The Baltimore Art Museum was strategically situated in the midst of the intellectuals of the Johns Hopkins Homewood campus, the avant-garde and LGBTQ communities of Charles Village, and the wealthy donors of Roland Park. Tonight a stream of gleaming limos and owner-driven luxury cars snaked around the circular drive. Valets in khaki pants and white polos opened car doors and zoomed away in emptied vehicles to off-site parking. It was a typical Baltimore August and attendees hurried up the marble steps into the air-conditioned haven of the museum.

"Have the invites?" Mary Margaret was starting to squirm.

"In the forty-year-old evening bag Mom lent me for this occasion."

"Ladies." A tall skinny kid approached when Rita opened the driver side door. Rita exchanged her keys for a claim ticket, which she stowed inside her mother's evening bag.

She and Smooth inched along the queue toward the greeters who would verify their invitations. Rita could see that Bunny Blythe-Cramer hovered like a mother hen around the invitation inspectors. In a shimmering blue full-length dress with sky-high heels and a side slit cut way too high for her age, Bunny was in her element. She smiled and waved and blew kisses and hugged and skittered from one arriving couple to the next.

"You love this," Rita said to Bunny as they handed over their vellum cards.

"Oh, ladies, I am so happy to see you." Bunny came from behind the greeter she was supervising. She hugged Rita and then Mary Margaret.

"You say that to all the girls," Smooth said.

"Sorry?" Bunny took Rita's hand and pretended to ignore the comment. She leaned into Rita and whispered into her ear, "I need to talk to you. I don't know if it's tonight, but very soon."

Rita raised her eyebrows. "Something wrong?"

"Well, maybe now is the best time. People are occupied. Bunched around the bar stations." Bunny wiggled her finger to encourage Rita and Mary Margaret to follow.

They stalked after her down a gleaming marble hall. The flow of guests dwindled as they proceeded, the crowd voices growing from a loud buzz and cackle to a dull hum. Bunny scooped a key from her own evening bag and opened an office door. With a quick glance to see if anyone had followed, she led them inside and relocked the door.

"Very cloak and dagger, Bunny," Rita said. "What's going on?"

"First—are you still working your RM Security Services?"

Smooth rolled her eyes and plopped down into a high-back desk chair.

"Yes," Rita said.

"I need you to be discreet. If what I'm asking becomes common knowledge, I'll be out on my ass."

"Gotta say, you have my attention." Rita said. "I will also say that I can sign an NDA if you would like."

"No, I trust you will keep this between us." Bunny sighed. She waved her hand toward a small conference table. Rita sat as Bunny slid into one of the chairs across from her. Smooth leaned toward them from the desk chair but did not move to the table.

"I started working for Marianne as her personal assistant about three years ago," Bunny began. Shortly after her husband's death, Marianne Whitlock created a charitable foundation which she stated would be to "give back" to the community and socially responsible causes.

"Marianne and I spent a lot of time with Guy Preston, the non-profit attorney, and his team, learning what we had to do. I was right there with her as we put together our own team for the board of directors and volunteers who were going to help. We had a great treasurer and were hands on in working out governance and controls."

"I'm sensing a 'something happened' event," Rita interjected.

"For sure." Bunny pursed her lips and shook her head. "Regina Greenlaw, who was the treasurer, got breast cancer and had to quit. Marianne was beside herself. We had lots of possible candidates, but Marianne was very picky and it was taking forever to fill Regina's spot. We attended the Non-Profit Marketing Conference a year and a half ago, where Marianne was quite taken by this woman named Louise Mercilus."

Rita leaned across the table.

"I don't trust her," Bunny blurted.

"And this is because. . . ?" Rita asked.

"Little things. Little things hard to quantify—at least for me," Bunny said.

"Such as . . . ?" Smooth interjected.

"There haven't been any audits since Louise came on board. We used to have them once a year, and our treasurer, Reginia, would likely spring one at a random point during the year. Louise claims she's been on top of things and there's no need to pay top dollar for a specialized non-profit CPA. And while she's overly protective of our books, I've seen at times that there's substantial cash in our accounts. That cash isn't on the income statements or balance sheets."

"You haven't discussed this with Marianne Whitlock?" Smooth asked.

"I've suggested that we hire a professional for a true-up. But Marianne appears to have complete faith in Louise, who is glued to Marianne, assuring her how well things are going. And I think Marianne is probably happy to be free of the drudgery tasks. After Bill died, she was up to her eyes in the transition of all estate concerns to her control and all the work needed to build a new foundation."

"So, she's out of the loop," Rita said as she glanced over at Smooth.

"For the most part, yes. Louise runs everything financial."

"Have any idea how you'd like us to proceed or would you like some suggestions?" Rita asked.

"I definitely need guidance on this," said Bunny. "And we need to keep it quiet. I could be dead wrong and there's absolutely nothing amiss. Public knowledge of a fraud investigation would kill the foundation—and me as Marianne's personal assistant." Bunny sat back in her chair and sighed.

"I get it. Complete discretion. No one should know or suspect, most of all, this Louise woman," said Rita.

Bunny nodded and, in that instant, a knock came on the door. When Bunny opened the door, in walked a substantial older woman in a sparkling, dove-gray, beaded and sequined, knee-length A-line dress. The bodice fitted perfectly over her ample breasts with a sheer yoke and three-quarter sleeves. She walked straight to Rita.

Kate Smith lives popped immediately into Rita's head.

"Louise Mercilus," the woman thrust her hand forward. "I've heard so many things about you."

"And I, you," said Rita.

♏

The Gallery at Harborplace, the 30-story building at Pratt and Calvert streets, included a trendy shopping venue, 265,000 square feet of office space, a 700-hundred room hotel and five-levels of underground parking garage. After years of success, tenants were now advised that absentee ownership intended to close up shop.

The Mall's Harborplace Tower had once been a sought-after business address. Ironic that the Greater Baltimore Committee, the force behind the excitement and promise of a thriving new addition to Baltimore's visionary shopping destination, presided over "now what?" plans from the top floors of a failed revitalization effort that had looked so bright in the '80's.

On the same floor was the office of The Whitlock Charitable Trust, dedicated to national grants and projects for children of underserved communities. Louise Mercilus worked from that office, along with a rotating crew of office temps. Louise advised the trust's benefactor, Marianne Whitlock, that she wanted to keep overhead low and could work with minimal support. This was one of the red flags Bunny Blythe-Cramer pointed out to Rita. The constant turnover of workers offered little opportunity for any one person to grasp the day-to-day operations or provide an overview of what executive direction Mercilus was taking.

Today Rita had chatted Mary Margaret into taking her mother out to lunch with a shopping spree at a more successful mall closer to Rita's house. Rita glanced at her watch; Louise Mercilus emerged exactly at the appointed hour as had been agreed.

Mercilus wore an unadorned light-weight pantsuit, beige with matching flats. Her blouse was a darker beige with a crew neck. The standout feature of the outfit was a gold cross which lay flat just above her breasts. Embedded in the cross was a sizeable diamond which Rita recognized as the real McCoy.

"Thanks for meeting me for lunch." Rita held out her hand. Mercilus draped a limp, damp palm over Rita's.

"I rarely go out for lunch. I pack my own and eat at my desk. Too expensive down here," Mercilus commented.

"My treat," said Rita.

"Oh, no. Marianne and Bunny wanted me to chat with you, get a sense of how we could work together. I need to take you somewhere you will enjoy."

"I'm open to anything so let's pick a spot you'd like." Rita was determined to force Mercilus to show herself.

"Well, I do sometimes pick up Chick-Fil-A," Mercilus offered. "Run by good people. I know it's not fancy."

"Chick-Fil-A it is." Rita joined Mercilus as they made their way along Pratt Street. The traffic was loud and they didn't talk along the way.

After ordering the two women sat at a tiny table to wait for their food. The table was near the back where there was less volume of lunch hour chatter.

"I understand Bunny has suggested to Marianne that you conduct risk assessments of our vendors," Mercilus said.

"Yes, we have contracts with quite a few Baltimore firms and out of state as well. Are you interested in talking to them about our performance?" Rita asked.

Mercilus hesitated as though she had not expected this response. "Oh, no, I'm sure your company does a thorough job. I'm just not seeing a need in our situation."

"Let me say up front this isn't about you not doing your job. I hear only glowing praise of what you've accomplished with getting Marianne's foundation on solid ground."

"I've worked hard on that." Mercilus' eyes locked on Rita.

"I get that," Rita said. "Really. I think the idea was to look at things like a provider's disaster recovery, their vendors, info security. Things like that. More about computer and network technology considerations."

"I see." A flicker of relief crossed Mercilus' face.

A young woman, smiling from ear to ear, approached the table and set down the food. "Have a blessed day," she said.

Rita popped open the container with her chicken nuggets.

Before she could reach for one, Mercilus spoke up. "Will you join me?" She held out both hands. "Let's say our thanks." Mercilus bowed her head. Rita watched with the slightest tip of her own head.

Mercilus' eyes were closed though her lids fluttered momentarily. She held to Rita's fingers with a frail grip. The prayer was softly spoken.

"How did you come to work for Marianne?" Rita stuck a fork in her salad.

"We met at a Christian charity event," Mercilus said.

"What was that like? I understood Marianne to be a practicing Buddhist."

Mercilus never hesitated. "She was attending because the American Christian Foundation provides grants and contributions to all kinds of organizations for youth and inner-city communities. I had the good fortune to be seated next to her at the opening day luncheon."

Rita dunked her chicken into a tiny pool of honey mustard and popped it into her mouth. She made a mental note to have a conversation with the organizers of the event.

"I have to admit I am not a regular churchgoer. How did you get interested and involved?" Rita noticed Mercilus had already consumed half her sandwich.

"I had an unfortunate childhood. I found comfort and acceptance in church and started volunteering, then I had job offers from Christian groups and churches. The rest is pretty straightforward." Mercilus sipped her sweet tea.

So few details, Rita thought to herself.

"And how did you come to be an investigative reporter turned detective?" Mercilus met Rita's eyes but quickly turned her gaze just beyond her.

"My father was a Viet Nam vet. Came home with PTSD and did what a number of guys did, he became a cop. I respected his work for order and justice. I armed myself against his mental illness and acting out." Rita watched for a reaction from Mercilus, hoping for elaboration of her "unfortunate childhood." Mercilus offered no further details.

"I see," she said though she showed no recognition in her facial expression. She was a blank slate.

Rita tried a different tack. "Went to school on my own dime. Worked to get a masters in journalism at American U in DC. Lucked into a job at the *Washington Star*. The rest you probably know."

Mercilus had almost finished her sandwich while Rita was still on the first of her chicken nuggets.

"How about you?" Rita asked.

"I attended a Christian college. I have a B.A. in business."

"Which school?" Rita pressed.

"In Kentucky."

Rita raised her eyebrows in expectation of further details.

Mercilus blinked several times rapidly. "Kentucky Christian."

"I've often wondered how a religious school is different from secular. My buddy, Mary Margaret, has regaled me with stories of growing up in Catholic school. Is it anything like that?"

"I don't know," Mercilus said, "I've always been a part of evangelical life and organizations. Look, I'm sorry to eat and run, but I've got mountains of paperwork that need to get in for grant requests."

"No problem." Rita stood and offered her hand. Once again Mercilus responded with a reluctant and quick touch. "I'm looking forward to working with you."

Mercilus had already begun to walk away. She turned just enough to face Rita. "Thanks. I feel the same." She made her escape into the lunch crowd and Rita watched as she quickly hoofed away outside.

"Hey, I'm calling from your fav place to eat," Rita said into her phone, popping another piece of chicken into her mouth.

"Did you meet with Louise?" Mary Margaret asked.

"I witnessed an eating performance that could rival Joey Chestnut on the Fourth of July."

"What are you talking about?"

"Louise Mercilus scarfed her sandwich like a freed hostage. She was not going to sit still and chat about her past," Rita said.

"I know you asked questions," said Mary Margaret.

"Sure did. That is one tight-lipped woman. She was nervous, didn't want to answer. She was sketchy, sparse on details."

"How so?"

"I don't think she could tell me her college off the top of her head. She seemed nervous about my proposed vendor risk assessments. Something is not right."

"But you have crumbs to follow?"

"Indeed, I do," Rita said. "And I'm gonna."

• ⟡ •

Chapter 7

"Hey, hon, I brought you coffee and some doughnuts." One meaty hand delicately settled a grease-stained bag onto the tiny table set up for eating. The other hand rested the two large coffees beside it.

"What time is it?" Diane still lay on the bedding space created by the pull-down banquette.

"Eight o'clock." The abductor released the lid from one of the coffees. "Come git yer coffee before it gets cold."

"It's too hot to drink coffee. I want to go home." Diane sat up. She was still wearing the shorts and t-shirt she had fallen asleep in. Her eyes were puffy from the heat and humidity.

"Don't you worry. We just have to wait out all the hubbub. Then we can go back and it'll be ok."

Diane studied her captor chewing on a jelly filled doughnut. For a moment, a wave of nausea swept over her. "I want water."

"Comin' right up." The kidnapper immediately was out of the chair headed to the RV's fridge. "Now don't you worry. I'm gonna take care of everything."

It was early, but the August sun already generated a steady, steamy heat. The salt marsh outside carried the scent of mud flats and brackish water with a hint of the devil's own sulfur. Wisps of escaping gases spiraled among the thickets of bulrush and cordgrass. A black duck slapped his wings and rustled skyward. God-forsaken, Diane said to herself.

She grasped the icy water bottle offered and took a swig. She eyed the door and glanced out the small porthole window. The quarters were too confined for a successful escape maneuver. Tears welled in her eyes.

♏

"This is where he lives? Not much room on this trail. Better not be scratchin' up my Escalade." Bev swept an arm toward the thicket of honey locusts with an almost indistinguishable dirt trail, barely wide enough for one car, running up the hill. Nothing but trees loomed beyond the dense wild growth.

"There's wide open farmland behind the house. Roswell is care taking this place for a guy who wanted to start a vineyard," Rita said. "When the vines kept failing, the owner decided to sell. He moved and is paying Roswell to babysit until it's sold."

"Who is this guy?" Annie piped up from the backseat of Bev's Escalade.

"A network guy, Mom." Rita answered.

"He's on TV?"

"No, Mom, computers."

"You sure about using this guy again?" Bev asked.

"Sure as shootin'." Rita responded.

"Yeah, now that's what bothers me." Bev inched slowly along the vehicle tracks worn into the wooded path.

Joseph Bronislaw Malinowski was the youngest of three siblings. His mother, Katrin, was the daughter of a nationally noted Maryland portraitist. She herself was an artist. His father had been a military pilot in the first Gulf wars and now flew for a charter service. It was his father who had nicknamed him "Roswell" as a kid.

The young Malinowski was into sci-fi and rockets and then into computers, building his first custom PC at eleven. At fourteen, Roswell, was in and out of custody after handily changing calculus grades for two friends on the Cristo Rey prep school lacrosse team. The Jesuits were not happy, but his father and Highlandtown's city councilman managed a reprieve. Later he wrote video game cheats for his friends. It was his mother who nourished his intellectual curiosity and steered him slowly to the right side of cyber law.

Rita and Bev walked on either side of Annie as they carefully picked their way forward on the uneven brick path leading to a pickled white painted door. Before they could knock, Roswell swept open the door and welcomed them in.

"Saw you from the cameras." Roswell was a hair taller than Bev with shaggy blond hair and sparkling blue eyes. "Come in. Too hot out there." He had on cargo shorts, a "White Hat Hacker" t-shirt and flip flops. His left arm was a sleeve of tattoos; doves, a spiraling tree of life and even the Little Prince, all suggested the spiritual life. Then there was "The Jester" tattoo, Roswell's e-sport moniker. He was rated number seven in the country for his Fortnight prowess.

Roswell's Jester was not Batman's Joker, whose disturbing appearance confirmed the violent psychosis that was his nature. Roswell's Jester was "The Fool" from card zero of the Tarot's Major Arcana, signifying unlimited potential, adventure and fearlessness.

Bev lagged a minute to scan the small porch and trees along the drive. "Must be gettin' old," she said. "I didn't see the cameras as we drove in."

"I think I did ok at disguising them." Roswell gestured to his tiny living room. "Have a seat. I made some lemonade."

When Roswell had brought out the glasses and an unopened package of cookies and everyone had settled, his demeanor changed. "Tell me how I can help you. Last time was fun!"

Bev rolled her eyes.

Annie spoke up. "This house is lovely, young man." She reached for the cookies first thing. "Can you afford all this?"

"Mom!" Rita turned to Annie.

"It's ok. My mother asks the same questions. I do ok with my security jobs, but I do extra special at gaming."

"You're a gambler?" Annie's eyebrows arched in surprise; her mouth opened ever so slightly.

"No, ma'am, I'm not a gambler." Roswell laughed. "I compete in video game competitions. I'm very, very good at it."

"That's where the trophies come from," Annie stated.

"Yep."

"And the cash," Annie said.

"Yep," Roswell responded.

"The world has changed too fast for me." Annie shook her head. "Is there a place I can go if I need to smoke, young man?"

Roswell pointed upward. "There's a wicker rocker out on the porch just for you—and an ashtray. Whenever you're ready. . ." Annie was already on her way outside.

"I'm being watched by the police." Rita cut in. "They think I had something to do with Diane Winter's disappearance."

"Diane. She's your ex as I recall," Roswell commented. "I read about it. Not surprised that the police haven't found her though. They are slammed with the crime jump we're going through. Missing persons don't always get priority."

"I need you to find the surveillance and neutralize it." Rita leaned toward Roswell. "I can't get into the search for Diane with their watching my every move. For them, it'll just confirm I'm trying to cover my tracks."

"Got it," Roswell said. "Want to come with me?" He motioned to a door designed for the hobbit height of an 1890's man. Roswell stooped and ducked inside. He stayed on the top step to help Rita and Annie, who had come back inside, on the sturdy but narrow and uneven steps.

"Is this a bunker?" Annie took Roswell's hand as she took a tentative step down.

"Uh, I think of it as my workspace."

Bev was the last to enter, taking a glance around inside and through the windows before she ducked and descended the steps into a cavern that had originally been a root cellar. The temperature dropped sharply as the group descended. Though long ago the walls and floors had been cemented, the hint of damp earth remained in the air. The room was bathed in a surreal blue light and cast long, distorted shadows.

"Star Wars!" said Annie.

"And so it is, though I've never gotten this room to warp speed." Roswell laughed.

The group stood in the middle of a dreamlike interior. Mounted at the top of one wall was an array of monitors, displaying a spy's eye view of the grounds around Roswell's temporary home. In the dim otherworldly light, the live video feeds were like a window into an alien landscape.

Roswell let the visitors take in the ultra-clean shining spectacle of his lab. There was a box of labeled mobile smartphones, tablets and motherboards. There were more monitors, eyes dark and unblinking, awaiting their command to spy. The walls were shelved and lined with books, manuals, photos and a host of golden trophies.

Bev walked over to the box of mobile devices. "You save all these?"

"They're for penetration testing. I launch simulated cyberattacks to discover exploitable vulnerabilities in computer systems, networks, websites, applications." Roswell sat in a high-back command seat, cushioned and outfitted with a solid lumbar support. The chair was black leather, supple with multiple jointed, moveable sections to accommodate long hours of focused scrutiny.

"And a fridge," Annie exclaimed.

"I spend a lot of time here." Roswell smiled. The smile morphed quickly into a face of serious determination. "So here I am inside your PC." Bev and Rita stepped closer for a better look.

"That was fast," Rita said.

"I know your ip address," Roswell responded.

"See anything?" Bev asked.

"I see Rita has FinSpy on her machine." Roswell pointed to a jumble of letters and numbers. "It's hard to find and generally obscured by spaghetti code or nonsense instructions. It can capture everything you do on your machine. I'm going to leave it there because otherwise the cops would know we're on to them."

"But how can I work if they're watching all the time?" Rita frowned.

"Well, we're gonna use air gap." Roswell swiveled in his chair to face Rita and Bev.

"Probably need to do the same for Bev's machine as well as yours, Rita."

"What is air gap?"

"Physical isolation from the internet and from any other device on your network. No air card, no connection to any mobile transmission type. Unplugged when not in use. Install USB port blockers and plug unused USB ports. Drives on the air gap machine should be SDD or solid-state drives. Everything encrypted in AES256."

"So how do I communicate with this kind of set-up? I still have to use my email and run my business," Rita asked.

"And what about phones?" Bev added.

"To move data between the outside world and the air-gapped system, you write data to a physical medium such as a thumb drive, and physically move it between computers. You'll have an end-to-end encrypted email system so when you transfer the data from the air gap, you can send sensitive information. Otherwise, if you're buying from Amazon, you use your regular wifi internet-connected machine."

"So, the cops will still see my machine and communications, apps, everything. They just won't see transmissions I want to shield."

"Got it," Roswell turned to Bev. "And I need to inspect your phones. I'm sure they are under surveillance also. I'll download an end-to-end encryption app like Silent or Signal." Roswell turned back to Rita. "And I need to sweep your house and office. Yours too," he said as he glanced toward Bev.

"This is freaky," Bev said.

"I need a smoke," Annie piped in.

"Yeah," said Rita with a frown. "I get that. I need to take all this in."

m

In the office the next day, Rita sat at her desk, eyes squinting with intent at her computer screen. Occasionally she tapped her keyboard to change the scenery. Once in a while she'd shake her head.

"When are we going to lunch?" Annie Mars came in from the reception area where Bev had set up a television for her so Annie had something to do while Rita worked.

Rita turned and stared as if still held in the trance of the cyber space she had exited. "Uh." Rita glanced at her watch which seemed to jolt her back to the moment. "Mom, I'm so sorry."

Rita stood up and motioned to Bev at her desk in the next room. "Bev, the time got away from me. We have to get something to eat."

"You do not take good care of your mama, girl," Bev said as she approached Rita. "Come on, Miss Annie. Ima take you down to Miss Shirley's and we are gonna have us a fine comfort food lunch."

"You're not coming?" Annie asked Rita.

"I have a client coming in thirty minutes. I need to get myself together to let him know where we stand."

"Don't you ever eat, honey?" Annie asked.

"No, she don't," Bev chimed in.

"Beverly Jean Hills!" Rita said with a stifled smile.

"I tell it like it is, baby," said Bev. "Ain't gonna lie to your mama."

"Now, Mom, that place is wonderful." Rita came around her desk and gave her mother a hug. She handed Bev a credit card. "You will love it—best desserts for a million miles."

When Bev and her mother departed, Rita went back to her PC. She clicked the mouse a few times and the screen went dark. Then before she could settle back into her chair, the office door opened.

A woman entered. Her scraggly, graying hair was partially contained by a hair clip. Her face had that ruddy, unvarnished look of a gardener. She wore long pants, once new and bright, now bearing dirt stains at the knees, a Smith College tee, and a pair of ancient Crocs, dusty and gouged in several places. Hard to believe this was the outfit of a stock portfolio and land holdings worth millions.

"Justine, come in," Rita said to Diane's sister. They hugged as if they were avoiding contamination, arms around but bosoms barely meeting and quickly pulling away. Rita had always surmised that Justine was somehow afraid Rita would become interested in her and Justine was out to ensure that would not happen.

"Mom said you stopped by," Justine said.

"She remembered?" Rita asked.

"She was not in good form but she did."

"Any news?" Rita asked.

"None. The police are hopeless about finding my sister."

"That's why I'm in their sights," Rita sighed. "Listen, I have a client coming in any minute. You want to talk, let's make some time." Rita went to her computer and tapped it back to consciousness. She opened her calendar.

"That's ok," Justine said. "I dropped by on impulse. Can you start looking for Diane?"

"I wasn't kidding when I said the cops are trying to pin her disappearance on me."

"You?" Justine's face betrayed her confusion.

"I think their reasoning is that I did something on the basis that if I can't have her no one can."

"For God's sake. That's absurd."

"You know that, Justine. I know that. They have no one else and they're going for the gold here," Rita said.

"How can we change that?" Justine asked.

"For them, a bird in the hand outweighs all else," Rita said.

"Please," said Justine, "please at least change your mind."

Rita was silent.

"Think about it," said Justine.

The outer door opened and a man walked in.

"I'm going," said Justine, "but please think about it. I know you of all people could find her."

"Maybe," Rita said. The last thing she needed was Justine blurting out that Rita was looking for Diane. It would only encourage Billy Bolton to use it for more intrusive surveillance.

"No 'maybe'," Justine said, turned from Rita and left the office.

Rita motioned to her next client, who had been waiting to enter. Damn, in the middle again, she said to herself.

M

That night Rita sat with her mother on her porch in the dark. The house sat on a hill. They could see across the Belfast Valley to car lights on the interstate, I-83. The hum of engines was just loud enough to register. Annie smoked and her cigarette glowed bright with every draw. A fox yipped far behind the house in the woods.

"It's a beautiful night," Annie said.

"Mom, I'm sorry I've had to spend so much time away." Rita looked over at her mother.

"Honey, I'm used to it. You and your father. Seekers. Chasers of the elusive. Always looking for something."

"'Used to it is not what either of us hoped for you."

"Can't be helped, can it?"

"I don't think so. There's always that call. Dad was compelled to answer and I can't break the power of that same compulsion." Rita paused. "I do love you, Mom."

"I know you do. And I love you. Each of us in our way then." Annie stubbed her cigarette out and stood. "Goodnight, my girl. I pray every night you can find some peace."

Rita stood at her bedroom window and watched a star streak across the velvet heavens. She listened to the chorus of crickets and katydids as she breathed in the sweet earthy scent of new-mown grass and dewy gardens. In that moment, her head was quiet and all was right in the world.

Chapter 8

The Milton Inn was a mere seven miles from Rita's house. The 281-year-old fieldstone building nestled on a four-acre property along Baltimore County's York Road. The house was originally a coach stop for Quakers who settled in an area just north of Baltimore City. For over a hundred years, Quakers came to worship at the New Gunpowder Meeting House nearby.

The Milton Inn building was purchased by John Lamb in 1828, who transformed it into a "classic" school for boys. Sons of prominent Marylanders attended Lamb's Milton Academy (named for *Paradise Lost* poet John Milton). The most well-known grad of the Milton school was the assassin, John Wilkes Booth, who supposedly had carved his name in the back wooden steps. The story lived on despite the loss of the carving. The Inn became a restaurant in 1947, flourishing under exceptional chefs since that time.

Rita had never met Bunny's boss, Marianne Whitlock, though she had seen any number of photos of the woman on the society pages of the *Baltimore Sun* and *Baltimore Magazine*. Marianne had been a widow for seven years with no constant suitor or partner that was apparent. She seemed to devote her time to sponsoring fund raising events for her charitable foundation as well as for other causes she deemed worthy.

Rita was eager to meet Marianne and assess if the funny money issues Bunny suspected were the work of Louise Mercilus or a well-played plan to extract Whitlock Foundation monies for an underpublicized short fall in the estate of the late Mr. Whitlock. There were rumors after all.

As Rita walked across the parking lot of the Inn, her phone sounded. "Hey, what's up."

Mary Margaret was on the other end of the line. "Where are you? Hoping you could have lunch today."

"At the Milton Inn. I'm finally meeting the Queen of Baltimore's charity circuit."

"Well, aren't you something. Will you still speak to me after this?"

"Have to think about it." A trickle of sweat escaped from Rita's temple and meandered down her cheek. "And God, I hate these panty hose."

"Panty hose? In this heat? And girl, you're living in the past."

"My mother made me wear a dress and I . . ."

"Are you hearing yourself? 'My mother made me wear a dress'. How old are you? Ten?"

"I hate arguing with her. Besides, I want to look like the other 'ladies who lunch' who are going to be here. I want to size up this Whitlock woman. Had a thought that maybe what Bunny senses is a money grab from Whitlock herself."

"What?"

"There were rumors the old man lost a chunk in crap real estate deals. Maybe what Bunny sees is a way to replenish the Whitlock coffers."

"I don't know. I didn't see it like that but then I didn't know about the rumors."

"I did some digging. And I'm bringing in Roswell to help me find things I'm not able to."

"I'm going to pretend you haven't told me about Roswell. I remember last time. I don't want to go through that again."

"Not to worry." A white Mercedes SUV slid into the parking lot and Rita recognized Bunny as the driver. "Gotta go. They're here."

"Bon Appetit." Mary Margaret's face disappeared from Rita's phone screen. Rita took a tissue from her dress pocket and dabbed her temples.

Inside the cool interior of the Inn, the main dining room was shaded from the brilliant August sunshine. The individual rooms ranged from rustic hunting lodge décor to the open airiness of French country dining. Rita followed Marianne and Bunny into the back area with French doors which opened to a cobbled dining space outside. Though it was open-sided and shaded by a louvered pergola, all the white wooden tables were empty.

When the women had ordered and their drinks sat before them, Bunny opened the conversation. "Rita, I talked so much about the work you've done to support other charitable work that Marianne wanted to meet you."

"Long before we got here, I remember your exceptional reporting. You were so far ahead of the actual investigation into the accounting manipulation of Texas Oil and Gas."

"I was lucky to have encountered the right sources at the right time." Rita reached for her iced tea and proceeded to enhance it with five spoonsful of sugar.

"Not luck, I think," Marianne said with a smile.

"I started speculating about their success after a tip." Rita watched the sugar swirl in her tea glass.

"From?" Marianne asked.

"A critical source." Rita taste-tested her tea. Perfection.

Marianne smiled. "No kiss and tell.".

"Not me." Rita smiled back.

"Actually, that is precisely why I wanted to meet you," Marianne said. "We've seen such an uptick in non-profit fraud that Bunny talked me into having you walk through an unofficial audit. I certainly have no suspicions and Louise Mercilus has been particularly careful with my money and the money raised for my foundation. I have to say, she is a refreshing change from the gentleman who my husband had originally hired when we first established the foundation. Too careless, too much hiring of old school friends who were looking to coast in a cushy, highly visible appointment."

"I have seen that crater or cripple organizations."

"For sure," Bunny said with a sidelong glance at Rita. "As Marianne says, we don't suspect anything, but it can't hurt to know where vulnerabilities exist."

"True," Rita agreed.

"And," Marianne added, "Bunny has been suggesting for a while we can bolster credibility and security if we have a vendor risk assessment process. I can't see us having fraud problems from our providers with Louise on the job."

Bunny froze at that statement. She didn't have a comeback.

Rita didn't miss a beat. "Third party assessment isn't just about fraud. We look at your vendors' information security, litigation against them that could taint your efforts, disaster recovery. Doesn't mean Ms. Mercilus isn't doing her job. Means you keep a watchful eye for unexpected events and conditions that can impact you."

The waiter approached with their food and conversation halted temporarily.

When he was gone, Marianne reached for her salad fork. "I had not considered those things when Bunny and I spoke. What you're saying makes sense to me. I'm new to this foundation work. I'm still learning."

"Talk to some of the non-profits you respect." Rita said. "One of the big issues is third party platforms for donation. What are their security practices? Are scammers posing as a conduit for donation to you, but they're keeping the funds? Let me repeat that I'm not here to challenge Ms. Mercilus work but to help her." Rita shot a look at Bunny who seemed relieved as she dug into her turkey club.

Marianne leaned toward Rita. "I want you to know that I am a woman who believes that status quo is not unchangeable.

My goal is to tinder change via access. That is the bedrock of my efforts. My focus is on making the privileged aware and asking clearly and directly for their help. Most of them, even with all their 'toys', want to feel good about their role in the world. Where we have opposing sides, I would like to find areas on which we can agree. All of this depends on our credibility. We cannot afford to be shaken by the unthinkable of breaches and rumor."

Rita nodded. "Absolutely." She looked into Marianne's eyes and waited for her to make the move.

At last Marianne spoke, "Bunny and I will work with Louise on a list of our vendors with contact info and a brief description of the work they do for us. She can help you set up interviews and run interference. If you get push-back, let me know."

"I will."

"And now, let's put aside the serious and enjoy wonderful food and engaging company." Marianne raised her glass of San Pellegrino to which Bunny and Rita raised their own.

After lunch and Bunny drove off with Marianne Whitlock, Rita sat in her Jeep. Can't stand this, she said to herself. As other diners entered and left, Rita sidled herself toward the dashboard, so that she could reach under her dress and pull the offending panty hose from her body.

Damn, neither Bunny nor Marianne had worn dresses. They had on summer weight linen slacks, breezy tops and sandals without pantyhose. Note to self: never take fashion advice from an octogenarian. When she could take a breath, she phoned Roswell.

"Dude, is it possible to get a view of the Whitlock Foundation money. The whole picture. I'm looking for shell companies in exotic places . . ."

"I know what you're looking for. And doesn't have to be exotic. Think of South Dakota and Wyoming too for tax evasion and laundering. Quite the little havens for stashed dictator and tax evader monies."

"True."

"I'm on it."

Rita called Mary Margaret after.

"How was lunch? Hope you didn't scuff your Mary Janes," said Mary Margaret.

"Nope, but I've ripped off the damned panty hose. "

"What did you think of Miz Whitlock?" asked Mary Margaret.

"She just did not set off my gut alarm. I know cons are good at their game, but for me, I got the impression that Whitlock is the real deal."

"So what direction are you headed now?"

"Smooth, I don't want you in this. I'll need you to bail me out if I get my tail in a wringer."

"Rita."

"Smooth." Rita could picture that worried face with pursed lips on the other end of the conversation. She could not drag Mary Margaret into something with a volatility rating as high as what she had asked of Roswell.

"Be careful," said Mary Margaret.

"Aren't I always?"

There was a heavy sigh from the other end of the conversation.

♏

Early the next morning in Rita's office, the sun blazed behind a smoggy cloud over Baltimore. When Rita and Annie had left Rita's house, the air was clear with the scent of dew on grass and earth. As they trundled down the Jones Falls Expressway, the residual heat from the concrete, gas fumes and density of living spaces held the previous day's stale breath unrelieved by night.

"Mom," said Rita. "I'm making some calls. Can I get you anything before I hop on the phone?"

"Coffee's perfect, honey. And I have my donuts. I love these lemon-filled ones you got me. Don't find them anymore. Takes me back."

"Good," Rita said. "I shouldn't be long."

"You said you had a crossword for me?" Annie asked.

Rita spanked a folded *Baltimore Sun* on the edge of her desk and it popped open. She pulled out the section with the day's crossword and jumble.

"Need a pen," Annie said.

"Got it." Rita handed her one off her desk.

"All set, honey. Thanks." Annie picked up the remote to the TV in Rita's outer office and clicked on the news. She settled into the big, comfy, upholstered chair nearby with her puzzle, coffee and donuts.

Rita went back to her office. She left her door ajar, so that she had line of sight to her mother and sat behind her desk.

"American Christian Foundation. How may I direct your call?" A polished voice answered.

Rita had a name for the director responsible for conference events which she gave.

"Is she expecting your call?"

"She accepted my invitation," Rita said.

"Thank you."

"Good morning, Audra Sanhedrin's office." A cheery female voice answered.

"This is Rita Mars. I had emailed Ms. Sanhedrin about speaking this morning and she agreed."

Silence of the other end briefly.

"Yes, of course. I'll let her know you're on the line."

Rita waited.

"Ms. Sanhedrin, thanks for agreeing to speak with me today," Rita began.

"And I appreciate the credentials you sent beforehand. Now can you review what you're asking about and why?"

Rita gave her a quick brief that indicated that, in her new capacity as risk management consultant, she was going to cover some basic questions about ACF's association with Whitlock Charitable Foundation, about vendors they shared and a few basics about ACF's relationship to Louise Mercilus.

"So, if you don't mind, let's do the easy stuff first," Rita suggested. The casualness and brevity of the Mercilus queries were designed to allow Audra Sanhedrin to give little thought later about the nature of the information Rita was after.

"Louise told me she actually met Marianne at your annual conference," Rita paused.

It was a question, Rita knew, that could seem inappropriate for the risk assessment she had offered up as a reason for her call to Audra Sanhedrin. It was also a test.

Audra could dive right in and start chatting. Audra could also tap the brakes when thrown this oddball personal question. Rita was going to steer her away from Door Number 2.

"Ms. Mars. Is there some other reason you're calling me? I do know you from your newspaper career and recognize you from the driver's license images you sent. Still, I'm . . ."

Rita chuckled. "I'm sorry and please don't misunderstand. I had lunch with Louise just the other day, and she mentioned she had met Marianne Whitlock at your conference in North Carolina a few years back. I like Louise and thought how lucky Marianne was to have met her by chance. Please don't think I'm here to sink Louise, and I certainly couldn't imagine her involved in any unlawful conduct either. I'm sorry if I gave that impression," Rita said.

"This isn't a legal probe?" Audra asked.

"No way." Not yet, Rita said to herself. She took a sip of cold coffee "Just a bit of small talk and curiosity on my part."

"So, Marianne Whitlock is lucky as you say to have met Louise. She's really bright. Gave us some great fundraising ideas. In fact, I thought we were going to hire her, but she told me she thought she would do better in a small organization. She's kind of shy," Audra responded with no reservation in her voice.

"Yes, she is," Rita agreed as she rolled her eyes.

"Anyway, Louise asked a favor that I seat her with Marianne at the conference luncheon. Of course, I did that. I'm pretty sure she used our Major Gifts program to scout a home for herself. Louise had donated so many hours to that program; I thought it only fair to help her find a spot."

"That was so good of you, Audra," Rita said casting for more information.

"It was the right thing to do and our CEO agreed. Louise is such an extraordinary example for others in how she lives a Christian life," Audra said. "I enjoyed working with her."

"She does set a good example," Rita said. "She told me she had a very rough childhood . . ." Rita waited for Audra to elaborate if she knew.

"Orphaned, she told me. Passed from foster home to foster home with some of them very ugly. The kind of places we'd like to eliminate with our work here at ACF."

"Well, I know it will be quite an education working with Louise." Rita sensed Audra was running out of time and desire to talk about a past volunteer. "So, I'm sorry for getting us off my reason for phoning. Let me share some of the risk assessment processes we're working on at Whitlock."

When the conversation was over, Rita phoned Bunny.

"What did you find out?" Bunny asked.

"I think that Christian group Mercilus worked for was her hunting ground and she believed she found a target mark in Marianne Whitlock." Rita shared with Bunny the information that Audra Sanhedrin had given her.

"We got her." Bunny's voice jumped with excitement.

"We have 'jack', Bunny. We need evidence. No judge would issue a warrant based on a request to sit beside someone at lunch."

"Damn." Bunny's voice sank with disappointment. "You're right."

"We have to play the long game," Rita said. "And we're only at bat in the first."

Chapter 9

Far from the heat-sucking swelter of Baltimore City, Rita's house nestled beneath the undulating green canopy of aging maples and one mammoth sycamore. There was a breath of breeze at this height of the day. It was always cooler out here in the northern part of the county where homes were far apart, separated by pastures and stands of locust, poplar and white ash.

"Honey, there's a big ole van coming up your driveway." Annie had just come in from a smoking stint on the porch.

Rita glanced out her back door as a black cargo van, newly washed and sparkling in the noonday sun, crept to the top of the drive, swung around and parked beside Rita's Jeep.

"It's Roswell, Mom. I'll get him settled and fix you some lunch." Roswell tapped on the screen door frame. Rita welcomed him in.

"Damn, it's hot." Roswell carried a full suitcase-sized hard plastic case. He wore his usual cargo shorts and sandals along with an Orioles baseball cap and a T-shirt emblazoned with Captain America. "What do I need to do?" Rita asked.

"If I can just have free access," Roswell answered. "I brought detection gear for eavesdropping and video surveillance. This one gadget is cool. It's a tool with a lens I look through and if there's a camera lens, it lights up as red."

"Well, I do have my outside cameras for security," Rita said.

"I'll check with your locations and make sure there aren't any extras. If it's ok, I'll just go from room to room. Any spots, I need permission?" Roswell asked.

"No, though my attic is going to be hell."

"No worries." Roswell settled his detection kit case gently onto the floor and began to set up his tools. "I don't expect to find cameras."

"And why's that?" Rita asked.

"You're not that high up in the threat chain."

"Ha. I'm crushed."

Annie, who had watched quietly from the corner of the kitchen, motioned to Rita. "I'm going to lie down. I'm tired."

Rita accompanied her to the guest room where a ductless AC unit would keep Annie's sleep safe from the heat. Rita watched her mother slide in under the sheets and throw off the summer-weight linen spread. Rita recognized her mother's sharp decline from the last time they'd spent weeks in the summer together, the slowing of a once vibrant body. Annie, never tall, seemed frailer than Rita had noticed before.

She was moved to walk to her mother's bedside. She smoothed Annie's forehead and touched her snowy hair. "Sleep well."

"Oh, you know me," Annie said. "Easy to fall asleep." She turned on her side.

Rita turned then and was unsurprised by tears that pooled in her eyes. She let them fall as she exited the room. "I do know, Mom. I do know you." Without a sound, Rita closed the bedroom door behind her.

♏

Before there were luxury condos, before the proliferation of shops for six-figure earners and upscale restaurants with endless variations of tempting flavors, Liberty Point was a blue-collar field of labor. This space had once been the Bethlehem Steel Liberty Shipyard.

The sons of immigrants had rolled up their sleeves at the Shipyard and worked around the clock to serve the U.S. war effort. They hammered out America's Liberty Ships which transported supplies and troops. And those immigrants made the money to give their children a life and opportunities they had never enjoyed.

Now, like all things that rise, the Shipyard had aged and outlived its place in time. Liberty Point became its new name and from it rose an opulent high-rise. Advertised as a "boutique" community, developers had repurposed it as a Sotheby's kind of residence. Diane's current interest, Laura Palomina, lived there.

Rita stepped off the elevator on the tenth floor. She tapped on Palomina's door. Nothing. She knocked harder.

"I know you're there. I need to talk to you." Rita listened. She thought she heard shuffling on a carpet.

The door cracked with a chain protecting against entry. "What?" Palomina's tone was sharp.

"I need to talk about finding Diane." Rita mustered control to keep her voice even.

"You killed her, asshole." But Palomina did not close the door.

"I did not, you idiot." Rita shot back. "And you damn well know that."

Palomina hesitated then closed the door to release the chain. She stood, arms folded, with an angry, disapproving expression. "So? What?"

"Look, I'd like your help. The police read me the note Diane left before she disappeared. I think I understand it—and I could use your help if you really want to find her before it might be too late."

Palomina's arms loosened a bit but she did not uncross them. "I'm listening."

"Did the police show you the note?" Rita asked.

"Yes. They asked me if I knew the 'Eddie' the note was addressed to."

"And do you?"

Palomina's voice was low with a tinge of hurt as though she had taken the note as addressed to another Diane suitor. "No."

"I think I do," Rita said.

Palomina said nothing. She waited.

"It's a nickname, my nickname. Diane called me that after a whacky character on *Saturday Night Live*."

Palomina threw up her hands. "Oh, sure. And this was her way of trying to get you back?"

"Stop. Just stop," Rita shook her head. "Can you get out of your own ego? Are you actually interested in finding her—alive, unhurt?"

Palomina seemed to think this over for a minute. She took a deep breath. "Sit down." She pointed to the breakfast bar and two counter stools. "I'm having coffee. You?"

"Sure." Rita sat and glanced around the gleaming kitchen as she waited. "Do you cook in there?"

"Never. Just for looks." Palomina set down a mug in front of Rita. She went back and took an almond milk creamer from the fridge and gestured toward Rita with it, but Rita shook her head. She stayed standing on the other side of the counter.

"Look, what I'm going to say will probably piss you off. Just cut through that and let's get to what we need."

"I'm ready." Palomina dumped creamer into her coffee. "Go," she said.

Rita explained her understanding of the note. She talked about Diane's need to be the constant seductress, how she flirted with people, some of whom she sought out as easy successes. They were shy women for the most part, women with low self-esteem who would be wowed by the attention of a high-visibility, wealthy woman.

"Well, that's not me," Palomina interjected.

"No, you're on the other end of the spectrum. You're one she'd have to work on. You are a trophy."

Palomina paused. Rita considered that Palomina was running that through her head, assessing whether Rita could be right.

"Ok, maybe," Palomina said at last. "What's that got to do with where we are right now?"

"The phrase 'voted most likely' is something I used to say after yet another triangulation of a third party into my relationship with her. The entire phrase is 'I vote you most likely to be killed by someone you've seduced and dumped.'"

Palomina opened her mouth. Stopped. "Go on."

Rita could see in Palomina's eyes that she recognized this behavior. "And 'Pay Misty for me' rang a bell . . ."

"The old Clint Eastwood movie."

"Exactly." Rita nodded.

"So, what do we do next?" Palomina leaned across the counter toward Rita.

"We?" Rita asked.

"Sure. I'm a news person like you were. I have connections. I might know things that I didn't realize could be important."

"If we're going to find Diane alive, this can't be *The Geraldo Rivera Show*."

"I know that," Palomina snapped.

"You have to know it and you have to act it. If stalkers aren't getting reciprocity from their victim or if they think authorities are closing in, they can unravel. They can turn on their victim. We have no idea what happened with Diane, even though we have the note and surmise she was kidnapped. Without a profiler's threat assessment, we are traveling blind—and that can mean mistakes with deadly consequences." Rita watched Palomina's face.

Her journalistic excitement about a news story drained with Rita's blunt assessment of the situation.

"Understood," Palomina said.

Rita shared what little she knew and what information she needed. "What do you think?" she asked when she finished.

"I'm in and I'll keep my own counsel."

They agreed to talk further after Palomina gathered the information Rita had requested. At the door, as Rita was leaving, Palomina touched Rita's arm.

"You know, you were the reporter I wanted to be," she said. "I was thrilled that you lived here. I even met you once. I was a senior in high school. You came for a Career Day presentation."

"That was a lifetime ago," Rita said.

"We're not that far apart in age." Palomina laughed and added, "I don't want us to be enemies."

Rita's body stiffened as Palomina unexpectedly hugged her.

♏

Days of unforgiving heat. Days of sweat and endless sun. Days waiting for the sun to cease in a swampy, low tide stench of brackish mud.

"I want a shower." Diane stood up from the bench seat, which had become her perch since the ordeal began.

No immediate response from her captor. "Been thinkin' about that."

"I want a shower. Now." Diane's voice was raised but shaky. "Not another minute here." She pounded her fist on the tiny counter in the camper. "Get me out of here."

"Ok. Ok." The hulk of Diane's abductor rose out of the lounge chair set up near a ceiling-mounted TV. "Lemme think about where we can go."

"I can't take this heat and this sweat anymore." Diane struck her fist against the wall of the camper. "I have to move. I have to be clean." Diane's head bowed and rested on the wall. Shuddering sobs seized her as she broke down into tears.

"Now, honey, don't you cry. I'm gonna take care of you." A big paw slid around Diane's shoulders and squeezed her into a gruff hug.

"I cannot take this." Diane offered no resistance.

Her abductor turned her around and pulled Diane closer so they were chest to chest. The stalker patted her back. Diane breathed in the strong, sour scent of body odor and mildew.

"I know a place. Been there a few times. Get yer stuff together. And yer sittin' up front with me in the truck." The stalker released Diane.

"Where?" she asked.

"Just up the road. Nice place. Let's git on the road. We'll stop and get us some breakfast. I got money." The stalker smiled at Diane.

Diane, resigned, nodded without a smile.

Inside the truck, the stalker yanked on a dirty white baseball cap and pulled the brim downward as Diane settled into the passenger seat and reached for the seatbelt. "You need anything else? Besides the shower—and breakfast?"

Diane shook her head. "No," she said in a whisper. She leaned her head against the passenger window and closed her eyes.

"I'm takin' care of you. I know this ain't your usual way of doin' things, but I will get you whatever you need." The stalker glanced over, then patted Diane's hand which was resting on her seat.

Diane did not respond.

"I know this ain't the way you thought it would be. I'm sorry we snuck off like we did."

Diane noticed a change of tone in her abductor's voice. Softer. Conciliatory. She sat up straighter. "Have to say I wasn't expecting it."

The truck sped up to pass a mammoth John Deere combine that was lumbering along the lonely narrow road that led from Blackwater Wildlife Refuge to the main north-south drag of Maryland Route 50.

"Course, that was the whole idea. Knew yer friends weren't gonna approve." The driver did not turn to Diane but kept a straight gaze on the road. "I don't talk like they do. I don't make that kinda money."

Diane listened. Were these confessions signals of a change of heart?

"I could see from the first time we met you were interested. I could feel it, you know? And I knew you didn't want to jump right into things. Damn, I couldn't sleep. Didn't have no appetite. And I knew them big shot women friends of yers would be tryin' to break us up. I could see 'em makin' fun of how I dress. I ain't fancy enough. All I could do was think of you, day and night."

Diane's hopes fell. This was not the revelation she was looking for. For a moment, she thought she might burst into tears, but she swallowed her fear. This was not the time to be weak.

A Route 50 sign whooshed by on Diane's side of the road. They were headed toward civilization and a main east-west highway. Traffic increased as they neared their turn-off. She sat up straighter to scout her surroundings. People. People in cars she could signal. People in convenience stores and gas stations she could leave a note for.

"We can go somewhere they don't know us. Start over." The abductor glanced over at Diane. "Been wantin' to tell you that."

Diane scanned the roadside and the vehicles around them. "What's your plan?"

"Mean where we goin'?" The stalker turned slightly but kept eyes on the road. No smile. Dead serious.

"Yes, where are we headed?" Diane asked. A van, loaded with kids and surf rafts strapped on top, cruised in the lane on her side of the truck. A grinning little boy waved at her. His mother barked something back and he faced forward.

"Haven't decided yet. Got some places in mind though." The van full of kids pulled off into a gas station.

"What about my job in Baltimore? I can't just up and leave. I need to turn things over. Find somebody to take my clients." Diane spotted a State of Maryland mowing crew. One man drove a yellow tractor with a long arm side rotor mower. Behind him was a gang of prison trustees wearing safety vests, spearing trash and dislodged clumps of brush with long-armed grappling tools. In their midst was a lone deputy, also wearing a safety vest and keeping a watchful eye on his charges.

"It'll work out. Don't you worry yer head about it." And the driver fell silent.

"Ok to roll down the window?" Diane asked after a while as she noticed the truck was approaching an intersection and almost parallel with the mowers.

"Don't you want the AC on?" Diane's abductor took her foot off the accelerator as they came to a slow rolling stop at the traffic lights.

"I want to smell something other than marsh," Diane said. Her eye was on the deputy and the trustees.

The mower driver had drawn up the cutting attachment which stuck up from the tractor like a mast without a sail; snippets of grass and weeds drifted off the blades to flutter away in the light breeze. The pick-up crew stood waiting for instruction. The deputy had walked to join his workers and stood in the median so close Diane could have almost touched him if she stretched her arm out her open window.

Diane shot a glance at the side mirror but she could not see her abductor from this angle. It was a long traffic light with strings of cars waiting to resume their travel.

Diane frantically beckoned to the deputy, arm dangling from the truck cab out of sight of the driver. A trustee waved. Then a second. One of them whistled. At the whistle, Diane's abductor checked the rearview.

"What's up with those guys?"

Diane paid no attention but continued to gesture a "come here" motion out of sight of her captor. The deputy stared at the intersection and said something unintelligible to his crew.

"Hey, baby, how 'bout a ride?" One of the trustees called. The deputy turned sharply and silently acknowledged Diane's gesture. He cocked his head.

"She wavin' at me! She wavin' at me!" shouted another trustee. With that, the crew started walking toward the truck with Diane and her abductor.

"Hey, get back here," the deputy shouted and started after his charges who were already alongside the truck.

As soon as the road crew drew close, Diane hopped out.

"What the fuck?" growled Diane's abductor.

"Hey, you give us a ride, baby?" The tallest of the road crew flashed an inviting smile. He was a handsome young black man. "Nice long ride?"

Diane's abductor leaped from the truck and charged around the front to face the trustees and the deputy who marched to the tall young man who had stepped within feet of Diane.

The light changed and now traffic sitting obstructed by the empty truck started to honk and shout for the driver to get back in the truck and get out of the way.

"Ma'am," the deputy said to Diane. "These guys aren't gonna get outta their cells again if you do something like this."

"Worth it." The young black man smiled. "Give us some excitement in this lame-ass garbage pickin' work."

"Get back in the truck." Diane's captor hissed in her ear. "Now."

Diane never hesitated. She slid back in. Prison trustees were not going to be able to help. She had no note to pass and who was going to believe an inmate on a work crew that she'd told him she was kidnapped?

"Goddamm, crazy woman." The abductor climbed back in the truck and gunned the engine. "What the hell you think you're doin' with a stunt like that?"

"Just stretching my legs," Diane answered as she glanced in the rearview where the deputy had herded his crew back to their job. She closed her eyes and drew in a long deep breath. She was too hot, too tired, too hopeful she might be recognized.

The light changed and the truck roared away from the intersection, putting increasing distance between them and the deputy who stared after the departing vehicle as he shook his head.

Chapter 10

It had been a drudge of a day. Annie and Rita sat side by side on the sofa. On the coffee table, a wide open, grease-stained cardboard box displayed the remains of a thin crust pizza heaped with extra cheese and pepperoni. Crumpled tomato sauce-streaked napkins mounded in front of each of the diners.

"Mom, Sarah is gonna kill me for feeding you this. It's a home-delivery heart attack!" Rita reached for her third slice, hesitated and drew her hand back.

"Sarah is a good egg, but I'm not planning to spill my entire dietary intake while I'm visiting. And I know durn well you're not gonna tell her either."

Rita shook her head. True that, she said to herself. My sister would read me the riot act. "Want me to get you a refill on that iced tea?"

"Yup, thanks," Annie said. "News is comin' on." She reached into the pizza remnant, picked off a pepperoni and popped it into her mouth. In seconds, she denuded an entire slice. "Hurry up or you'll miss it."

Rita opened the refrigerator door. She heard the WJX news theme followed by Laura Palomina's professionally cheery greeting to open the broadcast.

"You want mint leaves in your tea?" Rita called to Annie.

"Sure, thanks," Annie responded.

"And some excitement this morning as beach goers jammed the highways on their way to Ocean City," Palomina announced.

Rita gently muddled mint leaves with sugar and dropped it into her glass and Annie's. As she grasped the iced teas and looked up, Annie was in front of the television staring.

"Isn't that Diane?" Annie swung around to face Rita.

Rita's head swiveled to where Annie was pointing. Her chin dropped—and the video was gone. Palomina moved to national headlines.

"It was her." Annie still stood beside the tv. "I'd swear it."

Rita froze. For a few fleeting seconds, she stared at the screen, mouth open, saying nothing.

"My god," she said. Her knees jellied. She hesitated in taking a step. "My god," she said again.

"Gimme those," Annie said. "Sit down before you fall down." Annie took the iced tea glasses and rested them on the coasters on the coffee table.

"Diane," Rita said. "Mom, that was her." Simultaneously she wanted to run and sit down. Her hands trembled. "Where was that video taken?"

"Near Cambridge. Maybe Trappe," Annie answered. "Didn't hear a thing after I noticed that woman beside the truck."

"I've got to call Palomina." Rita's hands still shook as she punched the number into her cell phone. She left a message.

"Let's look," Rita said. "I'll bet the station posted the video to their site."

Rita took the steps two at a time up the stairs to her home office. She clicked through the state news section. Nothing.

"Find it?" Annie asked, trying to catch her breath from the stairs.

"No. I'm trying more local sites."

Rita pulled a chair over for Annie as she leaped from site to site. Nothing.

"And now we wait," Rita said. "We wait." She stared at her silent phone willing it to sound.

♏

Annie had been in bed for hours. It was after midnight. Rita paced the kitchen. She kept an eye on her phone screen. She checked to make sure the ringer was enabled. Every so often she went back to her computer to see if the video had been posted. Still nothing.

Rita's head raced. Over and over, she played that lightning strike recognition. Maybe it wasn't Diane at all. No, had to be. Rita was sure—and then she wasn't. Dammit, Palomina, where the hell are you? Why aren't you calling back?

Rita sat at her computer. She got up again. She paced.

The eye of the cell phone lit. Laura Palomina displayed across its face. The Marseilles ringtone blared.

"Damn, where have you been?" Rita tried to command the waver out of her voice.

"And good evening to you too," Laura answered with a certain tone.

"I saw her."

"What are you talking about?" A hint of annoyance was in Palomina's voice.

"That video you showed. The scuffle at the traffic signal on Route 50. It was Diane." Rita paused, waiting.

"No, can't be," Palomina's response was hesitant.

"Let's look at it together. I know it's late but you want to bring it to my place? I have some software to enhance images and video. I can't leave my mother by herself at this hour of the night."

Palomina sighed. "Ok. I'll be there as soon as I can. I'm finishing up prepping for tomorrow's news."

Rita went back to her PC. She knew police would be monitoring her outbound network traffic, but she was going only to the WJX web site. No video though. She had to wait for Palomina. She resumed her pacing.

Headlights swept across the kitchen, their reflection bouncing off windowpanes. An expensive and high-octane motor purred to a halt near Rita's back door. A car door closed quietly. Rita was already at the backdoor, screen held open for Laura Palomina.

"Hey," she said. Palomina stretched her arms to hug Rita then caught herself. "Habit."

"It's ok. Come in. Do you have the video?"

Palomina reached into the pocket of her shorts. She held up a thumb drive which she offered to Rita.

"Let's look. Come upstairs to my office. I have the computer set up and the image software booted." Rita led the way. "My mom's asleep so we need to be quiet."

"Got it," whispered Palomina. "Hey, you know there's some old lady out in front of the house next door with a flashlight."

Rita chuckled. "That's Loretta, my neighbor. She's looking for fairies."

"You're kidding, right?" Palomina asked as she sat in the chair beside the pc.

"She has Alzheimer's. You can't see him, but her husband is out there keeping her from straying too far," Rita said.

The women reached the top and Rita pointed to a room where the unblinking eye of a computer cast an electronic glow. Palomina shook her head as Rita plugged the thumb drive into her machine.

"This is raw feed from I think ten cell phones," Palomina commented.

Rita plopped into the driver's seat and grabbed the computer mouse. The first snippet was a jiggly view taken by a cell phone. Voices were unintelligible. The driver of the truck was already out of the cab standing stiffly in front of the vehicle and too blurred to see clearly. The focus in this clip was the young black man who had approached the woman who had jumped out of the passenger side. He grinned. The deputy approached him. The video snippet went black.

"We paid people for their capture of the event. Not all of them have the focus on the truck passengers," Palomina said.

"Ok, so let's see what the next one shows us," said Rita.

This clip never strayed from the pick-up crew and the response of the deputy. It did catch a glimpse of a woman's arm, but no more.

"Could be anybody." Rita punched in another video file. This clip started with a partial view parallel with the person who had jumped out of the truck to face the trustee detail.

"Yes," Rita said.

Palomina's jaw dropped. "It's her."

The women stared at Diane, who fleetingly appeared as the phone camera panned from the truck to the work crew. Rita rewound to the moment Diane came into view and enlarged the clip.

From this portion of the video and one other phone capture, it was apparent they could identify Diane. They could not identify the truck driver but were able to capture a decent description of the vehicle. No tag number in view.

Rita leaned back in her chair with her index finger to her lips. "We should probably send this to the police," she said.

"You sound unsure," Palomina said.

"I am." Rita stared at the screen.

 barm

Hours after Palomina left, Rita sat at her computer. It was deep into the night, dark and hot. She gulped iced tea as she worked. A ceiling fan turned lazy circles above her, barely stirring the humid night air. A fox yipped far up the hill, and her cat, The Great White Hunter, lifted his head, stood and stretched in a long low reach. He was going out to join the rest of the night stalkers. Rita walked with him to the door from which he sauntered to like a prowling lion.

"Get'em, dude," Rita whispered.

Back at her computer, she stared at the screen. Her eyes were scratchy and watering. She had been at the machine for hours after her mother had gone off to watch TV in her room and fell asleep. Her cell phone sounded.

"Roswell?"

"Yep."

"What are you doing up at this hour?"

"Practicing for my next tournament. I set up a notification to alert me about unusual traffic on your network. Yours has been buzzin'. What's going on?"

Rita told him about the Diane videos. Within half an hour, Rita could hear through her open windows the muffled roar of a motorcycle and the bumps and jingles of a vehicle climbing her driveway. No lights. She tiptoed to her mother's bedroom and peaked in.

The ceiling fan blades circled like a slow-motion merry-go-round. Annie was asleep on her back, a light coverlet over her. She snored like a charging rhino. Rita gently turned her to her side and the noise subsided.

"Hey, come on in," Rita said as she greeted Roswell at the back door. "I'm glad you're here. I want to show you those clips."

Roswell set down an outsized computer case. "Can I stick this in your fridge?" He handed Rita two bottles marked lemon-ginger.

"You drink this?"

"I love it. Kombucha keeps my head clear. Try it." Roswell handed her a chilled thermal tumbler.

Rita sniffed the offering. She touched her lips to the lid and sipped. She made a face. "Fruity beer."

"Yeah, kinda," Roswell laughed.

"I think I'm sticking to Coke," said Rita.

She touched her finger to her lips as she and Roswell started up to her office. She whispered, "Mom." Roswell nodded and together they crept up the old farmhouse steps.

Rowell spoke. "Did you have your wifi on? You know the police would have access to anything you pulled up or plugged in if you were connected to the public network."

"Damn. I think I was too much in shock. I forgot to shut down because I was checking the tv station site online to see the video shown on the news. Then I suddenly remembered what you told me about access." Rita leaned her head back and sighed. "I can't believe I screwed this up. But wifi is definitely off now."

Roswell pulled a sleek, ultra-thin laptop from his computer bag and sat down. "Let me check this out." His fingers skittered over the keys like a hummingbird.

Rita stared at the scroll of numbers, letters and symbols rolling on Roswell's screen and lurked behind him. "How are you getting online?"

He shook his head and continued to tap the keys without looking up.

"What are you doing?" Rita asked.

Roswell, without missing a beat, touched his finger to his lips and continued his keyboard dance.

"Sorry." Rita pulled up a seat to watch.

Roswell went through the same routine Rita and Laura Palomina had performed earlier. Rita had downloaded nothing to her machine from Palomina's thumb drive but had transferred it to her own external drive—as Roswell had instructed her when he found the police remotely monitoring her pc.

In only two clips were passengers from the abductor's truck captured with any sort of clarity. Diane, though grainy, was more visible and recognizable. The driver remained a mystery.

"Wish somebody would have gotten the license plate," Roswell said when he had exited the last clip.

Rita sighed. "Yeah." She shook her head. "As it is, I'm calculating roughly a day's drive on my map." She showed him the interactive map on her machine and the perimeter she'd marked out as roughly possible in one day.

"Lotta geography there." Roswell stared at the screen.

"Too much," Rita said. "But it has been a few days and whoever took Diane decided to stay and hide out here in Maryland."

"What's the plan with the news video?" Roswell asked.

"I need to keep a low profile on this," Rita responded. "I told Palomina to take it to the police."

"Good—and I've retrieved the capture from the far end."

"Meaning?

"Meaning the police will never see what their digital net snagged from your machine."

"They won't have knowledge about those videos until Ms. Palomina hands them the thumb drive?"

"Exactly." Rowell tapped his laptop and the screen went dark. "One crisis averted. Let me fill you in on the other search."

"Mercilus?"

Roswell nodded. "I've searched everything from the resume and background story you gave me about Louise Mercilus. I have drawn a blank. I scoured the Certified Financial Advisor Institute. I called the headquarters. No name on the rolls."

"How about. . . ?" Rita started.

"FINRA? Financial Industry Regulatory Authority had nada. And the state. The State of Maryland requires registration, but Louise Mercilus isn't registered—at least in that name anyway. I can show you." Roswell tagged his laptop to wake it once more. His fingers fluttered like hummingbirds across his keyboard.

"Wait!" Rita touched his arm.

"What? No one will know I'm there."

"I will," Rita said.

"And your point?" Roswell asked. "We've already got our hackles raised that this woman isn't who she says she is and she's hiding something. A big something. And I'm on a server hopping VPN. I'm damned near impossible to track."

Rita pursed her lips and nodded. "Go," she said and fixed her eyes on the glowing screen in front of Roswell.

"I'm in." He began to tap across his keyboard, his hands like hummingbirds, moving with speed and dexterity.

Rita stared at black screens with strings of letters and numbers of sometimes green, sometimes white, always pulsing. Roswell's fingers sped over his keyboard. Screens popped up, disappeared. Rita searched each fleeting scene for something recognizable. Nothing.

"How can you tell where you're going? I can't even tell where you are," said Rita. "Can they catch us here?"

"Usually takes weeks, sometimes months before a breach is recognized." Roswell leaned forward. "Name of that woman again with the spelling. I want to be sure."

Rita's mouth went dry as she spelled out "Mercilus." Her heart pounded as Roswell typed quickly, never a glance at his keyboard. She looked at her watch.

"Almost done," Roswell said.

Rita stared at the screen of constantly rolling code. And suddenly all was dark. Roswell's hands went still.

"Nothing at all under that name in the state registry or FINRA."

"Wonder if she's in there under a married name, an alias." Rita leaned back in her chair.

"You had given me her home and biz address. I searched those too. Nada." Roswell picked up his thermal tumbler and took a long drink. "She's freelancing?"

"Yes. This makes me feel Bunny has it right. And why would a person like Marianne Whitlock hire someone to manage her foundation without a background check?"

"Careless? Not used to managing this kind of financial operation?"

"No," Rita said. "Something more. Something hidden."

Chapter 11

Rita sat at her office desk. The complete lack of information on Louise Mercilus was as suspicious as if they'd found a trail of larceny and grift. No one is invisible on the web, Rita said to herself. She had spent the night in the belly of the digital beast and not a speck, not a crumb or a cookie, no Google mention, no Facebook feed. She glanced out her window where the blue-grey darkness of an impending thunderstorm crept across the city.

She picked up her cell. "Are you guys about done?" Bev had taken Rita's mother to the Lexington Market for a crabcake lunch at Faidley's Seafood and a fresh batch of Berger's decadent fudge and shortbread cookies.

"On our way back," Bev said. "We need to get to the office before the sky opens up."

"I can hear the storm gods clearing their throat," Rita responded.

"Your mom can move pretty quick when she's on the cookie hunt. I gotta keep an eye."

"She's like that," Rita laughed.

"Gotta bounce, girl."

Rita clicked off her phone. She had been on her computer all day in the recirculated chill of her office building's cooling system. She wanted to breathe in the smell of rain, the pungency of ozone from the coming storm and the blended flavors of city life. She threw off her sweater and headed for the street.

Outside, she drew in a deep draught of overheated sidewalk and bus fumes. Glancing skyward, she watched the thunderheads roll in from the Inner Harbor. It was after one o'clock and the streets streamed cars and cabs. Horns honked while buses grunted into motion, belching diesel as they lurched forward on their appointed routes.

Behind her, she heard a man's voice yell, "Hey." Rita wasn't expecting anyone and she did not turn around. "Hey" came toward her, louder but still distant. Then she heard the unmistaken whoop of a police siren.

Before she could react, Billy Bolton was in her face. "What the hell's the matter with you?"

"What?" Rita could barely get the words out. She took a step back.

"I been calling you." Bolton's face was red, his mouth twisted into unconcealed contempt.

"Nobody called me. I heard somebody yelling 'hey' for God's sake." As with every head-on challenge Rita perceived, the flint struck the steel in her chest and she rose to the fight.

"What the fuck. You're supposed to halt when a cop calls you."

"You never addressed me and you sure as hell did not identify yourself." Rita mentally patted herself on the back for not adding "asshole."

"You think you're so God-damned smart, don't you?" Bolton edged closer until he was inches from Rita's nose.

"Apparently smarter than some." Rita stood her ground.

"People like you make me sick," Bolton snarled.

"What's that mean?" Rita's smarter self called a hurried time out. Is he trying to bait me? Is Bolton trying to play me into an arrest?

"You think you're so much smarter than everybody else. Well, we know you tried to block us from investigating you. You got something to hide and I'm gonna prove it."

At that moment, a small happy voice called from behind Bolton. "Hi, honey. We're back." Rita could see her mother walking briskly ahead of Bev. Suddenly Annie Mars stood beside her daughter.

"Whadja do, call your mommy?" Bolton smirked.

"Leave her out of this." Rita stretched her arm out in a protective block in front of her mother.

"Who is this?" Annie asked. By this time, Bev caught up. Wearing periwinkle linen shorts a white racerback tank and a pair of Nikes, Bev stood ready at Rita's left elbow.

"Baltimore's finest, Mom." Rita dropped her arm and gently moved Annie behind her. "Here to protect and serve."

"I'm calling for back-up." Bolton yanked his handheld radio off his belt. Rita heard "10-16" which she knew as the code for backup. Instantly a siren fired from an unseen but nearby patrol car. This was a set-up.

Bev took a step forward. Bolton drew his weapon.

"This cowboy cop is not worth it, Bev." Rita touched her arm. "He's out of control."

"Honey, are we going to jail?" Annie's voice wavered.

"Not you." Rita handed her the keys to the office. "Go to my office, Mom. Call Patrick and tell him what happened. He'll find me."

A patrol car screamed to a halt at the curb.

♏

Separated from Bev at Baltimore's Central Booking, Rita was still handcuffed with her hands behind her back. She walked with a female correction officer who held Rita's elbow with a piercing grip. The officer, short and stocky, looked straight ahead. The handcuffs cut into Rita's wrists, and she tried to keep her hands and arms still to keep from getting gouged.

The correction officer jerked Rita to the right and approached a fortified guard station deeper into the Booking Center. Rita winced with the sudden motion and another steel-toothed bite into her wrists. Her brain flooded with raw fear. She countered the rush with deep breaths, long and slow. They were a minor impediment to her instinct to fight but she held herself together. Though she had been detained as a reporter before, that fear of capture and caging had never been tamed. Her only recourse was discipline.

Arriving at an empty holding cell, the corrections officer, still not having spoken, halted. She turned Rita around and unlocked her handcuffs. Rita started to turn to her but the officer secured her elbow and lightly touched her back with a small push.

"Inside." These were the only words she'd spoken.

When Rita had cleared the cell door, the woman closed it with a definitive clang. The sound and knowledge of no escape sent another volley of distress from her brain. The officer was already far down the narrow hallway. Shouted comments from other inmates, which had evaded perception during the walk to the cell, crept into Rita's consciousness. She shook her head as if to throw them off. She hesitated and tried deep breathing. The air was thick with the fetid mix of vomit and bleach and the stale breath of too many people in a confined space. With brute strength, she wrestled down the panic of someone buried alive.

♏

"That boy be bat-shit." Bev's once pristine outfit had not escaped the handling and the accommodations of the Baltimore City Intake and Booking. Her white tank top was smudged in several places and her shorts had a streak of blood. "And that screw in there put a bruise on this beautiful face." Bev gently touched a swollen dark mark under her left eye.

Patrick Dwyer sprung Rita and Bev. They gathered at Rita's office where her mother waited. The thunderstorm passed during the incarcerations. Brilliant sunlight sliced through the clouds.

"Rita, my dear, this Billy Bolton detective is out for blood," Dwyer said. "Mine is not a casual comment. I've been privy to his personnel file—and his Internal Affairs history."

Annie, who had been standing by her daughter, put an arm around her waist and held tight. Rita reciprocated. Inside, she trembled, but she was not going to reveal her feelings. She needed time to collect herself.

"Got that right," Bev said. She disappeared into the back room and returned with a cold washcloth on her cheek. "I better not be havin' no black eye."

Rita had yet to speak, reluctant to betray a shaky voice and the residuals of her terror at being locked up.

"What can we do?" Annie asked. "Mr. Dwyer?"

"Patrick, please," Dwyer responded. "Keep as low a profile as you can. Let them handle the missing Diane case. Stay away from it and stay away from him."

"Hmm." The gauntlet cast, jitters fled and Rita's fight response fired.

"I know that 'hmm'." Bev rolled her eyes.

"Bev, I think Mom's had enough excitement for the day. And we need to bathe the stink of jail off of ourselves."

"True that." Bev turned her attention to the smudges on her outfit. "Never get the stains outta these clothes." She shook her head. "Damn."

"Are you ok?" Rita touched Bev's arm.

Bev clasped her long manicured fingers over Rita's hand. "I will be. Don't you fret, sister. I been up against it since the day I came out a black boy into this world."

For an instant, Rita thought she saw a tear, but Bev patted her arm and drew away.

♏

Rita swung into her driveway and the Jeep trundled like a tired soul up toward the house. Annie had dozed on the way home but sat up once they made the turn.

"Honey, it's been a day. I must have fallen asleep." Annie yawned.

"Mom, I'm sorry for the horribleness of it all." Rita slid out of the driver's side and went around to help her mother off the Jeep's side steps.

"Married to your father, following your reporter job, I am not always surprised, but I'm always prepared."

"I'm sorry." Rita wrapped her arms around Annie. Tears, fiercely dammed through the day, rushed down her cheeks.

"You just let it come," Annie said. "I used to tell your father, 'Every day is not the crusades and you're not St. George.'"

Rita buried her head in her mother's neck and held her tight.

♏

In a few hours, Pratt and Lombard streets would fill with baseball's Baltimore Oriole fans. They would swarm the sidewalks and stream through alleys and side streets from off-site parking. Some would stop and buy pennants and peanuts for their kids. Some would clutch their pre-event beers. Kids would chatter and run ahead in excitement. Moms would caution and dads would keep an eye.

In this early hour though, it was a different Baltimore. This was a city waking and going to work. Shopkeepers swept the leavings of the night: the discarded drink cups, beer cans, food wrappers, vodka shorties, sometimes a needle and newspapers. Bikers on their way to desk jobs weaved through light traffic. Far out in the harbor, a clean-up scow herded harbor trash for disposal.

Rita walked the five-minute route from her office on Gay Street toward Gallery Place and the administrative offices of the Whitlock Charitable Foundation. She was meeting with Louise Mercilus this morning. Bunny would be there. Just the three of them. Today Rita would begin her duties—real and surreptitious.

"Morning," Rita said as she entered the reception area. The door that opened into Mercilus' office gave Rita a clear view of her target, who, upon Rita's entry, appeared to quickly close work on her computer.

Immediately the outsized gold cross around Mercilus's neck captured Rita's eye. The cross was plain but conspicuous. It was a badge of sorts, a symbol of association. It transmitted recognition of the like-purposed in the same manner as a Mason's ring or gang colors.

"Good morning," Mercilus said. "I've set up the projector in our little conference room. Thought it might give us room to work without being crowded." She stood and started out of the office.

Something she doesn't want me to see in here? Rita asked herself. "Looks like you've got a great view from here. Mind if I take a peek?"

Rita kept her eye on Mercilus who stiffened briefly in response to the request. "Of course not," Mercilus said. "Come in." She stationed herself between the windows and her desk. Rita walked to the windows.

Gallery Place Tower stood perfectly positioned as a prestige address for both business and residential tenants. The panorama of the Patapsco harbor sprawled center view on the south side of the building—where the Whitlock Foundation was housed. To the west was Camden Yards, home to the Baltimore Orioles and the NFL Ravens. Toward the east, one could see the Pier 6 concert pavilion with its 6-mast tensile roof a la Sydney Opera House. The Tower had been a dream location until the owners defaulted and ceased upkeep. Now there was talk of shutting the entire building down, apartments, offices, shopping.

"Great view," Rita said. At that moment, Bunny Blythe-Cramer walked into reception.

"I don't spend much time on scenery," Mercilus said. "Let's get started now that Bunny's here."

The three women sat at a long boardroom table. On the screen at the far end of the room projected the home page of the program Whitlock Foundation used to manage its operations. Mercilus sat at the controls on her laptop while Rita and Bunny sat next to each other, one chair between them and Louise. Bunny turned an anxious face to Rita who purposefully ignored acknowledgement.

"Where do you want to start?" Mercilus asked.

"Just walk us through each section to get familiarity," Rita responded. "I need to get an overview of how things work."

"Fine," Mercilus said though the tone did not sound as if that were true. She clicked the remote and the screen slid to the home screen of the Foundation's vendor management system.

"How long have you used this system?" Rita asked.

Mercilus did not look at Rita but answered, "I upgraded when I got here."

Bunny poked Rita under the table and out of sight of Mercilus.

"I see. What was the problem with the other system?" Rita asked.

"Old, out of date. I wanted Marianne to have the most current and best software." Mercilus still refused to directly address Rita. Her eyes were on the screen.

"Let's take a look at the performance section," Rita suggested. "Like to get a snapshot of the current status of your vendors."

Mercilus clicked through to that part of the database. She offered no explanations.

Rita asked to see several vendors so she could drill down into details. From there she asked for the section on agreements. She wanted to see current and past contracts for service.

"Who are the admins for this software?" Rita asked.

"I am." Mercilus said.

"No one backs you up?"

At this point, Mercilus turned to Rita. The gaze was steady and hard; her nostrils flared. Her tone was imperative. Rita returned that withering expression and held it until Mercilus looked away and back to the screen at the far end of the room.

In that moment, Rita's memory plucked an image from her past. Fourth grade, Mrs. Steadman, with that similar matronly body type, not shapely but substantial. The bulk conveyed a sense of unwavering adherence to a set of rules and woe be unto anyone who behaved carelessly and colored outside her lines.

"Are we finished?" Mercilus asked.

"Just a couple more sections," Rita said. "Let's take a look at Receipts and Invoicing and then Master Planning."

Mercilus hesitated, started to speak, but instead clicked on that menu item. Her lips tightened and she squeezed the remote to the first requested section. Rita made no comment.

"Who has access to this system?" she asked.

"I'm the admin and there are other, lesser permissions for certain people."

"You are the only person with full control and access?" Rita continued.

"I'm the one who has the big picture and the software knowledge. Too many people making changes can create unforced errors. I keep the data up to date," Mercilus said.

"Louise, thanks for your time this morning. I know you have a lot going on. Please give me admin permission so I can work on the vendor risk assessments." Rita waited for a response.

"Not sure you need full admin." Mercilus clicked off the projection. "I'll set you up with the highest role-based level."

Rita was going to settle this here and now. "I am going to need full admin access."

"I'll have to talk to Marianne." Mercilus sniffed.

"Uh, hate to butt in here," Bunny said in an apologetic tone. "Marianne suggested you share that authority for now." She stopped and then added, "Just til the vendor assessment is over anyway."

"I'm still going to speak with Marianne," Mercilus replied. "I spent a lot of time fixing errors when I got here. I don't want it screwed up."

"I make the commitment that I will not change anything without your knowledge. I'm not a newcomer to info security."

"Fine," Mercilus said. "I've got to get back to work. You can show yourselves out." She stalked out of the room.

"She doesn't sound happy," Bunny said as she and Rita stood to leave.

"She's not supposed to be happy. Just compliant," Rita said. "It's hammer time."

•———◦৩৲৹◦———•

Chapter 12

It was one of those August afternoons. After blistering weeks of sticky haze, the rain gods decided to make a statement with a skirmish at the end of each day. They assumed control of the sky and marshalled towering thunderheads to lead the charge. The sharp metallic scent of ozone mixed with the sweet smell of water. A rumble now and then signaled the approaching storm. While the heat had subsided, the air was still heavy, hard to breathe and cloud-to-ground lightning rippled on the far southern horizon.

"Storm's comin'." Annie stood at Rita's open front door and looked out across the valley.

Rita had come down from her home office. "I shut the upstairs windows."

"I used to love storms when I was a girl," Annie said. "Excitement. Thunder. Lightening. Like the cavalry coming to beat back the heat."

"It is like that. Didn't know you were a poet, Mom." Rita glanced at her watch. "Bunny Blythe-Cramer, the lady I'm working with right now, is stopping by after work tonight. You know, on the Whitlock Trust thing?"

"I remember." Annie turned away from watching the distant flashes of light. "I'll hang out in the living room and watch tv while you talk."

Bunny arrived in a waxed and gleaming SUV that dwarfed her frame. Rita shook her head as she watched the woman gingerly step on the vehicle's running board. Rain was still far off, but the wind had picked up.

Rita held the door as Bunny entered, umbrella in one hand, briefcase in the other. "I feel like a spy," she said as she rested the umbrella against the door frame.

"We are spies." Rita closed the door and pointed to the high-backed stools along the breakfast counter. "Can I get you anything? We have chocolate cake, ice cream, Bev made homemade cookies and I have a fresh pot of coffee."

"How come you don't weight 200 pounds?" Bunny stepped on the rung of one of breakfast bar stools and swung herself up into the seat.

"Cuz, I don't keep this stuff in the house when my mother isn't here. How about coffee? Or I have Coke and iced tea."

"Coffee's good. Can't believe it was desert hot out there just a few hours ago. Now it's turning chilly."

When coffee was in front of Rita and Bunny, it was Bunny who started the conversation. "Where are we right now with anything you've found? Louise has been bending Marianne Whitlock's ear since our little review of our system."

"We set up the Trojan Horse. Marianne has allowed us to force Louise to roll it into her gates. Now I have to find if there's a real steal or if this woman is simply mismanaging her responsibilities."

Bunny sighed and took a sip of her coffee. "Marianne has so much faith in Louise. I'm in a tight spot. The more Louise harangues Marianne about being watched, not trusted; the more I'm concerned that she's going to win the war of words and we're going to be stonewalled by the very person we're trying to protect."

"I have to produce some evidence pretty quickly," Rita said. "There are a couple of areas that I'm particularly interested in. According to the latest fraud studies, financial crimes of asset misappropriation and bribery or corruption are the top two." Rita sipped her coffee.

"Say that in ways I understand. What does that mean?" Bunny leaned toward Rita and stared.

"Let me give you examples," Rita said. "Skimming falls under the asset misappropriation category. So, tell me how you take in funds. Just cash donations or do you ever accept real estate or cars for resale? And have you ever checked that the cash donations fully match monies pledged?" Rita stood and walked to the doorway into the living room.

Annie had fallen asleep on the sofa as Joe Namath exhorted viewers to "get all they deserve" from Medicare. Rita went back to the breakfast bar.

"Well, no, I've never personally checked those things. I'm not savvy enough to understand all the ways we turn real assets into Trust money. We do accept real estate though." Bunny frowned. "I know it's a mixed bag of how we get in possession of real estate."

"Tell me," Rita said.

"People turn over buildings directly. Usually they need a tax break and that's one way to get it and the donors don't have to pay capital gains. Sometimes we get property through trusts. That's complicated. The donor sells to us. Proceeds go into a trust and over a set period, the donor gets distributions from profits the real estate generates. When the designated period is over, the property becomes part of the charity, in this case Whitlock's, portfolio."

Rita nodded. "Louise manages all this by herself?" She got up and retrieved a plate of cookies from the kitchen.

Bunny nodded. "There are three people involved in these kinds of donations: Marianne, Louise and a financial planner that Louise hired about six months ago."

"Definitely something for me to dig into." Rita picked up her coffee mug and stuck it into the microwave to warm it. "How about Whitlock's vendors? Are you involved in any vendor selections or vendor performance reviews?"

"Not really. I mean I know some of the local companies, but I don't know every single one." Bunny squirmed in her seat. "You are scaring me."

Rita rejoined Bunny. "Warm up?" she offered, but Bunny shook her head even though her coffee had cooled and the milk had filmed over its surface.

"I'm guessing Louise handles all the vendor relations as well?" Rita said.

Bunny nodded.

"I'm not here to scare you as much as educate you. What I've covered tonight are areas I'm going to spend time on in your system. Is everyone legit? Do the numbers match between donation and reporting?"

"If there's fraud, Marianne will be devasted. The Foundation will collapse. No one will ever trust us going forward." Bunny chewed her lip and lowered her head.

"Let's prevent that from happening," Rita said.

"What about the horrible PR, the fallout from finding fraud?" Bunny asked.

"We haven't found it—yet. Let's look. I have to tell you that I might not find anything."

"Do you think that is a good possibility?" Bunny asked.

"No," Rita responded, "I don't."

"Didn't think so," Bunny sighed.

"I need you involved, Bunny." Rita reached for a homemade chocolate chip.

"I have to be honest. I don't know how to navigate the non-profit management program. I handle all the event planning, Marianne's personal and organization schedules. I am rarely involved in financial meetings or decision making."

"Not a problem. I want you to keep an eye on Louise. Keep tabs on who visits, where she goes and who she meets with." The room was darkening now. The storm's front running cloud cover cast a deep shadow between the earth and the sun. Warning rumbles grew louder. The wind stiffened.

"What if I mess up, miss something?" Bunny rubbed her hands together.

Rita reached over and placed a reassuring hand on Bunny's worried gesture. "You don't have to find everything or know everything. Keep an eye out. Ask about people you don't know. We'll talk every week unless something really out of the ordinary happens—then you contact me. Remember, you're not in this by yourself."

"I know," Bunny replied, "though I keep thinking I should not have poked this hornet's nest." A fat rain droplet and then another splatted on the nearest kitchen window."

"You need to get out of here before you have to swim to your car," Rita said. It was only six o'clock in the evening but the sun was gone, obscured by advancing thunderheads.

"I gotta go," Bunny slid off her stool and grabbed her umbrella by the door.

"Be careful out there," Rita called after her. As she heard the thunk of Bunny's car door, a resounding crack heralded the storm's arrival. Her 100-year-old farm kitchen lit up in a blaze of light and dimmed as rapidly. A fat droplet splatted on the windowpane over her sink.

In seconds, Rita could see nothing but crushing sheets of rain cascading across the parking area. She watched Bunny's car lights go on as the SUV inched toward the drive and downhill to the main road.

"Across the Rubicon," she murmured to herself.

♏

The storm washed the sky to a brilliant blue. Pillowy snow-colored clouds, absent in Rita's early morning hours, now lazed on the horizon. The choking heat had lifted and across the surrounding pastures, water droplets glistened.

Where Bunny had sat the night before, Annie assumed possession. "As long as the earth endures, seedtime and harvest, cold and heat, summer and winter, day and night will never cease."

"Mom, that sounds very poetic." Rita poured Annie's coffee and asked, "How about scrambled eggs this morning. Bev bought me some buckboard bacon I can put in the oven for you. And I got some sourdough for toast. I'm gonna throw the bacon in now." She went to the fridge.

"What the heck is 'buckboard' bacon? And it's Genesis." Annie sloshed cream into her coffee until it was a rich caramel color. She dug into the sugar bowl next.

Rita watched as Annie transported spoon after spoon into her cup. "Jesus, Mom. Stop. "

"Tastes good," Annie responded. "Perfect," she declared after five heaping sugar servings were dumped and stirred.

"Genesis," Rita asked, "like the Bible Genesis?"

"Yep. Not like Phil Collins, for heaven's sake." Annie rested her coffee cup on the counter.

"Well, excuse me." Rita turned so that her mother would not see the smile.

"I'm old, girlie. Not dumb." Annie sniffed.

"I see that," Rita said. "Mom, I have to interview people today about the Whitlock Foundation situation. I'll take you with me into work and you can spend time with Bev. Can we do that? I'll come back to the office as quickly as I can."

℠

Rita picked up her phone and reviewed the lists of vendors she'd created. Today she was interviewing those vendors Louise Mercilus had scuttled soon after her coming on board at the Whitlock Foundation. Rita had chosen them because they were also vendors who previously had substantial, and apparently competent, histories with Whitlock. Each one had been with the old man's financial advisor practice for more than ten years. Why had they been jettisoned so quickly from the Trust organization?

Rita checked the addresses. A long morning loomed. The service companies she needed to visit were scattered across the city and two were at opposite ends of Baltimore County.

"Damn, I'll be driving all day," Rita said to herself. She punched on the radio in her Jeep. Bruce was singing "I'm On Fire." She poked her satellite radio button again. The London Philharmonic performing Debussy. Rita stomped on the gas.

After three hours of driving, four cups of coffee, multiple pit stops and consistent but vague responses from business owners, Rita had little. The owners had been surprised and hurt when told their contracts were terminated. Two indicated that

Mercilus had told them their work was unacceptable over a period of two to three weeks. To a person, they had asked what could be improved. They got vague answers about late arrivals or employee insubordination or their work wasn't suitable for a charitable organization. One tried to sue, but Mercilus had a non-Trust attorney quash that.

Holabird Industrial Park had to be Rita's last stop for today. She had to get back to the office and Annie. She had promised. She tried to suppress the consternation she heard in her sister's voice as her projected disapproval played in the imaginary conversation roiling in Rita's head.

Rita rolled through the blue-collar neighborhood looking for Portal Street. The homes were small here, older, some pre-WWII. The population was mostly working class white. It was a neighborhood rooted in the '50's.

This area had once been the proud home of Fort Holabird and started as Camp Holabird in 1918 as the Army's first motor transport training center and depot. It was at Camp Holabird in the 20's that the very first Jeeps were developed and tested for the military.

Later as a federal facility, it guarded federal witnesses and defendants such as John Dean, E. Howard Hunt and Charles Colson from the Nixon years. Over the next 30 years more than 230 acres were transferred to Baltimore City for development into Fort Holabird Industrial Park.

Rita rolled into the park, a maze of two-story white brick office buildings and long, squat warehouse structures with roll-up doors and loading docks. Architecture was severely utilitarian with little aesthetic in the steel and concrete design. Trucks zoomed around unlandscaped roads and there was a constant thump and whir of machinery.

"Your destination is on the right," GPS announced.

"And so it is." Rita pulled into a visitor space in front of a one-story brick building with two truck bays that backed into substantial warehousing space. She parked in front of the office where "Domingo Cleaning Services" was stenciled on the glass door.

The reception area was spare with a chest high counter and a literature display rack with individual flyers explaining types of services offered, a rack of business cards and a dusty arrangement of plastic pink roses with baby's breath. The receptionist area was bathed in light via an oversized industrial window reinforced with an exterior mesh of woven steel wire. Behind the counter was a desk with a computer monitor and an empty swivel chair tucked neatly flush with the desk.

Rita looked for a bell or a house phone to summon help. Nothing. She noticed a camera blinking in one of the corners. Real or merely a deterrent? She had no idea.

To her right was a steel door that Rita assumed led to storage and staging areas. She listened but heard no activity on the other side. She was about to pull the door open to see if there was anyone inside working when it swung outward and a handsome young Hispanic man almost collided with her.

"I am so sorry," he said. "We're short-handed today and I was helping unload cleaning supplies." The young man smiled. "I am Ernesto, Jr. Please. How can I help you?"

Rita explained who she was and why she had come. The young man's smile melted and his face followed into an expression of sadness.

"Come into my office," Ernesto said with the slightest lingering Spanish accent.

Rita followed him through the warehouse doors to a cubby hole where two desks faced each other. The room smelled of pine oil with a hint of ammonia. Walking room was narrow. Boxes of carpet shampoo and disinfectants, assorted mop heads, cleaning machine parts and manuals littered the floor. No windows, only harsh fluorescence lit the room.

Ernesto settled into a worn leather office chair and Rita sat in his visitor chair. Behind him, the wall was a gallery of framed and dusted photos of weddings and christenings and confirmations, summer softball teams with "Domingo Cleaning Services" patches on bright blue uniforms and a brand-new yellow Corvette. Above them all was a slender wooden cross with a crucified bronze Jesus.

"You know," Ernesto began, "when this woman, Louise Mercilus, told my father our company was fired, he cried. My father is the strongest man I know. When we first moved here and had trouble with a gang who hated Latinos, he guarded our building. He had no gun. He faced them again and again with only a baseball bat. He was fearless. But this act, this firing brought him to his knees."

"Why so emotional? Companies lose contracts all the time," Rita said.

"He and Mr. Whitlock were close. My dad would personally check on Mr. Will's office. Nothing out of place. Always spotless. They got to know each other because my dad would often go with the crews and help clean to make sure it was done right. My dad took pride in his work."

"And so what, according to Louise Mercilus, was the problem, the cause for ending your contract?"

Ernesto swallowed hard. "She told my dad that the work was sloppy. Trash cans were not emptied or a floor was left unbuffed. My father immediately started going every night with the crew assigned to the Whitlock offices. He would come home satisfied everyone had done their job. The next morning, he would get a call that someone had forgotten one thing or another to do. In about a month after Mr. Will was buried, so were we."

"I see," Rita said. "I'm sorry."

"This Louise woman gave the contract to a church group in the city. My dad never speaks about it, but he was not the same after." Ernesto leaned across the desk toward Rita. "Mr. Will and my father were friends. They had gotten to know each other. My dad was often invited to the Whitlock boat, even to their house. My father was so excited when Mr. Will invited our family to his wedding to Marianne. My whole family went, my dad and mom, me and my four brothers."

Ernesto shook his head and sank back into his chair as if recalling a memory.

"What do you think happened?" Rita asked.

"Maybe this Mercilus woman does not like Latinos—I kept tabs on who they hired, not just our replacements but other companies who came in after she took over. All white, all church related groups."

"Or maybe it's a management thing—you bring in the people who know you, who're loyal to you." Rita offered.

"Maybe," Ernesto said half-heartedly. "It just felt bad and there were no good reasons."

"I get it." Rita glanced at her watch. It was time to meet back up with Annie and Bev. "And I make you a promise. When my review of all this is over, I will share my findings with you."

Ernesto raised a skeptical eyebrow.

"*Te prometo la verdad, mi amigo.*" Rita stood, shook hands with Ernesto and left.

Chapter 13

The Helmund Afghani restaurant on Charles Street had its origins in a love story. The twenty-two-year-old son of an Afghan parliament member was living in Washington D.C. in 1970 and being tutored in English by his landlord's daughter. The young man attended American University by day and worked in DC's most glorious culinary venues, learning the business of food, by night. Eventually he married the landlord's daughter and they dreamed their dream together.

One of those dreams was Helmund. Tonight Rita was treating Bev and Annie to the wonders of Aushak, Banjan Laghatak and Kaddo Borawi with tender lamb marinated in cilantro and lemon and turmeric. Annie had been skeptical. Bev was thrilled. Rita wanted peace and pleasure and Helmund was a favorite.

"I love the pictures," Annie remarked as the waiter led them to a table.

Briefly Rita scanned the menu. She already knew what she would order. It was lamb chops, the same every time she came here. And she had been here often with Diane.

Helmund was one of their favorite places. They came without friends or family. It was their romantic getaway spot, their refuge from a hectic workweek place. They would meet here and linger over dinner and coffee and a shared dessert. They renewed themselves and each other here.

It had been a long time since Rita had braved returning to this place. She was determined to dissolve the held memories and the denied pain. Stop, Rita's head shouted at her consciousness. Take that deep breath. Stay in the moment.

"I have no idea what this menu is saying to me." Annie lowered her menu and stared at Rita over the frames of her glasses. She broke the grip of Rita's memory.

"Mom, think of something you like and I'll find it's equivalent on the menu. No surprises. No tricks."

"Deal." Annie lowered her menu. "I want dessert. I'm getting older and life is uncertain."

"Good try," Rita said with a reprimanding glance at Bev who was chuckling quietly behind her own menu. Bev straightened her face and rested the menu beside her plate.

"Lamb chops, Mama? Mighty good. That's what I'm gettin'." Bev raised her eyebrows as she offered her suggestion.

"I like lamb. How about potatoes?" Annie asked. "Nothing all mixed up with things I've never heard of."

"I'll ask if we can get Pakora," Rita responded.

"Sounds too exotic." Annie made a face.

"Think of it as a twist on french fries." Rita signaled the waiter.

"Ooo. Yeah, french fries," Annie smiled. "Ok then. But I still want dessert."

"And you shall have it," Rita answered.

The waiter took their order, came back with a covered dish of warm Naan and departed to the kitchen.

"Finally, a few minutes away from it all," Rita said.

"Well, look who's gonna join us." Annie said, grinning from ear to ear. "Miss Mary Margaret."

Rita swiveled in her seat, muttering to herself, "This cannot be good."

Smooth marched to the table. All eyes were on her. When she reached the table, she put an arm around Rita's shoulder and bent low to speak softly into her ear.

"There's a search warrant for your house. Bolton is on his way," Smooth said. "You need to be there with your attorney."

"What?" Annie's tone was sharp, insistent. "What is it?"

Bev stared at Rita. She said nothing but waited for instruction.

"I have to go. Nothing much but something I have to deal with. Bev, can you stay with Mom through dinner? Bring her home when you're done?" Rita stood.

"Sure, baby." Bev reached out to touch Annie's hand. "It ain't nothin', Mama. She does this all the time. Don't you be worryin'."

"I want to go with you." Annie started to stand.

"Please. I will not be long and I'll meet you at home. Everything's fine. Promise," Rita said with a weak smile. Smooth smiled too as if to reassure Annie.

"I lived with your father for over thirty years," Annie said. "I know 'fine.' And this ain't it." Still she sat back down, a deep frown darkening her face.

Rita walked around the table, gave her mother a hug for futile reassurance and followed Smooth out of the restaurant and onto the Charles Street sidewalk. On a warm summer evening, tourists and locals crowded the streets, going into or coming out of this hub of upscale eateries. When they were out on the pavement, Smooth and Rita stood for a moment beside The Helmund's door.

"I'm on my way to a retirement party in Fells Point," Smooth said. "I have a notification set on your name, so when the warrant popped up, I came over here immediately."

"I spend most of my life feeling like I've been shot out of a cannon," Rita said.

"You stole that line," Smooth said.

"Molly Ivins nailed it." Rita sighed. "Go to your party. I'll call Patrick on my way."

"Keep your cool." Smooth touched Rita's arm. "This cop is a loose cannon."

"Don't I always?"

"Don't fuck with him, Rita." Smooth's voice was sharp and straight like a gut punch.

"I love you too." Rita held open her arms and enfolded her friend for a brief but powerful hug.

"I'll be at Max's on Broadway," Smooth said. "Text or call if you get in a bind. Bolton's boss is my old boss and he's a good guy. I can call him, but only as a last resort. I need to have a low profile to be able to help you going forward."

"Got it." Rita nodded.

"Ok, I'm outta here. In about an hour, I'm gonna be fending off hands grabbing my butt," Smooth laughed.

"Yeah, but they know you're gay," Rita said.

"Don't matter to a roomful of guys who're blind drunk and blowing off steam."

"So true."

As Rita approached her house, she saw the strobing blue and red of police cars shooting skyward from behind. She had her windows open, and the closer she got, she heard unintelligible commands from police radios. They shattered the soft silence of a perfect quiet evening.

Out of habit, she glanced over at Loretta Mondieu's house. It seemed every light in the house was on. She did not see either Loretta or her husband, Leonard. Her headlights lit up a silhouette at the top of her drive. The figure held up a hand to indicate he wanted her to stop.

"I'm sorry," said the policeman who leaned into Rita's driver side window. "Police activity here, and we aren't letting anybody in unless they're connected to this case."

"Does being the homeowner qualify?" Rita's tone was smirky and sarcastic.

The policeman seemed surprised. He didn't speak but waved her on up the drive.

"My attorney will be here and I expect you to let him enter also." Rita hit the gas without waiting for a response. In her rearview mirror, she watched as he stood looking after her charge up the hill and swing into the parking pad behind her house.

"YooHoo." A familiar woman's voice trilled between radio bursts. Loretta had stationed herself at Rita's back door. On one side of her was Billy Bolton and on the other side was her husband, Leonard.

"Loretta?" Rita slid out of the Jeep and approached the people in front of her back door.

"Is this your house or not?" Billy Bolton raised his voice just below a shout. "This woman here keeps telling me it belongs to her uncle. She's been here since we came."

"Tell him," Loretta said in a determined tone. "This is Hodge's house. Been in our family forever." She crossed her arms in emphasis.

Rita could hardly hear her over the crackle of police radio transmissions. The strobing red and blue gumball lights twirled like a carnival side show.

"Officer Bolton . . ." Rita began when a Rolls Silver Spur flashed onto the scene. "Jesus." Rita spun around to watch a portly Patrick Dwyer throw open the back door of his car and snap to attention. He was wearing black satin pajama bottoms, a Cannes Film Festival t-shirt and a pair of handmade leather huaraches. He marched to Bolton.

"May I view your warrant, please, officer? I am this young lady's attorney. You may remember me from our most recent interview on your behest." Dwyer held out a hand. Bolton swore something unintelligible under his breath but he handed over the warrant. Dwyer beckoned to his driver and whispered in her ear. She retrieved a small led flashlight from the Rolls' glove box and shone it on the document.

"I see here you state you have probable cause that this property contains information regarding a missing person. To wit, you believe this information is contained in written communications or electronic devices. Have I stated this accurately?" Dwyer locked eyes with Bolton who refused to back down.

"That's right." Bolton started to reach for the warrant, but Dwyer wasn't giving it back.

"May I continue?"

Bolton drew back his hand. Dwyer stood parsing the warrant with a perfectly manicured finger while his driver held the flashlight. Rita came to stand by her attorney.

"More distraction on the way," Dwyer said softly to Rita without lifting his head from the paper.

"Distraction?" Rita asked. Out of the corner of her eye, she caught a convoy of vehicles on the road below her property.

"Hey, Bolton," called the policeman at the top of Rita's driveway. "Bunch of news people here."

Billy Bolton pursed his lips in anger and stormed over to his patrolman. With raised voices, they argued with each other. Rita backed away from Dwyer to watch the activity at the top of her driveway.

She heard a woman's voice, also raised, now countering what seemed Bolton's refusal to allow entry. Rita then heard a definitively loud "No." More arguing followed from the assembled reporters.

There was no mistaking Bolton's voice above the fray. "Fuck."

He waved in the vans and SUVs on Rita's drive. Like vultures descending on roadkill, they swarmed onto the sizeable blacktop behind Rita's house. Cameramen hopped out and hoisted broadcast cameras onto their shoulders. Feature reporters tested their mics.

"Saddle up," Bolton called to the accompanying patrolmen as he slid behind the wheel of his unmarked. His windshield red and blue flashers went dark as did all the roof-mounted gumball lights. The waiting policemen settled back into their cruisers and inched through the parking area to sail down the driveway.

Clear that no further police activity or breaking story was in the works, the news crews shook broadcast cameras off their shoulders and repacked them in the back of their vans. Reporters stowed their mics and waited for crew drivers to transport them back to their respective stations or newsrooms.

Laura Palomina, mic in hand, walked over to Rita. "What is going on here? I got a call from Patrick Dwyer, mob lawyer extraordinaire, who was supposedly giving us a tip about a big time bust."

Rita shook her head and held up a finger indicating that Palomina should hold that thought. She walked over to Dwyer. "That . . . was an amazing move."

Dwyer chuckled and threw an arm around Rita. "The whole secret lies in confusing the enemy, so that he cannot fathom our real intent.'"

"I get the Sun Tzu thing but how did you know it would work?" Rita asked.

"People like Bolton succeed only in the shadows. The light of day—or tv lights—exposes them and renders them ineffective."

"Understood. Thank you, Patrick." Rita turned and hugged him.

"And please, next time, try to schedule these ineffectual forays against you so that my connubial bliss is not on the line." Dwyer patted her back and broke from her embrace.

"You're a trip, my friend," Rita said.

Dwyer headed back to his Rolls. His driver had the Silver Spur purring and ready to move out. Before he entered the back seat, he turned once more to Rita. "I know the judge from whom Officer Bolton secured that warrant. He's not a fool. And he is a friend. I am inviting him to lunch this week for a chat about this incident and about Bolton." With that he turned, waved a hand in the air to signal goodbye and sank into the luxurious leather of his ride. The Rolls dipped out of sight.

In almost the same instant, a gleaming white Escalade roared onto the parking area. Before Bev could apply the brakes, Annie Mars opened her passenger side door. Rita heard Bev say something unintelligible.

Rita stood beside Laura Palomina as Annie lowered herself to the asphalt from the SUV. "My mother," Rita said to

Palomina. "We were out to dinner when I got word of the impending search. Left my assistant and my mom to finish the meal while I raced back here."

"What were they searching for?" Palomina waved to her cameraman. "Meet you back at the station," she called to him. She had driven her own car tonight.

"According to the warrant, I had secreted information involving the disappearance of Diane Winter and may even be holding her here," Rita said.

"That's absurd," Palomina said.

"Sure is." Annie cut in and took Rita's hand. "They didn't search, did they?"

"No, but I need to thank Loretta." Rita caught Loretta and Leonard as they were making their way back home.

While Rita was thanking the Mondieus for their intervention, Bev came to stand beside Annie and Laura Palomina.

"That girl right there," Bev pointed at Rita across the way, "is a non-stop adrenalin rush."

"She comes by it honest," Annie agreed. "Her father was the same. Always on to the next case—there was never a drought there."

"Was her father also a reporter?" Palomina asked.

Annie laughed out loud. "No way. He was a cop. He was not a fan of what he called the 'damn news machine.' He was a Viet Nam vet. Rita marched to end the war. His first response to adversity was physical. Rita tackles with her head by thinking things through. Lloyd believed that people can't change. Not Rita. She believes she can make a difference."

"She's tough alright," Palomina said, looking toward the woman who was now hugging Loretta.

"Now let me tell you something." Annie's face turned serious. "All that 'tough' is the armor she straps into every day. You see what she wants you to see and she has perfected the art of camouflage. It is her protection. But in the heart of the night when no one is around, her feelings, like lions on the hunt, come out. She fears them. She feels them with exquisite sense and believes they can devour her."

Bev nodded.

"And picking up a phrase I learned from my husband—'not on my watch'." Annie's voice was strong, determined.

Laura Palomina looked away. The reference was pointed. She started to leave.

"Wadja bring me? I am famished after all that." Rita jogged to her waiting confederates in the night's excitement.

"I should be going," Palomina said. "I'm actually off tonight."

"Well, good," Rita put an arm around her and said, "Come on in." She started toward her back door. "I need an MRE. For the rest of you well-fed troops, I've got coffee and an infinite supply of dessert." With her arm still around Palomina, she stuck out an elbow for her mother to join. "And you too, Bev. One slice of chocolate cake is never gonna hurt that incredible figure of yours."

Annie turned to Palomina when they were inside Rita's kitchen. "Not on my watch," she repeated.

140

Chapter 14

The temporary respite from oppressive heat evaporated. Rita woke up. The light was still that ethereal blue when the sun approached but has not breached the horizon. She ran her fingers through her hair. Damp from sweat. Out of the bathroom, she tiptoed to her mother's room. Annie had turned the AC on low and closed her windows. She was bundled and asleep.

Rita dressed in her running shorts and singlet and pulled on her new kicks. Downstairs she selected a Gatorade from the fridge and placed it into an insulated bag which she then stuffed with ice packs. Before she left to run, she checked her emails.

Nothing from Roswell. Without a direction in which to hunt, he had nowhere to go. Rita shook her head. "I have to find a way," she said out loud.

She picked up her hydration bag and a towel and went to her Jeep. Outside the Great White Hunter was engaged in a game Rita immediately recognized. She crept up behind him to see a small rabbit, terrorized, shivering and unable to flee his captor.

"Sorry, Dude," Rita said. She grabbed the cat with her towel so that he couldn't scratch. He howled. She walked back to the house with the cat exerting all his strength wriggling against her hold. She deposited him inside her back door and went back to the Jeep.

For a moment, she rested her head on the steering wheel. The rabbit was a reminder. Somewhere out there was Diane. Was she feeling like trapped prey? Was she trying to escape. Rita had wanted to stay out of the search; she always said that to herself and she never meant it.

I can't do this now, Rita thought. Keep moving. And make up your damned mind.

The trail Rita ran on was an old railway bed. This corridor of the Northern Central Railway dated back to 1832 and served towns between Baltimore and upstate New York. The service ran for 140 years until flooding from tropical storm Agnes obliterated the railbed in 1972.

She came here every morning, fair weather or foul. It was her refuge and therapy. Here her mind rested from its pervasive pursuit and questions, remembrance of things past that she wished to lay to rest. Here she was free and that freedom allowed answers to bubble to consciousness, problems to find perspective, stress to release its grasp.

Rita locked her Jeep and prepared for her run. It was quiet here on this crushed gravel surface, except for the crunch of running shoes or bike tires on the stone. She sailed out two and a half miles then turned to complete her usual five miles.

Rita grabbed her Gatorade and stood leaning back on the side of her Jeep. Still not many cars in the small parking area. She'd passed only one bike rider on her route. She took a long deep swallow of Frost Glacier Cherry. Piercing yet only a whisper of cherry flavor, it was perfect for pushing back road dust and refreshing a runner. She drained the plastic bottle halfway.

As she returned the half empty container to her small cooler, she grabbed the towel she brought, swiped her face and tossed the towel onto the passenger seat. It had come to her at mile four. She wasn't going to follow the rules. She was going with her gut. She would phone Roswell and send him on an expedition.

♏

Rita and Annie spoke little on the way to the office. Annie was exhausted after the previous day's adventure in diversion by circus. As she drove, Rita glanced over and saw her mother nodding. Rita fidgeted in her seat. Her mind was spinning with her new ideas and she was like a ready racehorse.

"Get ahold of Roswell," Rita said first thing when she and Annie walked through her office door.

Annie's eyes popped wide. Bev stared.

"You got a hunch," Bev said, shaking her head.

"I have an action plan," Rita countered.

"Oh, Lord." Bev waited for the plan's unveiling.

"The cops are doing a crap job, if anything, to find Diane."

Rita poured two cups from the office coffee maker. She handed one to her mother who was half sitting, half reclining on the office love seat.

"Don't do this," Bev warned.

"I am not going to continue this dumb game with Billy Bolton. He'll be in my face forever if I don't find Diane. I'll always be the suspect and he'll always be hassling me. Doesn't matter if he has zero evidence of that. He's going to keep coming."

"That's what they do." Bev nodded. "But I think you're playing with fire. He could hurt you."

Rita paused and then stated. "Silence becomes cowardice."

For a moment, neither Bev nor Annie spoke.

Rita turned to Bev. "Please, get hold of Roswell."

"On it." Bev turned back to her PC.

♏

Rita and Annie were finishing up lunch when Roswell arrived. Bev was out and Rita had opened her office door so that she had a view into the waiting room.

"Hey, I can come back," Roswell offered when Rita motioned him into her office. Annie started gathering her sandwich and soda. Today Roswell had on a black T-shirt with a stark white imprint of "I'm In."

"Mom, don't move. It's OK," Rita said and pointed Roswell to a chair beside her mother.

"Roswell, I need your help." Rita pushed the remains of her turkey club to the side and leaned toward him. "I wanted to stay out of the search for Diane Winter. I can't at this point . . ."

"Cops were all over you the other night." Roswell rested his arms on his knees and leaned toward her. "What do you need?"

A fleeting expression of surprise rippled across Rita's face. She resumed with determination. "I want us to find Diane. I want to go all out. And I need your skills and your buy-in."

"Hacking," Roswell said.

"Unsanctioned search." Rita met his eyes. "I talked to Diane's assistant a while back. She didn't have any names of recent acquaintances, no stalkers or new admirers. Knowing Diane, I still believe that is where we will find answers."

Roswell sat back and struck a thoughtful pose as he considered this approach. "Email," he said at last, "I need to access her email accounts. Business as well as personal."

"The cops have her laptop and phone," Rita said. "I can't get those."

"All I need are her email addresses—all of them," Roswell said. "Makes it a little more difficult and time consuming, but never impossible. People never read the fine print that comes with free email services. Pretty much you give away all your privacy. In exchange for 'free', your email provider has full access to all your emails and that includes IP addresses, cookie data, your browser and version and on and on. They tout this as a way to personalize your experience, but it's a malicious hacker's dream. Combined with uneven server-side security, it's not a matter of 'if', it's a matter of 'when' you'll get compromised."

Annie cleared her throat. "I have no idea what you just said."

Roswell laughed. "Miss Annie, think of it like politics. Pols will tell you anything you want to hear. Some of it's so complicated most people won't bother to look into how it's gonna happen—or if it even can happen. It's too much to wrap their heads around."

"Now that I get," Annie said.

"What's your exposure?" Rita asked. "I have to protect you."

"I'm good," Roswell said. "You let me worry about me. I have to be in a Fortnight tournament at the end of the month. I'm gonna be there and I'm gonna have those email senders for you before then."

"Roswell, I'm counting on that." Rita stood to signal the end of the meeting. "At any hint of trouble, you have to let me know so I can help you."

"Not to worry." Roswell stood, his six-foot four frame hovered over Annie and he reached down to hug her. "I'm quicker than they think. Let me know when we have a place to play."

With Roswell gone to await further input, Rita picked up her cell. "Sorry to call but this isn't a text or email request."

"Ok . . ." Laura Palomina was curious.

"I have a way, I think, to find more than the cops—about Diane," Rita began.

"I'm listening."

"When we first broke up, I had a few emails from Diane. I need to confirm that she still has the same carrier and address," Rita said.

Palomina gave her Diane's most current email address. "What are you doing?"

"If I tell you, you could get into trouble. You don't need that." Rita doodled a barred window on her note pad.

"I want the story when it's over," Palomina said.

"I can't promise that. If the tactic works, I won't be able to explain how I got there without putting myself at the mercy of Bobby Bolton. He's jonesing to take me down."

Palomina on the other end said nothing for a moment.

"And I need you to keep what I've just told you under wraps. Doesn't matter I haven't told you everything. Too many people with knowledge can kill the effort—and me. Are you with me?" Rita asked.

"I'm with you," Palomina said without hesitation. "But you know I'll want a story."

"And a story you shall have. I promise it," Rita said. When she'd finished her call with Palomina, she phoned Lakshmi, Diane's assistant.

"Sorry to jump right in here, but I need some help. First I need your commitment." Rita paused.

"That sounds ominous," Lakshmi's voice betrayed reluctance.

"It may be." Rita took a deep breath and began. "Here is my proposition and what I'm asking. I'm going to conduct my own off-the-record hunt for Diane. The police keep hounding me. They even came to search my house. I am telling you I had nothing to do with her disappearance. What I need from you can only come from your belief that I was not involved. My question up front to you is: do you think I did some harm to Diane?"

Lakshmi answered immediately. "Of course not."

"I want you to be sure of that answer. Do you need time to be clear in your own mind? I hate putting you in a difficult position but I need to know."

"You're scaring me."

Rita had not wanted to step off the cliff without a chute, but she was going to have to take her leap. "I need access to Diane's emails—all of them. A lot of execs have multiples to manage the daily barrage. I know Diane had several based-on priorities for responding. I do know her personal email but not the work-related ones. I need those to sniff out anybody who could have taken her. I don't have them, and if I do get them, the police might want to try and accuse me because I have that knowledge and because I've been searching them."

"I see." Lakshmi seemed to be considering what Rita had told her.

"It's a lot to ask," Rita said.

"Yes." Lakshmi paused.

If Lakshmi declined, it would be troublesome. Would she keep this conversation to herself if no police officer inquired? Would she bend if Bolton questioned her about other email addresses. In her head, Rita riffed through the successful defensive tactics she had used before in her newspaper days.

"I'm with you," Lakshmi said at last. "I've thought it through. I accepted your investigative work when you were still a reporter. I know that Diane trusted you. And I certainly believe you more than that arrogant cop."

"I'm grateful," Rita said with a sigh of relief. "I will keep you informed, Lakshmi. I won't let you down. I may not be able to find Diane, but I will not expose you."

"I want you to find Diane and if there are more things I can help with, I want to know."

"Thank you, Lakshmi." Rita closed her eyes briefly in gratitude.

With the conversation over, Rita sat back in her desk chair. Annie, with a full belly from lunch and extra cookies for dessert, had put her head back and fallen asleep. Her Styrofoam sandwich box rested at an angle on one knee.

"We're off and running, Mom," Rita whispered though she knew Annie would not hear her.

♏

At the same time, a pick-up with two female passengers pulled up to a gasoline pump. It was dusk now, the rush hour flood of the homeward bound had slowed to a trickle. Diane rested her head on the passenger window. Her eyes were closed.

"I hate havin' to move every minute," Diane's abductor said. "Wouldn't have to be like this if you'da stayed in the damn truck them few days ago. Now we have to keep on the run. Stay off the main roads. Sleep in shit motels." It was clear anger was kindled by every statement of complaint.

"I'm sorry." Diane sat up and opened her eyes. She glanced toward the convenience store connected with the gas station. A workman exited the store with a six pack of beer.

"That don't help us with havin' to be more careful. Ziggin' and zaggin'." The driver struck the steering wheel with an open palm. "Only good thing is seein' that shot of us less and less on the evenin' news."

"Um." Diane studied the store front. On the plate glass window beside the door, down low and in small signage was a notification that restrooms were inside. "I need to go to the bathroom."

"Well, you'll hafta wait til I get the truck filled. Ain't lettin' you go in there by yourself." With that comment, the kidnapper slid out of the driver side, closed the door and walked back to the gas tank.

Diane's stalker came around to the passenger side and opened the door. "Well come on if you gotta go."

"Thanks." Diane slid out. There was only one car parked in front of the convenience store now. She didn't want her abductor to notice her looking around, so she learned as much as she could by using just her eyes.

Impossible to leave a note on a car with her jailer striding alongside and almost dragging her along. No cops stopping by for a quick coffee for the road. Lights went on inside as did the lot lamp poles and fluorescents by the gas pumps.

Diane reached for the door handle. A meaty hand firmly grasped Diane's with her fingers wrapped around the handle.

"Don't try nothin' stupid," the kidnapper said in a low growl.

"Wouldn't think of it." Diane tried to pull back the door. The over-sized hand stayed in place and allowed the door to open only a few inches. "I ain't foolin' around."

"I have that etched in my brain," Diane responded. "Indelibly."

Chapter 15

Monday morning meetings. Rita hated them. Always had. Back in the day when she was a working reporter, editorial meetings were a mix of nodding off and sassing back. Doughnuts and deadlines. Fighting for the stories you wanted to chase and dodging assignments you thought were boring. She pictured herself at the round conference table in the *Washington Star* and, without bidding, a smile lifted the corners of her mouth.

"Louise will be here in a sec." Bunny entered the room. Her voice burst the memory bubble for Rita and she turned her attention to the attendees.

In the chair at the head of the table was Marianne who was reading emails on her iPhone. At the right-hand side was an empty chair. Rita assumed it was for Louise Mercilus. To the left of Marianne, Bunny settled into her seat, glancing at her watch. Rita had left that chair available for Bunny. Entering together immediately after Bunny were a man and a woman Rita had never met. The entire right side of the conference table belonged to Louise. She would be one facing many.

Let's see how she dances, Rita said to herself.

Marianne looked up. She seemed to have finished reading her emails and was ready to engage in the meeting. She glanced at the door, then her watch. Seven minutes after the hour appointed for this event.

Rita sent a text to Bunny who was still scanning emails on her phone. "Is it always like this?"

Bunny tapped back. "Whenever somebody new comes in. An authority figure, our accountant or attorney. Anybody Marianne respects."

Rita started another text and then stopped and laid down her phone as Louise Mercilus entered the room, arms full with a notebook, iPad, smartphone and folders. Bunny cut a sideways glance of annoyance at Rita and shook her head.

"Louise, are we cutting into something important?" Marianne asked. "We can reschedule if you need to."

"Oh, no," Mercilus answered. "I've got it all under control." She smiled the smile of an inquisitor with a captive infidel. Rita watched Mercilus take her time in placing her tools on the conference table, slow, deliberate, reinforcing her importance and command.

When she finished and sat down. She leaned toward Marianne and placed a hand on her arm. "So sorry to hold you up," Mercilus said, basking in Marianne's approval.

Bunny turned to Rita. Rita did not respond but kept her eye on Louise. Rita would be an observer here, a behaviorist learning the ways of this woman, Mercilus. She would step back from engagement and focus with the lenses she had honed over her years as an investigative reporter. She needed an answer: insecurity or criminal intent?

Mercilus, her hand still on Marianne's arm, said quietly but decisively, "Let's begin as we always do—with a prayer." She bowed her head. Clearly this was a part of every meeting as all attendees followed her lead.

Mercilus gave forth in a pastoral cadence. "Father, your word says that where two or three are gathered in your name, you are in their midst. Thank you for being with us today at this meeting. Let this place be full of your glory. We come against the spirit of division in the name of Jesus. Amen." No one echoed the amen.

"Oh, and before we get started," Marianne said, "I'd like to introduce Rita Mars who is going to be doing vendor risk assessments for us. Rita, can you tell us a little about yourself before we jump into the meeting?"

"Rita Mars is a household name," Louise Mercilus announced before Rita could begin. "She's the gal who broke the story on the big oil broker accounting scandal. She's a former big name with the *Washington Star*. We are lucky to have her here in her capacity as head of RM Security Services." Mercilus threw out an arm in a sweeping tv wrestling ring announcer gesture toward Rita.

Rita smiled her knowing smile. First shot across the bow is upstaging. She glanced at Marianne who was beaming. Bunny's head was lowered as if she were studying some imperfection in the conference table. The man and woman turned in their seats to view the woman who drew this effusive introduction from Marianne.

"Not sure I live up to the hype," Rita began but Mercilus cut in.

"Don't be so modest. Please." Mercilus' eyes glinted like the sharp end of a spear.

"I was a reporter," Rita said. "I did a lot of reporting, as Louise has mentioned, about crime. My company now works on security issues for other organizations. Doesn't mean something is amiss. Mostly management brings in a consultant for a safety check. In the case of the Whitlock Foundation, we're reviewing vendor practices to confirm they have solid security practices in place. It's a way of checking to make sure they don't have problems that could lead to issues for you. I am grateful to be here, and I'm looking forward to working with you all."

Bunny finally raised her head to look at Rita. Rita gave away no hint of mindset, no frown, no raised eyebrow. A perfect poker face.

"Thanks for that," Louise said, still standing and still in charge. "I have an agenda here." She passed out a single page of items to the group.

The meeting turned to the affairs of the Foundation. The man, who Rita surmised was the accountant, announced to Marianne and the other attendees that ninety cents of every dollar was going to Foundation efforts.

Rita jotted a note on the legal pad she'd brought. She looked up from writing and saw that Mercilus was watching her.

The woman spoke next and indicated that donations had taken a slight dip from last year. She was the lead on fundraising. She also expressed some concern about a lower average gift amount and average fundraising amount. She recommended they review plans for their development teams to shore up the decline.

Rita picked up her pen to make that note. She caught that blatant stare again from Louise Mercilus. It was a challenge. Rita gave her attention fully to writing her note and ignored the look.

"I'll catch up with you later," Bunny said to Rita when the meeting adjourned. "I have a deadline and I'll call." She scurried after Marianne. Louise was gone and the accountant and head of fundraising had departed first.

Rita headed for the ladies' room. As she washed her hands, she heard the door behind her open. Instinctively she looked up to see who had entered. Louise stood behind her. Their eyes met in the mirror.

"Why are you really here?" Louise was a good three inches taller than Rita and outweighed her with a stolid matronly figure. She took a step forward as Rita turned to face her. Immediately Rita conjured up Mrs. Gillis, her fifth-grade teacher who wielded her imposing body weight over the skinny little miscreants in her class.

"Whoa, Louise," Rita said, "I'm doing just what I said back there in the meeting." Rita stood her ground. She smiled and squared her shoulders.

"I don't think that at all," Louise hissed. She inched forward. Rita did not move. She could feel the rounded rim of the sink against her butt. She wants to pin me like a science class bug, Rita said to herself.

"Not sure why you would think that." Rita detected the scents of peppermint and coffee emanating from Mercilus.

"That little busybody, Blythe-Cramer, hasn't liked me from the start. She's jealous and she's spent every day trying to break the tie I have with Marianne Whitlock." Rita expected Louise to shake a finger in her face the way old Mrs. Gillis used to do.

"Let's not get paranoid," Rita said.

"You think I'm paranoid?" This comment was a waved red cape to Mercilus. Deep furrows grooved her forehead and her lips were taut in a clenched jaw.

"Didn't say that." Rita shook her head.

"I'm on to you." Mercilus' manicured and red polished nail stabbed Rita's shoulder.

"Don't touch me again." Rita glanced at Mercilus' hand and then gripped her opponent with her eyes.

The two women stood braced, knees in a slight bend. Each awaited a sign from the other at opposing sides of their established battleground. Mercilus pulled her hand back, turned and walked out of the bathroom, flinging the door back on its hinges.

♏

Bunny Blythe-Cramer's office was an expansive room with a window view of Baltimore's Inner Harbor Marketplace. Sunlight streamed in. The wall directly across from Bunny's desk exhibited a photo gallery of family and Whitlock Foundation events. The bookshelf behind the desk supported a few books and a collection of personal awards, more photos and grandchild crafted tchotchkes.

"Got a minute?" Rita stood in the doorway.

"Sure," Bunny said. "Sorry I couldn't talk right after the meeting."

"This woman, Mercilus, is quite the performer." Rita felt her body still rigid with the fight response from her encounter with Louise. Her mouth was dry as she spoke.

"My world." Bunny sighed. "Did something happen?"

"She accosted me in the ladies' room. Threatened me."

Bunny sat back in her chair as she considered Rita's comment. "What did she do?"

"She was in my face. She used her physical advantage to try and intimidate me," Rita said.

"Wow, she's never tried that with me." Bunny's face betrayed her apprehension. "I've been on the receiving end of her pushing for my buy-in on projects. She's insinuated some ugly things about me, about my being Jewish. When I've spoken to Marianne, she's had us in for a three-way meeting. Louise always insisted I've misunderstood her. In the sessions we've had like this, she plays the victim."

"Does Louise follow up with more threats after these meetings?" Rita asked.

Bunny leaned forward. "Oh no. She knows she's won if Marianne seems satisfied with her explanation of the misunderstanding. Later if we pass in the hall or the restroom, she says nothing. But it's the smirking, the silent gloating that gets to me. Louise knows that as long as she can sweet-talk Marianne into believing she can do no wrong, she has the upper hand here." Bunny shook her head.

"So what's your approach?" Rita asked.

"I minimize my contact with her. I state my case if I object to something Louise proposes, but I never engage like I used to." Bunny sighed. "I'm a coward—and that's why I brought you in. I don't have the stomach for this fight. I don't have the wherewithal."

"I've dealt with her type before," Rita said, her mind riffing through the greedy execs, the cons and the self-serving politicians she'd exposed in her career. "I have some thoughts."

"From your lips to God's ear," Bunny said.

"For all the righteous spouting and cross wearing, there is nothing Godly in this woman's behavior. The crux for me though is not the fanaticism, it's what she's hiding behind this ultra-religious façade." Rita looked at Bunny. "The issue you brought me in to find."

"I'm praying that you do, if you'll pardon that expression," said Bunny.

"I've fought in these trenches," Rita replied, standing from her chair. "I'm armed. And I'm dangerous."

ℳ

"Mom, how about lunch in Annapolis today? You loved the Spa Creek Café place last time we went." Rita settled her briefcase and laptop behind the driver's seat of her Jeep. "I'll put the top down and we can cruise on over there."

Annie rested her insulated tumbler of coffee on the passenger side floor then latched on to the interior grab handle and hoisted herself into the seat. "And who's the appointment with after lunch?"

"Mom," Rita said, swinging herself behind the wheel.

"Rita."

"You know me too well," Rita said with a grin.

"I know you better than that." Annie took a swig of coffee. "You're your father's child."

"Meaning?" Rita touched the ignition.

"I went on Sunday afternoon rides and tours through unfamiliar neighborhoods and quick stops at the police station after a romantic dinner. Always in the name of justice or the greater good." Annie slid the passenger seat belt across her chest and clicked it to lock.

"Means Dad wasn't after justice?" Rita poked the ignition and the Jeep hummed. She shifted into reverse.

"Your father was going for justice," Annie said, "no mistake about that. But he lived for the chase. That was his other drug, besides the alcohol."

Rita guided the Jeep down her driveway to Belfast Road toward the expressway into Baltimore City. "I like the chase."

"I know you do, honey." Annie paused. "So where are we really going today?"

♏

Rita and Annie enjoyed their lunch at the waterside café. Though it was late August, the smothering humidity was low today. A sail boater's dream of a breeze fanned gently across their faces as they ate while the sun cast golden gleaming sparkles on the creek.

"Ready?" Rita asked when the check was paid and the waitress was clearing plates.

"I'm always ready," Annie laughed.

The Maryland Secretary of State's Charity Organizations Division was on Francis Street in Annapolis. The street was named for Sir Francis Nicholson who, in the late 1600's, designed the city's layout. He copied ideas from European capitals that featured circles with radiating streets to create focal points such St. Anne's Episcopal Church and the State House, the colony's seat of government. It was a design carried over by L'Enfant to Washington, DC.

The Secretary of State offices were housed in a modern no-frills brick structure, functional without aesthetics. Cast aluminum cutout letters mounted over the entrance modestly declared this was the Wineland Building. The street was as narrow as it had been when first constructed for horse traffic and both street and sidewalks were worn brick. Francis Street was a spoke off the circle which ringed the State House, visible at its east end.

Annie decided she would stroll Main Street and the shops while Rita spoke with the director of the Charity Division. Rita made sure Annie was headed in the right direction and then entered the office building.

She spoke to the receptionist and was guided to the office of Shane Smith, assistant secretary of state. Rita followed the receptionist through a maze of cubicles and the low buzz of multiple phone calls in progress.

Shane Smith's office was graced by a window overlooking Francis Street; strong yellow sunlight streamed in. The office walls were glass with shades that could be lowered for privacy. Her desk was a photo gallery of Smith with awards, Smith with State execs, no family, no friends, no pets. As she entered, Smith thrust out a hand to shake.

Shane Smith was a woman who had probably been a career civil servant. She was tall, slender and wore a dress suit and heels. Rita speculated the outfit had nothing to do with her but was chosen for an earlier meeting with higher ups. The woman wore makeup, but it didn't hide the weary lines around her mouth or the crows' feet at the corner of her eyes.

Weariness carried over in her voice. "Ms. Mars, I used to read you in the *Washington Star*. I read your email about your foray into scammy charities. You're looking to go back to your investigative days?"

Rita had purposefully crafted her appeal for a meeting that did not specify any one organization or person. She left it open as if she were generally interested. With the skill of scammers rising in the digital age, she leveraged that trend to enable a meeting where she could learn more by revealing less.

"With my new line of work in security, I have a client newsletter and occasionally a webinar which deals with the ways crime is changing and how to protect yourself and your company. With the trend of using a charity for a front, I want to start understanding more about fraud on non-profit."

"How do we start?" Smith asked, already tapping into her database.

Rita explained that she was interested in a database for sanctions, settlements and convictions. Smith tapped on the keys to her PC. "I have to get permission from the Secretary of State's office for that access. If you get turned down, the counteroffer will be for reports. You'll need to be very specific about what you want."

"I appreciate this." Rita stood. "Any other guidance you can give me about what you've seen, the tricks used, the hard to prove cases?"

"I think the hardest case we had was a few years back. A group of so-called cancer charities out of Tennessee ripped off about a hundred ninety thousand dollars. A family affair with a family member representing several divisions of the charity. It was disgusting but, with the FTC, we stopped it."

"Repayment?" Rita asked.

Smith sighed and shook her head. "With frauds like these, the thieves usually have spent the money on cars and vacations."

Rita paused. She'd seen this kind of greed chewing its way into the heart and muscle of trust and the desire to help. "I know every state has an organization just like yours. How do scammers hide their theft? "

"In this case," Smith said, "the thieves hid their siphoning of funds by claiming in the mandatory reports that they were receiving high volume of 'gifts-in-kind'. This allowed them to present a more efficient distribution of monies than there actually were."

"And they went to jail . . ."

"No. They were barred from creating or participating in any further fundraising ventures." Smith glanced at her watch.

Rita stood. "I appreciate your time." She held out her hand which Smith shook.

"It's futile," Smith said as she gathered a notebook and cell phone from her desk.

"Going after the people who do these things?" Rita walked with her as she exited the office.

"It's insidious. Always the next one comes along."

Rita watched Smith walk down the hallway to her next meeting. She thought of Mercilus, the encounter in the ladies' room, the haughty righteousness. The more she thought about it, the angrier she felt—and the more committed.

Chapter 16

Sunday afternoon. Summer. For Rita it conjured days of the past. Annie would be in the kitchen frying her family's famous chicken. Rita could hear an occasional pop of hot oil. Cubes of boiled potatoes sat cooling in a big ceramic bowl with happy yellow sunflowers garlanded around the edge. Annie's creamy potato salad dressing awaited dispensing in a quart Pyrex measuring cup. Rita's sister, Sara, helped her mother with the prep work.

In the living room, Rita sat with her father, eyes on the television. The Baltimore Orioles were playing. The sound came from the tv with only a now and then critical remark from Lloyd Mars. "No pitching," he'd grumble. Rita would nod. "Guy couldn't hit the broadside of a barn," he'd complain when the side struck out. Rita would nod again.

Rita came to think of those times as the 'soft days.' Sweet peace with no bickering. Her father took Sundays to heart. He didn't talk about work. He didn't talk about catching bad guys. Rita often wondered now if it required his brute strength to quell that urge for the hunt. If it was a feat of that magnitude her father never let it show.

Today was that kind of Sunday. The exception was Rita's expecting company. No ball game. No fried chicken. And today, unlike those Sundays of the past, the hunt was on. Roswell was in Rita's office setting up his laptop on a folding table. Laura Palomina was sitting beside Roswell with her laptop. Annie was outside on Rita's porch, smoking and drinking coffee.

"I appreciate both of you coming over to help out today," Rita said to Roswell and Palomina. "I know this was your one and only day off this week, so specially to you, Laura," Rita said to Palomina.

"Happy to help," Roswell said. He took a slug of his Kombucha. Rita felt that sourish carbonation in the back of her throat as she watched Roswell drink. Involuntarily her face puckered with that remembered taste.

"If this can help find Diane, I'm in," Palomina said.

"I have lists of email addresses we need to view today," Rita stated. "I've had Diane's assistant go through the business-related addresses already. Since she already had access as her assistant, she also was familiar with the content from almost all those people. While there were a few with sketchy comments about other people, none were about being friends, asking for a date, getting too personal. The major list then is done. We still have over six hundred that need an eye."

"What if we can't figure out who owns that email." Palomina asked.

"We put those in a separate list for further investigation," Rita replied. "I've downloaded the addresses into spreadsheets.

As you recognize the name, type that in the column beside the address. Roswell is going to review actual emails from any addresses that seem like outliers."

"Mission impossible." Palomina shook her head. "Are you sure we're going to find the kidnapper this way?" Her brow wrinkled and mouth turned downward as if she were going where she didn't want to go. Was that a headshake that followed?

"Hell, no," Rita said. "I don't. What I do know is how Diane operated." She avoided looking at Palomina when she said this. "I believe this is fertile ground for a start. If either of you has an approach they think works better, say so. This isn't a time to quibble about affronted egos and that means mine too. I'm open." Rita looked from Palomina to Roswell. "Then let's get on it. We don't want to be here all night."

After two hours, Rita's attention took on a life of its own and sneaked a peak out the window. Still sunny. Still the inviting breeze. She stood up.

"Let's take a break before we start screaming in boredom." Rita stretched. "We need some sugar to spark our brain cells."

Roswell chimed in "Sugar makes you think you need more sugar. It impairs cognitive function."

"You've never been eighty-five," Annie said. She'd come inside from her smoke break. "Wait til you're my age, young man," Annie said to Roswell and then to Rita, "I'll make a snack tray, honey." She started down the stairs to the kitchen.

"No sugar?" Laura Palomina asked Roswell. "I don't eat a lot because I watch my weight but sugar cane is surely vegan."

"They use bone char to make it white," Roswell said. "I use brown rice syrup or monkfruit for sweetener." He grabbed the backpack he'd brought and pulled out a reusable bag which he tilted toward Palomina. "Try one and see if it doesn't satisfy your sweet tooth. These are peanut butter cookies I made."

"Not bad," Palomina agreed as she chewed. She stood up then. "I think I'm going to exercise my legs. They think I died."

In the kitchen, Annie had taken several snack bowls from Rita's cupboard. In one she had poured corn chips, in another pretzels. Now she was working on the main attraction: Double Stuff Oreos and homemade chocolate chip cookies which she and Bev had baked.

"Oh. My. God," Laura laughed. "I haven't had Oreos in forever."

Rita glanced over. Laura was a good eight years younger. She had kept herself well. She was slim. Had terrific legs that ran upward into a snug but not skin-tight pair of cut-off jeans shorts. She wore a v-neck t-shirt which hinted at cleavage.

Stop right there, Rita said to herself. She looked away and caught Annie watching her. She could feel the blush bloom to her cheeks and could not stop it. Annie, with a frown, slowly turned her head the merest of movement back and forth in disapproval.

"Help me take these upstairs." Annie shoved the cookie plate at Palomina. "You pour the iced teas," she directed Rita.

"Your mom is still sharp," Palomina said as she watched Annie march out of the kitchen.

"She's hanging in there—and she's tough." Rita pulled the iced tea pitcher from the refrigerator and held it under the ice maker for a quick burst of cubes. She walked over to the counter to grab napkins, passing close to Palomina.

As she stood finishing up the iced tea tray, the soft bright scent of perfume stole her attention. The fragrance was floral and she recognized jasmine mixed with a hint of vanilla.

"Can I help you with that?" Palomina asked. Rita's tray was full and a plastic cup tumbled to the floor. They both bent to pick it up.

"I'm good." Rita met Palomina's eyes. She quickly averted her focus to keeping her serving tray stable. "What is that you're wearing by the way?"

"These old jeans?" Palomina laughed.

"The perfume. It's nice," Rita said lamenting how pathetic her compliment sounded.

"Chance," Palomina answered. "Chanel makes it."

"Ahh. Interesting name," Rita replied.

"Very," Palomina said with a laugh.

Rita cleared her throat and turned her attention back to the tasks at hand.

"I'm not the enemy," Palomina said as she and her plate of cookies departed the kitchen and left Rita to her juggling act.

What does that mean, Rita asked herself.

Upstairs in Rita's office, Annie had found a chair and was happily devouring potato chips with mounds of onion dip. Roswell was checking his email and thoughtfully chewing his vegan peanut butter cookies. Palomina, with her earbuds in, tapped her smartphone keys with squared French nail tips.

Rita placed the iced tea tray on her desk. She offered a chilled cup to Annie, then one to Palomina as she ended her phone call. Roswell held up his container of Kombucha to indicate he was passing on the tea.

"I feel like I'm making good progress," Rita said, sliding down into her desk chair and eyeing the work she'd accomplished on her list of emails. "What about you two?" Rita looked from Roswell to Laura Palomina.

"I've gone through more than half the personal emails you gave me," Laura responded. "I know most of these and I made a list of people I didn't recognize and emailed them to Roswell. There were only two out of a hundred and twenty or so."

"I haven't checked the ones you sent me yet," Roswell said to Palomina, his eyes never leaving his screen. He had departed his email and was now booting up his battle game of choice. Suddenly a lush topographical map burst onto the screen in vibrant green and gold and purple. Roswell paused the screen action and turned to Rita.

"I have no outliers on my list so far. Almost all were verified by Diane's assistant. I also did sampling of the actual messages. Business only. Doesn't necessarily mean they couldn't be part of the kidnap but the likelihood is very, very small."

"Yeah, I'm not looking at a business relationship in this case," Rita mused. Her eyes were lowered and still as her head processed her thought.

"Did you send those outliers to Rita too?" Roswell asked Palomina "They could be old relationships, old friends that she'd recognize and you might not."

"Good point." Palomina hovered over her laptop and tapped out an email to Rita with the names. Roswell had set up an alternate wifi route with a hotspot that evaded police scrutiny.

"On my list of personals, I have three names I don't recognize. I also have one that I do recognize but it was someone who has been problematic in the past—an aggressive type who was pissed that Diane broke off their fling." Rita shot a sideways glance at Laura Palomina to detect any reaction. No verbal response, but she spotted a quizzical expression.

"What the heck have you got there?" Annie had walked over to stand beside Roswell who had unpaused his game after Rita finished speaking. She squinted at the speed freak action on Roswell's laptop screen.

"Fortnite," Roswell answered without a hesitation in his online action.

"What is that?" Annie edged closer for a better look.

"It's a survival game," Roswell said as he blasted a figure who had bounded from above. "The idea is to be the last man standing. On that quest, you collect or 'forage' for weapons, healing items and things that can protect you or potentiate your power." As he spoke, Roswell's dashing masked character launched into a high arching leap. He blasted his over-sized automatic weapon as he flew.

Rita joined Annie to watch. Palomina moved behind Rita's shoulder to join Roswell's audience. He deftly guided his leaping on-screen figure in dizzying speed, collecting helpful forageables as he careened from one high point to another. His eyes never left the game as his fingers skittered over the keyboard.

"I'm gettin' dizzy watchin'." Annie shook her head. She stepped back and resumed her interest in the Oreos.

"I could never follow this," Palomina said, putting a hand on Rita's shoulder.

"Nor could I," Rita said. "I've slowed down since my misspent youth."

"I'm sure you'd want your adversaries to think that." Palomina patted Rita with the hand on her shoulder.

Roswell halted his game and exited. "Back to work," he said. "I have a security gig tonight." He checked his watch.

Rita sighed. "Yeah, let's get back to it." She took a last longing look out of the window at a perfect Sunday summer afternoon that was slipping away. "I still have to do my five-miler."

"Want some company?" Palomina asked. "I think I can keep up."

"Uh, well." Rita looked past Palomina and noticed her mother's trademark face of disapproval.

"No problem if you'd rather go it alone," Palomina said. "I had planned to go to the gym after this anyway."

"Thanks," Rita said. "Running is my think time, my alone time. Sorry."

The room fell quiet then except for the occasional clicking of keyboard keys. Shadows crept across the floor as the sun sauntered on its arc toward the horizon. In short order, it would touch the tops of the locust trees that bordered the far end of Rita's property. The pale face of a waxing moon appeared, waiting to take center stage in the night.

"Done." Palomina declared in an hour. She leaned back from her laptop and stretched. "Two more names for us."

"And I have two," Rita said.

"I have one to add," Roswell turned in his seat and reached for his backpack. "I gotta get going to my next gig."

"One sec," Rita said. "Make sure I have everything you two have collected. I believe we have nine we decided to investigate further. One of these," Rita pointed at Palomina, "we can cross off immediately. She drove her classic Trans Am into a bridge a year ago. And another one I know is living in the UK. I'll verify that but looks like we have seven left for serious consideration."

"Lucky seven." Roswell slung his backpack over one shoulder. "Don't email them to me to review." He drew a thumb drive out of his backpack. "I downloaded them. I'll see what kind of messages they've been sending and get back to you." With thumb drive stowed, Roswell saluted Rita, hugged Annie and waved a goodbye to Laura Palomina.

"What a day." Palomina did a long slow backward stretch in her chair.

"You missed it," Annie said. "At least I got to enjoy the sunshine and the breeze."

"This needed to be done," Rita said. "If you're hunting, you take your pleasure in all that it requires. Today we identified our possibles. Now we whittle it down, one by one."

"What if we don't?" Palomina sat up straight. She was looking to Rita for an answer.

"I'm betting we will," Rita responded. "Our lead is in this list of seven. I feel it."

"Sure hope you're right," Palomina said. She shut down her laptop and closed the lid. "I've talked to the cops or my police contact every day. They have nothing."

"I think Bolton has let his ego take over. He's so intent on punishing me, he's left Diane's disappearance on the back burner."

"On that I couldn't agree more." Palomina packed her laptop and stood. "Gotta go to the gym." She turned to Rita. "I sure as hell hope this goes somewhere fast. It's been a week now with nothing coming from that initial sighting. I get worried that the crazy who has Diane will hurt her or even kill her."

"I think of that every minute," Rita said. "Never out of my thoughts."

Palomina departed and the house was quiet again. Annie started gathering the half-empty snack bowls and iced tea glasses.

"Mom, just rest. I'll take care of cleaning up." Rita stared out the window that overlooked the front of her property and her driveway. She watched Palomina's car roll down the asphalt and shoot onto the main road.

"I got this," Annie said. She disappeared down the steps with an armful of dishes.

Rita joined her in the kitchen with the plates and napkins and glasses Annie had been unable to carry. "I printed out the list of the magnificent seven. Wanna see?"

"Sure." Annie sidled up to Rita who had laid a sheet of paper on the counter.

"You dated that girl!" Annie pointed at a name.

"Yep."

"Oh my." Annie turned to Rita. "And is that the same . . . ?"

"Sure is. The very same Chris I left. I met Diane the next month. Chris still holds a grudge and thinks I was cheating on her with Diane."

"Not true." Annie shook her head.

"Try telling her that," Rita said.

Chapter 17

Chevy Chase Recreation Center. Where else would you see a warning sign that high heels damage rubber play surfaces or have the luxury of folding chairs to watch a softball game. And nowhere else would you play ball on real grass with a field shaded by old growth trees. Almost every other softball site run by DC Parks and Rec was a bald, parched patch with metal bleachers and no haven from afternoon sun.

"Isn't this lovely." Annie slid out of Rita's Jeep.

Just a few yards in front of them was the field where a tall blonde pitcher stood atop the mound hurling underhand warmup pitches to her catcher. At each pitch, the woman would eye her target and then suddenly windmill a screeching throw that thunked securely into the waiting catcher's mitt.

"Lookin' good, baby." The catcher was a black woman with a roll of flesh that yanked on her game shirt and lopped over her shorts. She removed the ball from her glove, and with the grace of a prima ballerina, the catcher sprang from behind the plate. With uninterrupted fluid motion, she launched a perfect throw squarely into the pitchers' waiting mitt. The agility of a woman carrying that baggage always surprised Rita.

Rita glanced toward each dugout. Women in red and white pinstripes were huddled on one side as a player-coach in the middle of the circle assigned starting positions. On the opposite side, women in blue shorts and white t's milled about, chatting in groups of three or four. Rita motioned to Annie that she was headed to the players in blue. Annie sauntered over to a wooden folding chair in the most shaded area behind the diamond.

"See you ladies haven't gotten any more organized since I left," Rita said as she approached the dugout. A grin lit up her face.

"Oh, my god," said the redhead with a catcher's mask hugging the top of her head.

"Come back to watch us win?" Another voice chimed in.

"Came back to see the pride of DC women's softball." Rita ducked into the dugout. She knew a few of the women playing, but there were a lot of new faces, younger faces. For a moment, Rita felt a pang of sadness. Softball, the fun, the togetherness of her team, all behind her now. She would not be going back.

"Angel!" Rita called to a dark-haired woman at the far end of the dugout. She was a hint taller than Rita, but not as thin. She was also younger. Her arms tightly defined with daily workouts. She had her ball cap on backwards and was busy changing sneakers to cleats. She had not noticed Rita's entry.

"Girl," Angel said, "it's been a long time." She held out her arms and the two hugged. Angel smelled of sweat and beer and Juicy Fruit gum. "Heard you quit the *Star*." Angel held her friend by her shoulders even as they broke from the embrace as if inspecting her friend for changes.

"Time to do something different." Rita looked into Angel's face. "Need to ask you some questions."

"I heard about Diane." Angel released her hold on Rita and sat back down to change her other shoe. "Any progress on that?"

"Nada." Rita picked up Angel's mitt and punched it a few times as she waited for Angel to finish.

"Really? No suspects at all?" Angel stood and held her hand out to recover her mitt.

"That's why I'm here actually," Rita said.

"I'm a suspect?" Angel's voice went up an octave. "You think I had something to do with her disappearance?" Angel slipped her hand into the ball glove retrieved from Rita. With short blunt blows, she struck the leather pocket like boxing jabs.

"Not really," Rita said. "But I know Diane made overtures toward you."

Angel turned her face away from Rita. She stared out though the dugout screening across the ball field.

"I'm not here to embarrass you or accuse you. I'm hoping you might know of anyone that either I didn't know about or somebody you know who might have carried a grudge about being pursued and dumped." A whistle sounded at home plate.

"Walk with me," Angel said and led Rita out across the infield. Her voice resumed a normal volume without her earlier defensive edge.

"Do you know anything? Anything at all," Rita asked. "The cops think I did her in. Been dogging my every move."

"Well, that's just absurd," said Angel.

"I need your help."

Angel, head down, turned just before she and Rita reached the team gathered around home plate. "Diane started calling me just after you two broke up. Invited me to dinner. I'd heard the stories. I went." Angel raised her face to Rita though she looked past her instead of meeting her eyes. "If I had wanted to go out with somebody, it would have been you."

Rita felt the flush creep upward from her neck and she looked away. She could see Annie relaxing in the spectator chairs beyond the backstop. She took a breath. "Thanks, Angel."

Angel gave a short, embarrassed grin and held out her arms. "Take care of yourself, baby. If I can help, I will. I want you to know that," she said as the women wrapped arms around each other in a quick hug.

"You have my cell number?" Rita asked.

"I got your number," Angel laughed. "Stay for the game. We can have a beer after."

"Got my mom with me tonight." Rita pointed to Annie. "Stay in touch."

Annie had leaned back in her folding chair and closed her eyes. Spectators rambled in and began to fill the seats around the softball diamond. Rita waved to a few she knew as she made her way to her mother. Softly she touched her mother's arm.

"Oh, sorry," Annie said with the groggy voice of sleep. "Musta dozed off. Find out anything?"

"Yep. Found out I gotta move on to the next one." Rita glanced back at Angel who had taken her position at first base. She'd never suspected Angel's attraction.

♏

Rita and Annie rode in silence. The orange August sun washed the horizon in a farewell blaze of color. Annie was getting tired. Rita could tell by the way she slumped in her seat.

"Mom, this won't take long," Rita said.

"Takes what it takes," Annie yawned. "Can you stop and get me a coffee and a little sugar before we make your next stop? Need a little pick me up."

It was the last, late flow of rush hour. Even Rita had that nagging weight of late afternoon fatigue. At her desk at the *Star*, she'd kept a bag of Chips Ahoy for moments like these. She smiled to herself as her image of working at her desk in the newsroom wafted into her memory. She suddenly jolted into the present when Annie joyously pointed and announced a sighting.

"Dunkin' Donuts." Annie's thin, arthritic hand, finger extended, almost grazed the windshield.

"Dunkin' at three o'clock," Rita said as she dodged into the right lane. She rolled the Jeep into the drive-through. "Know what you want?"

"Small coffee, cream, three sugars. Two crème filled donuts." Annie ducked forward so that she could read the menu board near the order microphone.

"Mom, let's do one donut. Those crème things are a heart attack with powdered sugar on top. We're going to eat dinner when I get finished with the next interview."

"I'm savin' one." Annie had shaken off her listlessness and was energized by the prospect of a big dose of sugar.

"You have to promise to save it for later." Rita spoke her order into the small metal box from which a blurred voice announced its uninspired offer of service.

Rita punched an address into her GPS.

"Where we off to?" Annie had devoured her first donut and was sipping her coffee.

"Down into Baltimore City. Waverly." Rita nudged her accelerator to 70. "I promised our next interviewee I'd be there before seven o'clock."

"Anybody I'd know?" Annie stared wistfully at the lonely crème-filled at the bottom of her bag. She took a sidelong glance at Rita whose eyes were focused on the road and traffic.

"You met her a few times. Kate Miller. The nurse?" Rita was wishing now she'd arranged to meet Kate tomorrow. The drive back from DC was going to be a grueling trip on I-95. More than an hour later, she eased into a parking space two blocks from Kate's house.

The Waverly neighborhood stood at the north central perimeter of Baltimore City. In the early days of the city, the area was a tiny village along York Road known as Huntingdon. Wealthy residents began building summer cottages there in the late 19th century. To avoid confusion with other places using the Huntingdon name, the village was named for Sir Walter Scott's novel Waverly.

The Waverly neighborhood is deeply woven into the history and nostalgia of Baltimore. The third oldest public high school in America, City College, a secondary school for boys was founded there in 1839. On the east side of the community is Ellerslie Avenue, former site of Municipal Stadium, the football stadium where the great Johnny Unitas and the Baltimore Colts played in their glory days and later Memorial Stadium which both the Colts and the Baltimore Orioles baseball team called home field. Hardly a mile to the west are the offices of Johns Hopkins University.

The neighborhood is and has always been in the forefront of activism and counterculture. It was Waverly which hosted Baltimore's first Gay Pride Day celebration. Even now residents call the main street, Lavender Lane, where a thriving population of women live.

"Mom, we're a couple of blocks from where I need to go." Rita turned from the steering wheel to face her mother. "I don't like leaving you out here by yourself but we'd have to walk."

"I'll be OK." Annie unclicked her seat belt. "And it's too durn hot to sit in the car."

Together the two trudged up the block. Rita linked her arm in her mother's. "Tupac used to live one street over."

"Two packs? I don't even finish one cigarette." Annie gave an evil eye look at her daughter.

"Tupac, Mom. Tupac Shakur, the rapper."

"And you would think I know him, why?" Annie kept up her brisk pace to match Rita's stride.

At last Rita stopped in front of a two-story rowhome. The houses in this area were built in the early 1900's, reminiscent of English working-class neighborhoods. The difference here was that the houses were wider, had porches and windows in every room that permitted far more daylight than their earlier, dark counterparts.

A woman in splotched painter pants and a paint-streaked white t-shirt opened the door to Rita's knock. She had been baking. The sweet smell of cake wafted to the front door.

"'Bout gave you up," said the woman. "Come on in. I can't talk too long. I need to get to hospice while Cyn is still awake."

"Kate, this is my mom," Rita said. "Think you two met way back when."

"I remember you," Kate said to Annie as she gave her a hug.

"And I'm sorry to hear about Cyndi," Rita said. "I just needed to touch base with you about whether you had any contact with Diane in the last week or even the last month. Police aren't making much headway."

"Rita," Kate said with fatigue heavy in her voice, "I've been taking care of Cyndi and that's all I've been doing. She's been in hospice for four days now and not much time left."

"I understand. Just trying to run down a lead somewhere. We have nothing and with time passing, I worry we're never going to find her." Rita felt the words stumbling out of her mouth. This woman's partner was dying of breast cancer and Rita was here bugging her.

"Diane and I had a thing once," Kate said as she beckoned for her visitors to follow her into the kitchen. "Once is what I want to emphasize. Before you. She was a little too calculating for me though and that was that." Kate had already frosted her cake. Now she cut it in half and nestled one portion into a foil tent. The remainder she settled onto a glass cake plate and rested its matching glass dome on top.

"I know I'm a noodge, but any shred might be important. A person, a comment, anything even if it seemed at the time to be nothing." Rita could feel herself tiptoeing around the edges of coercion and badgering. She swallowed hard.

Kate was packing up, including the cake she was taking to her partner. "Rita, the only person I heard say anything about Diane was your ex, Chris. We ran into each other grocery shopping after the news about Diane's disappearance."

Rita held her breath. Annie's attention gravitated to Kate like a magnet to steel. "What did she say?" Rita could not stop the tremor in her voice.

"She said that it served Diane right. Said she had no sympathy and hoped she was never found." Kate flung a backpack across her shoulder and picked up the canvas bag which she'd packed with the foil wrapped cake on top.

As Rita and Annie were on their way back home, Rita had to remind herself to stop punching the accelerator. Chris Killigan refused to speak to Rita for more than a year after their break-up. She was a woman with a short fuse, an activist for the homeless, a person who could hold a grudge, a strategist who embraced the concept of scorched earth.

"Think Chris's a likely candidate?" Annie asked as Rita swung the Jeep into her long, uphill driveway.

"I'm thinking a lot of things," Rita answered. "Chris took to heart that saying 'if they won't see the light, make 'em feel the heat.'"

"I never knew she was like that." Annie clasped her crème donut bag as she waited for Rita to unlock the door.

"I saw plenty of it." Rita swung the door open and waited for Annie to enter.

"Like what?" Annie asked.

"Like when the Baltimore City Council voted down some measures Chris and her group wanted passed, she organized night gatherings at the homes of the members who voted no. People sang or chanted all night. It was miserable for everybody and it just made the nay-sayers dig in."

"Oh, my," Annie said as she put her donut bag on the counter and peeked in.

"Let me get you a decent dinner and then we'll have dessert in front of the tv." Rita pointed at the grease-stained bag.

"Weren't you afraid of her—a little bit?" Annie rolled the top of the bag to close it again.

"No, not really. Whatever crazy revenge she's taken on politicians, it's never been about physical violence." Rita pulled salad makings out of the fridge.

"I'm hearing a 'but' in your tone," Annie observed.

Rita said nothing yet a reservation had sprung from her subconscious into the arena of possibility. *This is your life, Rita Mars.* She reconsidered the women she'd met with that day. Years compressed to mere minutes of meeting like walking the gauntlet. In that rear-view mirror of memory, the intensity diminished to an emotional speck and it made her want to cry.

Chapter 18

Another Monday meeting at the Whitlock Foundation. As usual, Marianne was the first to arrive. Rita noticed in prior sessions Marianne would come in almost an hour early and sit in the empty conference room. She would read notes she'd already made and sometimes edit what she'd established as topics for discussion. She was a tea drinker, an Earl Grey fan, and Marianne would go through several cups as she sat alone to prepare for her staff meeting.

Louise would still be in her office, door closed. Today, Rita heard voices as she passed. One voice was young, eager. She surmised it was the ambitious and newly graduated assistant to Louise. Rita heard the words "chance to shine" and then Marianne's name. She thought little of it and walked on down the hallway to her closet of an office space.

It was another dog-day morning with a heated haze already draped over the city. She glanced out of the window to watch two homeless men attempting to negotiate breakfast money at the McDonalds on the corner. Inured to the ubiquitous presence and begging, streams of customers looked through the two and entered without acknowledgement. Rita turned back to the cheap metal desk Louise had acquired for her use. She unpacked her computer bag and settled to make her own notes about exploring the companies the Foundation employed.

Rita settled into the world's cheapest desk chair. First and foremost, Mercilus had purchased a model with limited height adjustment. Rita's feet dangled and she knew that after an hour or so, her feet were headed to pins and needles. There were no armrests, which made it tiresome to spend any extended time working at her laptop. Rita reminded herself that she needed to order her own desk chair. She wouldn't be cowed by this cheap trick played by Mercilus.

In the meantime, Rita planned to scour the existing Foundation contracts and make a list, with contact information, of the current vendors. From her first pass at research and feedback from previous suppliers, she'd determined that the entire body of services companies had rapidly turned over once Bill Whitlock passed away and Mercilus had taken over as Marianne's Chief Operations Officer.

Rita's exploration and cataloging came to a halt when she heard Louise and her protégé rustle past her door on the way to the Monday meeting. She started to leave the laptop working, thought again and shut it down. She picked up her machine and took it with her to the meeting.

Marianne smiled and nodded as Rita entered. Mercilus, sitting at her right, presented herself as oblivious and did not acknowledge Rita. Mercilus' protégé avoided direct eye contact as Rita seated herself beside Bunny. However, Rita did see the young woman cast darting glances at her.

Something is running under the surface, Rita said to herself. Time to be still and observant.

Louise Mercilus opened the meeting with her usual update on the state of donations and finances. She mentioned overhead as a contributing factor to reduced donation strength. When she was finished, Louise motioned to the accountant who confirmed Mercilus' comments about the cost of the Foundation doing business. Donations were trending down and some pledges had been adjusted in that same direction.

"I'm going to ask you." Marianne indicated everyone sitting around the conference table. "We have a strong base with people dedicated to supporting our approach to fundraising and to the projects we have in progress. Where is the disconnect?" Marianne looked from one attendee to another.

Rita kept an eye on Mercilus who seemed to be above this discussion as Marianne glanced from the accountant to the head of development.

"I have to dig into this," said Marianne's hand-picked lead on fundraising. "I haven't seen any decline in willingness to donate, so I'd like to know more about who's scaling back and why. I feel that I've been on top of our efforts, so this takes me by surprise. I will work on this today and report back to you in the morning," she said to Marianne.

Marianne skipped over Bunny, who was her personal assistant and had no working involvement in raising money. She also skipped over Rita. The young man in charge of social media gave his update. He reported that he'd seen no negatives about the Foundation and that the donor follower numbers actually grew in the last quarter.

It was then Louise's assistant cleared her throat. Rita still had her eye on Mercilus, who she saw nod ever so slightly at the young woman about to speak.

"Why don't you share what you've been working on," Louise said to her assistant.

"I've been doing some work on this as I've noticed the downward shift," the woman said as she stood to report. "We have a lot of people on staff now, full timers. That's a lot of operating expense. Just the kind of thing non-profits struggle with."

"And you think you might have a solution?" Marianne asked. "Let's hear it." Everyone swiveled in their seats to offer their complete attention.

"Over time, I've been making a list of thoughts about a situation like this." Mercilus' assistant reached into the folder in front of her and pulled out the exact number of pages as attendees. She distributed them around the table.

"Why don't you stand," Mercilus advised as her helper began to explain the five items on her list. The young woman grinned and rose from her seat.

Rita read the list the woman had prepared. She pulled a pen from the notebook she'd brought with her to the meeting and started annotating the "ideas."

"So, at the top, I have stated the obvious—we stand to save a significant amount of money if we move from employees to volunteers for administrative functions." The young woman looked up to see response.

"What percentage—or dollar amount—of existing overhead does that savings amount to?" Rita asked. Bunny's foot touched Rita's and Rita caught her approving smile.

"Well, I haven't gotten to an exact amount. I was waiting until I got approval before I started doing the math. I do know that by using volunteers for more administrative functions, non-profits in this country have been generating as much as a 20% savings boost."

"And the risk factors involved?" Rita's voice was even. She wasn't going to provoke a pissing contest.

"Can we get through the list before we begin the pros and cons?" The protégé was impatient and eager to finish her personal performance for Marianne.

"Absolutely." Rita scribbled again on her copy of the money-saving recommendations.

♏

Bunny Blythe-Cramer's main office was in the home of Marianne Whitlock. From that location, she managed Marianne's calendar, arranged her travel and herded all the cats that came with Marianne's life of money and responsibility. Bunny also kept a small office in the suite which housed the

Whitlock Foundation administration. She and Rita convened there after the staff meeting.

Rita settled into a brocade wingback beside Bunny's desk. A four-panel room divider with a Van Gogh cherry blossom print sheltered Bunny's personal space from a sunny, wide-open room which lead to Marianne's flower garden. Prominent on Bunny's desk were individual photos of her two daughters, each with husband and children.

"I saw you taking a hell of lot of notes." Bunny rested an over-sized canvas tote beside her desk and turned to the coffee maker behind her desk chair.

"I have to give credit where it's due." Rita nodded as Bunny held up an extra mug in a suggested offering of coffee.

"What does that mean?" Bunny switched the coffeemaker's "on" button. "From the perspective of my ignorance about the recommendations presented, I kept thinking these seemed like good resource management. I started to doubt my suspicions about Louise."

"And that was the whole point of that performance," Rita said with a cynical smile.

"Performance? I hope you're going to explain that."

"First," Rita said. "I need to let you know that I overheard bits and pieces of a conversation between Louise and Ms. MBA." Rita leaned back in the chair beside Bunny's desk. She repeated the words she knew she'd correctly recognized as she passed Mercilus' closed door.

"Ok, but how does that make you more certain of your

suspicions? It seems like a conversation any mentor would have with a favorite newbie."

"Of course it did." Rita laughed. "But I will tell you that you and I witnessed one of the most artful pieces of Kabuki I think I've ever seen."

Bunny stood to prepare the coffees. "I want to hear this explanation. Let's get our coffee first."

Coffee in hand, Rita resumed her seat and took a sip before she dissected what she had dubbed "theater" to Bunny. She opened her notebook and drew out the talking points paper Louise's assistant had handed out.

"Item one," Rita began, "is the hook. Louise tells us via her assistant that admin cost is dragging down the amount of money that actually gets to charities. Every legitimate charity's goal is to maximize funds going to programs while minimizing the expense of raising those funds. Financial efficiency is the name of the game."

"Yes, but that seems pretty conventional to me."

"The second item is a recommendation: engage volunteers to perform more administrative functions."

"Non-profits do that though."

"Which brings us to item number three," Rita said. "The assistant introduced episodic scheduling. The presentation did not mention whether these recruits are local and on-site or whether they are virtual. The bottom line though is that in performing work piecemeal, broken into slivers of a program or just a day or two of keying input, no one person has overall knowledge of a program or how it fits into the

Whitlock mission or if transactions are on the up-and-up. Additionally if the volunteers work remotely, this is even more cover for fraudulent actions. An easy divide and conquer scheme."

Bunny sat back in her chair. She said nothing. Rita could sense the gears whirring in Bunny's head.

"I would have had no idea unless you explained," Bunny commented in a quiet voice, shaking her head as she spoke.

"That's the whole point," Rita said. "And one more thing. This was an incredibly smart move on Mercilus' part. She talks her assistant into making the suggestions. That way if Marianne doesn't like it, it reflects on the presenter and not on Louise."

"Never even thought of that," Bunny said.

"That might not have occurred to me either if I hadn't overheard the conversation before the meeting." Rita took a sip of her coffee.

"I'm trying to wrap my head around this." Bunny looked to Rita. "Do you think Louise has done this before?"

"I'd bet the farm on it. It's too smooth, too polished not to be."

"I'm afraid to ask about the last two recommendations."

"In item four, the assistant suggested 'in-kind' compensation," Rita stated. "That action makes employees out of those volunteers according to tax law and the Foundation would find itself in IRS hot water. The last suggestion made is an accounting trick that in essence fudges the Administrative Expense Ratio—pretty much it's lying about the amount of money that actually gets to the charity."

Bunny took a deep breath. "What do we do next? I'm not sure we can convince Marianne of the situation at this point. She's too trusting of Louise—and too reliant."

"If we go to Marianne now, I think she'll ask a few questions; Louise will smooth things over and that will be the end of it. No, this requires hard evidence we don't have yet. That's why getting the assistant to pimp those recommendations was genius. Louise can slough off any of our suspicions as way too harsh on a new employee still learning the ways non-profits work but nonetheless trying to help the organization."

Bunny nodded. "I see that. But what do we do to keep Louise from burning down the house before we get ourselves in position to stop it?"

"I've been thinking about that," Rita said. "One question— how long has Louise been Marianne's most trusted advisor?"

"She's been here for about fourteen months." Bunny leaned across her desk.

"Then the con should be rising to a crescendo," Rita said. "The average con has legs for about eighteen months before it implodes. Right now, today, we saw some of the first wobbles in this house of cards. She's moving to the end game."

"You're scaring me," Bunny said. "Can we get ahead of this?"

"You have to trust me on this," Rita cautioned her. "You can't start signaling little telltale warnings to Marianne or making insinuating remarks in private or in meetings. Mercilus is focused on me right now as someone who just might start saying the empress has no clothes. If she thinks we all know, she'll bolt. We want to shut her down and leave no opening for her to escape. Are you with me on that?"

"I am." Bunny held up her coffee cup in salute. She thought for a moment.

"But . . ." Rita noted the hesitation.

"Not sure it's a 'but.'" Bunny held Rita with her eyes. "What if she gets away with it? What if she runs off and drags the Foundation down with the bad press if it gets out? What if . . ."

Rita stood. "There are a million possibilities. We're aware of them. Our greatest risk is if we do nothing."

"I know. I'm just nervous?" Bunny asked.

"'If you know the enemy and know yourself, you need not fear the result of a hundred battles.'"

"Wow, did you just make that up?" Bunny asked.

"Not me," Rita laughed. "And I have to get out of here. I need to get back to my office."

♏

Rita slid into the driver's seat of her Jeep. The parking garage had filled since she arrived. The concrete was already soaking up the August sun. Though this side of the structure was shaded, the air was thick and sticky. She switched on the A/C and then the radio to an oldies station.

Tears for Fears was singing "Everybody Wants to Rule the World." Rita shook her head. She wished she felt as warrior confident as she'd portrayed to Bunny. Louise Mercilus had pulled this trick before and Rita suspected many more times than once. She speculated that Mercilus had perfected her act, much the way an elusive serial killer adjusts and tweaks until he gets his butchery just right. She had been on hunts like this. She'd won many. Still there were opponents who had slipped the trap whether by misstep or by happenstance.

Rita nosed the Jeep out into traffic. Keep the faith, Rita thought to herself. Every case she'd ever battled to win began with a question to herself: Is it possible there was no nefarious activity and she'd simply misinterpreted the situation? Once in the trenches, she would rise to the task and questioning herself would fall away. The thrill of the chase, the belief she could win, would take over her head and nothing would deter her will.

Chapter 19

There is a universal smell to cheap motel rooms. Pine oil disinfectant, old carpets and stale air from aging HVAC room units. Outside is the incessant rumble of highway traffic with the occasional blast from an eighteen-wheeler's horn.

Diane's eyes opened. Without turning her head, she glanced to her right. Her abductor was buried under the bed's cheesy comforter. The A/C, which had chilled the room all night, had given over to a dwindling effort. The room had warmed and Diane speculated it would be too hot to stay inside as the day wore on.

She had to pee. She was still wearing the shorts and camp shirt that were the only change of clothes in the suitcase she brought with her. Could she get up and make a run? Her abductor had lodged the room's desk chair under the doorknob as extra security. Diane estimated she'd have to fling the chair back and flee in one desperate move.

The figure in the next bed shifted but did not rise. Diane held her breath as she waited to see if the kidnapper was going to get out of bed. The longer she waited, the more she needed to get to the bathroom.

Damn, Diane said to herself. I've waited too long. She slid out of her bed. It was only one step to the bathroom in this tiny space. She decided to see what her chances might be now. She did not flush but instead edged close to the door to look out into the room. The body in the occupied bed seemed not to have moved.

Diane squeezed her eyes tight as she inched the door open. The motel room faced east and daylight had seeped in between the slats of the big window. Slivers of evenly spaced sun betrayed years of wear across the carpet. Luck was with her. The shabby hollow door to the bathroom made no sound as it swung back softly on its hinges.

Diane stepped off the tile onto the coarse old rug. She tried not to think of that scummy, crunchy surface on her bare feel. She had decided against shoes—too much time to retrieve them and too much added motion in the room.

She reached the window. Now she was within one more step to the door. Instinctively she shot a glance over her shoulder. No movement from the occupied bed. Diane reached for the doorknob.

"Not goin' out, are you?" The lumpish figure under the comforter still had not changed position.

"Looking outside," Diane answered. She fought to keep her tears to herself and her voice from wavering.

"Good thing you're not tryin' to leave. Come on over here." The body in the bed turned.

"I need to go back to the bathroom," Diane said quickly. "I forgot to flush."

"Don't try anything," the abductor said. "I ain't asleep. And when I am, I'm a mouse whisper from wakin' up."

"Got it." Diane retreated to the bathroom where she sat on the toilet, head in hands, and let a hot stream of tears roll down her face.

♏

Rita dipped her Jeep onto the underground parking ramp. The afternoon sun had toasted the interior of her vehicle and the short stint from her office parking lot with the A/C at full tilt had done little to mitigate the heat. The Jeep sidled down the concrete corridor as Rita kept an eye out for an open spot. She rolled higher tier by tier. Mercifully she was able to dart into a slot before being forced onto the open roof's last-ditch chance to park.

"I'm sweating like a pig," Rita grumbled. She slammed the Jeep's door and walked to the garage elevator.

"Afternoon, Mz. Mars." The middle-aged black doorman in khakis and white polo grinned and grabbed Rita's hands in both of his. "Happy to see you, sweetheart woman. Been too long since I see you."

"Ajani!" Rita said. "Too long! I hope you are well and that your girlfriends are beautiful."

"Mz. Chris says bad things about you to me. I don't believe them. She can be *wahala*."

"Yes, she can be trouble. But she did agree to see me today. Not sure what to expect though."

"She working from home today. You need help. You text me. I come up and interrupt for you." Ajani laughed. "Save you from the devil." He laughed again.

"Hope I don't need that," Rita said and hugged him.

Rita walked through the high-rise lobby. Air conditioning was full on here and she shivered. There were no restrooms in the lobby—they'd been removed to dam the tide of homeless humanity who had nowhere to go out on the streets. Rita pulled a ragged tissue from her pants pocket and dabbed her face. She glanced at her wavering image cast on the mirrored brass walls of the elevator and sighed. She was sweaty, her camp shirt clung to her breasts and her khakis had all the crispness of wet laundry.

The elevator ride was slow and hesitant. It sparked memory of the joy of first moving in with Chris. All smiles and stolen kisses. The happy thought though soon morphed to Rita's moving out. The last ride down to the lobby. The anger. The tears. The pain.

Rita stood at what used to be her door to home. She swallowed and steadied herself. She knocked. Chris had been waiting, expectant, as the door opened instantly.

"I'm working," Chris said with the slightest waver in her voice. "I have a conference call in an hour." She turned as if she assumed Rita would follow. She did.

"Coffee?" Chris asked. "Just made some. It's good Sumatra."

Rita's favorite of coffees. A fleeting thought: was this special for me? Or maybe this is the coffee her new partner likes?

"How have you been?" Rita walked into the tiny kitchen and poured a cup. She took a breath of that deep earthy aroma.

"So, you only gave me a few sentences on what you're here for. I heard Diane got herself kidnapped. What's the back story? Revenge? Jilted lover? Ransom?" Chris ignored Rita's question about her welfare.

"I'm meeting with some women who knew Diane and who we all used to hang with."

"You mean women who had more than enough reason to want her scalp?" Chris watched Rita squirm.

"Yes." Rita's voice was firm in spite of herself.

"And you honestly think I would do an insane thing like take out a love rival?" Chris shook her head. "Do you really believe me capable of violence? After all the time we lived together. After every damned self-doubting secret of my soul I shared in pillow talk? Tell me. Look me in the eye and tell me you think I could be the person who could do harm to someone else." Chris held Rita's gaze with a commanding look like a mad scientist pinning a specimen.

"No." Rita could feel the heat of embarrassment flushing her neck and rising to her face. "No, I don't. But you know well enough that in any search, you follow every single sign, even if you find it low on probability of success. Every detail counts, even if it's to rule out a possibility."

Chris looked away.

"I'm not accusing you. I need your help." Rita swallowed hard. "I know you're angry with me. I don't deny I didn't try as hard as I could have to put us back together." Involuntarily a tear welled in Rita's eye. She swiped it immediately.

Chris looked down. She blinked as her eyes seemed to mirror the gears shifting in her head.

"And I was pissed that you didn't want to do the work. I let my anger take over. I wanted to punish you." Chris looked straight at Rita with those words. "I wounded us beyond repair."

"I'm sorry for my part," Rita said. The tear returned and once again, she brushed it away.

"The biggest mistake of my life." Chris walked to the high-rise window, away from Rita.

"Touching another person's life seems so easy at first." Rita approached her former partner. "We jump in with excitement and energy and expectation."

Chris nodded but did not turn around. Rita stood beside her and put a comforting arm around her shoulder.

"And all that passion, like a four-alarm fire," Chris said. "When the dust settles, sometimes that's all that's left—the dust."

"I'm so sorry for causing pain," Rita said and turned Chris to face her. Rita pulled her close. No holding back the tears now.

"And I am too." Chris's voice trembled with her weeping. "And at this point, we've both moved on." The last words choked out.

Rita held Chris close as they both let themselves feel. Rita opened her closed eyes. A high-flying seagull meandered across the roof tops of nearby buildings. It was alone, soaring actively now and then gliding on the thermals. Would it were that humans had no gift of personal thought, Rita considered. It is our heads, the emotional life with which we were imprinted that rule our responses. People believe they have free will but the more humanity Rita encountered, the more she believed people trick themselves into assuming they are in command.

"My nose is running onto your shirt." Chris gave a little laugh. She started to pull away from Rita's embrace, but Rita held her.

"What's a little snot between friends?" She squeezed Chris tighter. That pressing against familiar flesh ignited memory. Lazy Sundays drinking coffee and reading together on the sofa. Sunny days at the beach. Long summer nights with windows open and the songs of locusts mixed with whippoorwill calls. For just a moment, Rita wanted to jump the track, go back and try again.

Chris pulled away and went to her coffee table to return with a box of tissues. She took some and offered the box to Rita.

"Didn't mean to get all teary with you." Chris's voice was softer now, losing its combative tone.

"Don't apologize," Rita said. Her head regained balance, restoring her to the here and now.

After much sniffling and blowing of noses, Chris spoke. "I honestly don't know how I can help you with the Diane business. I hadn't even seen her since we broke up—until about two weeks ago."

"You saw her?" Rita's attention pivoted to the news. "Where? Was she with somebody?"

"Saw her down at the Inner Harbor on the promenade. She was walking with some hulk of a woman." Chris sauntered into her kitchen to dispose of the tissues.

"Not somebody you knew?" Rita asked. "Can you describe the woman?"

"Big ole girl. I saw her and thought 'rugby player'. Definite butch." Chris stopped. "You think that person kidnapped her?"

"Let me make notes." Rita slid her cell phone from her slacks pocket and pulled up an app. "Any guesses on height, weight?" Chris described the woman with prompts from Rita.

"You know," Rita said, "you just might have opened the door to finding out what happened to Diane." She saved her notes and slid the cell phone back in place.

"If I have," Chris ventured, "does this mean I won't see you again?"

Rita reached for her hand and drew her close. She could smell the flower-scented shampoo in Chris's hair and buried her face in its fragrance.

"It does not mean that," she said, all the while seeing herself as ambivalent and not a woman who returned to re-try feats of failure.

Chris, with Rita's prompts, recalled as much as she could from the day she'd spied Diane and the accompanying woman strolling around Baltimore's Inner Harbor. That woman was tall and heavy and towered over the tiny frame of Diane. As she said several times in her attempts to remember, this person was not the usual type Diane had been known to pursue.

♏

"I've got something." Rita was breathless as she blurted into her cell phone. From the moment Chris had revealed she'd seen Diane with a stranger, Rita had been antsy to hurl herself into tracking down the identity of that stranger.

"Who? What? Slow down, baby," Bev advised her.

"I was checking into the next to last person on my list of women to question. I saw Chris . . ."

"Chris? Like as in your ex twice removed?" Bev asked.

"Yeah, yeah," Rita pushed on. "She saw her with somebody."

"Who saw who with who?"

"Diane. Chris saw an unfamiliar woman with her—with Diane. I gotta find out who that was. It could be the link."

"The link to finding Diane?" Bev was trying to confirm what she thought she was hearing.

"Yes." Rita was impatient with Bev's inability to grasp what she was saying.

"Hey, I'm trying to get this straight."

"I'm sorry. I'm excited. This could be a big deal. This could be a breakthrough." Rita spoke more slowly.

"What can I do to help?" Bev had been through these drills before. She knew she would be the even hand, a steadying influence.

"I'm on my way to Diane's office. I want to sit down with Lakshmi again, run the description by her. And I'd like you to touch base with Diane's sister, her mother. I'm texting the stranger's description to you."

"How 'bout Miz Six O'clock News?"

"Yeah, I'll touch base with her." Rita said quickly. "I gotta go."

"No theatrics," Bev said.

"None," Rita promised. She punched the keyless ignition and the Jeep screamed backward out of the parking space.

♏

"You gonna be in there all day?" Diane's abductor growled as she stood by the motel room's bathroom door.

Diane opened the door, and as she did, a paw of a hand pushed hard. Diane was caught unprepared and the corner of the door barely missed her big toe. She lay on her bed on her back. She stared at the cheap fiberboard ceiling tiles above her head, all the while wondering if she had the time to unbolt the outside door and flee.

Before she could decide, the woman emerged from the bathroom and came over to sit on Diane's bed.

"Hey," the abductor said as she traced the outline of Diane's face with a calloused index finger. The woman leaned down for a kiss. Diane, eyes open, turned her face away.

"Come here." The woman gripped Diane's chin in a forceful hold. She bent down and pressed her lips against Diane's.

Diane closed her eyes and pulled against the powerful grip but her abductor was too strong. "I'm not ready," Diane said.

"Oh, yeah?" Her captor spit at her. "You were plenty hot for me when we spent all that time talkin' in the garage." She referred to the conversations Diane had engaged her in when they'd first started talking in the underground garage below Diane's office building.

For a split second, Diane debated whether to say she'd never meant things to go far. She decided against it in favor of her physical safety.

"I'm just not ready," Diane said. "We're still getting to know each other."

"Well, you'd better hurry up and know me," the captor muttered. She yanked Diane's chin so they faced each other. "Yer gettin' to be more trouble than you're worth."

Chapter 20

Rita launched the Jeep onto St. Paul Street. Traffic was light but slow. A restaurant supply truck usurped a lane as the driver hauled the evening specials into a tiny vegan eatery. She inched along on the one open lane of St. Paul until she, cursing to herself as she drove, sped beyond the bottleneck. She checked the time. Not the eternity she had expected.

"Thanks so much for seeing me on short notice," Rita said as Lakshmi invited her inside her office.

"You said you had something to go on?" Lakshmi rose quickly from her desk. "You have a picture or a name?" She pointed to the love seat where Diane's clients and associates would wait for their turn to meet with her.

"I have a description and only that. I'm hoping that will spark a memory of somebody who might fit it." Rita sat on the edge of the loveseat, eager to the edge of desperation.

"I'll try," Lakshmi said with some hesitation in her voice.

"It's a woman . . ." Rita started.

"A woman? Oh." Lakshmi's brows furrowed into a frown.

"You haven't seen her with anyone you didn't know or at least recognize?" Rita asked as she slid her cell phone out of a back pocket.

"No, at least I can't think of anybody. You don't have a picture?"

"We don't have that luxury," Rita responded. "Bear with me on this. I want you to give thought to the details I was able to extract from the person who saw Diane two weeks ago with an unknown."

"Is this description of the person who snatched her?" Lakshmi held a plastic water bottle that she twisted open and closed over and over without taking a drink.

"I don't know, Lakshmi, but we have to follow every single possibility. Think of it as a thousand-piece jigsaw puzzle. One by one, we eliminate the pieces that don't work and every discard brings us closer to the right piece." Rita flashed her phone on and pulled up her notes app.

Lakshmi squeezed the half empty water bottle until the plastic crinkled from the pressure.

"Ok, I'm going to read them to you. Picture each detail. Let it set in." Rita saw that Lakshmi's face was drained, lips tight and her long slender fingers continued to punish her water bottle.

"You can do this," Rita assured her. "And if you will, sit back in your seat. Close your eyes. Picture your favorite spot in all the world. Let the tension in your body relax."

Lakshmi nestled in the corner of the small loveseat and rested her head on the back cushion. As Rita started to speak, Lakshmi shot upright. "What if I'm wrong? What if I miss something? It'll be my fault if something happens to Diane." Lakshmi's eyes were wide, face taut as if she were the one in danger.

"Calm. Being calm will help. Sit back. Think of the special place; close your eyes and take three deep breaths. Tell me when you're ready." Rita reached out and relieved her interviewee of the now crushed water bottle.

"Where's your imagined place?" Rita asked after a few quiet minutes, and she could see the knots and ropes of tension had receded from Lakshmi's arms.

"Hmmm. Walks with my nani in the park near where I grew up." A smile dawned across Lakshmi's lips.

"I want you to think of that place. You are there waiting for Diane to join you. The sky is clear and there is a soft warm breeze. In the distance, you see two women approaching, one very much taller and heavier than the other one. You know immediately that the smaller woman is your boss, Diane. I'm going to describe the other woman to you. Lean back and observe. Don't speak, just nod, if you're ready." Rita watched for the sign.

After a further brief but intricately detailed introduction to the forest environment. Rita segued into the appearance of two women walking side-by-side, holding hands, approaching Lakshmi directly.

"Picture the woman with Diane as a big woman, tall, stout like a football player. You recognize Diane."

Lakshmi nodded.

Rita went through the descriptors provided by her ex, Chris. She spoke slowly with no urgency. Softly without pressure. After each feature, she paused to let Lakshmi set each characteristic in place. When she came to the last identifier, Rita sucked in her own breath. This piece was so definitive that she'd believed all along it would be the identifying detail that would be "the one."

"Lakshmi, you are doing great. I have one last item for you to attach to that figure you've created and then we're done."

Lakshmi nodded.

"It's a tattoo. It is on the left forearm of the woman you've created. It is a heart with a dagger through it. The heart is a Valentine heart, plump and red with a single blood drop. Take a good long look in your mind's eye. If you can visualize the heart, just nod for me." Rita's head raced like a freed dog from a pen. She steadied her voice so as not to disrupt her subject's mental artwork.

"The dagger is gold. The hilt is jeweled and the penetrating blade is silvery."

Lakshmi bolted upright from her reclining position on the loveseat. "That weird girl from the garage?"

Rita involuntarily leapt to her feet. "What girl? What's her name?" She realized she was zoning into that giddy pursuit of discovery. She sat down. Her entire body hummed like a downed wire.

"I don't know." Lakshmi's eyes teared. "I don't know her name."

"The woman with the tattoo works in the garage. The garage under this building?"

Lakshmi nodded. "But I haven't seen her in a while."

"Perfect," Rita said. And she was sure she was on the scent now. "Where's the management for this building?"

♏

Rita discovered the garage was managed separately from the commercial tenants of Diane's building. She was on her way to interview the supervisor for the parking facility. It was late in the day by now and traffic began to build. She didn't have far to go though as the offices were only six blocks over.

Howard Street was once the shining crown of Baltimore retail. Named for a past governor, the address to which Rita now headed was surrounded by noted venues such Johns Hopkins University, The Baltimore Museum of Art, Meyerhoff Symphony Hall and the Maryland Institute of Art.

In years long past, ladies whose husbands lunched at the Mercantile Club would take the streetcar to Hutzler's or Hochschild Kohn or Stewart's to shop. They could browse the fashionable shops of Howard's Antique Row. They could dine at the best of Baltimore at nearby Marconi's, once the haunt of H.L. Mencken, Sinclair Lewis and Lily Pons, or the exotic Brass Elephant, once hailed as the most beautiful restaurant in the city. Those wealthy buyers and sellers are gone now, some buildings never rented, never repaired. Some remained empty shells, left to decay with collapsed roofs and interior walls—homes for rats, crack pads for addicts, signposts of urban decay.

Rita spied an SUV departing a parking spot in front of her destination. She slid the Jeep along the curb, locked the vehicle and was, in minutes, in an elevator on the way to Piedmont Parking Management. She exited the elevator car. The hallway was silent as she padded down the corridor. She paused in front of a door with a frosted glass panel on which was stenciled the company name.

She was immediately in a small waiting area. No one sat at the reception desk and it appeared that it had not had an occupant for some time. No computer screen. The phone was silent. She heard the low tones of a phone conversation through the door to an inner office. She knocked.

"Just a minute. I'll be right with you," called a man's voice.

Rita waited. She studied the black and white photos on the wall that recorded samples of old Baltimore: a perspective shot of the once-famed rowhouse white marble steps, Memorial Stadium, the original food mecca of Lexington Market.

The door to the office opened.

"Mr. Cohen, thanks for agreeing to meet me. I'm Rita Mars. We spoke briefly about twenty minutes ago."

"Come in." Len Cohen was in his forties, Rita gauged. He was fit and stylish in his slim leg cargo pants, a white polo shirt with the company logo, and a pair of grey merino sneakers.

Rita seated herself in front of Cohen's desk. "As I said on the phone, I've been retained by the Winter family to try and locate their daughter, Diane." Rita pulled her Maryland PI license from her wallet and leaned forward to present it.

Cohen took a few minutes, checked the back as if he were familiar with what he was looking for. He nodded without comment and returned the license.

"How can I help you?" Cohen's desk phone rang and he touched a button. "Let me put these calls on silent for a few minutes."

"Thanks." Rita continued as she slid her investigator card back in her wallet. "One of Diane Winter's co-workers saw her about a week ago with a woman identified as an employee of your garage management group. I'd like to speak to that woman about anything she might know regarding Diane's taking off." Rita decided she would couch her interview in terms of Diane's disappearing on her own. She feared the situation could get messy if Cohen knew this was already a police matter.

Cohen did not hesitate though. "I know of the Winter family. Old money. I'm sure they want to be discreet."

"Yes," Rita agreed with relief. "They do."

"You need—what about this employee? I have some concerns about doling out personal info from personnel files."

"My thinking is that Diane might have told your employee something about her state of mind or where she was planning to go to," Rita said. "I certainly understand your reluctance about personal information. I would feel the same. Still, I can't find this needle in the Baltimore City haystack without an assist. Time is of the essence in situations like this. Her family is beside themselves." Rita paused to let her comments settle.

Cohen looked at Rita as though he were assessing her worthiness of trust. Rita said nothing and let the pressure of silence work.

"What's the name, I'll look them up." Cohen touched his PC keyboard.

"Well, here's where I hit the wall. I don't know the woman's name. I was hoping someone who supervised her could give me a name. I have one detail that I hope is distinctive enough for someone to recognize."

"Sounds like a long shot." Cohen's face told Rita he was skeptical. "I don't know everybody like my dad did when he started and ran this business."

"It is," Rita agreed. "The detail I wanted to share though seems unique enough for someone to remember. It's a tattoo." Rita reached for her cell phone. "I found one similar on the internet that I want to show you. According to Diane's co-worker, it was etched on the employee's arm." Rita pulled up a page on her screen. Cohen reached for the phone.

"Yeah. Hard to forget one like that," Cohen said. "I'm not a fan of tattoos but this bleeding heart with the dagger—hard to forget." Rita's heart began to pound.

"Do you remember the name of the owner?"

"Charlene something." Cohen tapped on the keys. "Lived in Highlandtown. Worked here about three years before she took off."

"Any trouble with this person?" Rita asked.

"Not any real trouble. She was kinda odd though. Claimed she was working on a criminal justice degree at University of Baltimore. She didn't seem that sharp though to the guy who supervises our garages for that part of the city." Cohen hit the print key and the laser in the corner zipped out a single sheet of paper.

"I should ask for a subpoena." Cohen retrieved the printout. "But if I were in the same situation as the Winters, I'd want this handled on the quiet."

"True," Rita said, hoping to escape the office with the paper before Cohen thought about it more.

Cohen handed over the personnel file of Charlene Zawaki.

♏

"Smooth, I need your help." Rita mashed the Jeep's accelerator as she launched onto the Jones Falls Expressway headed for home.

"Oh, I thought you might be checking in on your best friend," Mary Margaret said with a laugh. "'How are you, Mary Margaret? How about lunch this week, Mary Margaret?'" she taunted Rita.

"Very funny. You know I'm in over my head with this Diane thing—and my mom—and the fraud stuff."

Mary Margaret sighed. "Just pullin' your chain. And you're too damned easy to fire up."

"Sorry, I'm . . ." Rita started.

"Yeah, I know you're just doin' your job." Mary Margaret paused. "What do you need?"

"I need a background and any rap sheet on a Charlene Zawaki."

"Holy prayer beads, batgirl. You giving this name to Billy Bolton?" Mary Margaret asked.

"What do you think?" Rita asked with a hint of sarcasm.

"Why do I ask?"

"Because you think you'll 'save' me?"

"Yeah, right." Computer keys tapped on Smooth's side of the call. "Damn, girlie, I don't want Bolton breathing down my neck either."

"You won't let that happen. And you outrank him."

"A draft has been saved in our shared email account. Go forth and conquer."

Rita and Mary Margaret shared an email account where sensitive materials and information were passed by saving missives within the "Draft" folder. Unsent, untraceable, unaccounted for in email traffic. No one would ever see it except for Rita and Captain Mary Margaret Smooth.

As soon as Rita ended the call with Smooth, she used her VPN app to bring up Zawaki's Facebook feed. Involuntarily she shook her head as she scrolled through entry after entry. The most recent was a photo of the exterior of Diane's house. Zawaki crowed that she was moving up in the world and would soon be living in this "almost a million" dollar property in northern Baltimore County's "My Lady's Manor." The area acquired its name from the 10,000 acres presented by Charles Calvert, the third Lord Baltimore, to his fourth wife. A community over 300 years old, it was an enclave of long-established estates with extensive grounds, sprawling horse farms, celebrities from sports and commerce—not usually affordable by garage attendants.

There was a photo of Diane's car, her aging BMW 700 series. There were photos of Diane taken from afar at the My Lady's Manor annual steeplechase. Another picture featured a business news announcement that Diane Winter won Fund Manager of the year. A snapshot of a birthday card signed by Diane to "CharleyZ" with a twenty-five-dollar gift certificate to Panera. The first in the long string of Diane-related posts was taken inside the garage where Charlene was beaming as she stood with her arm around a petite Diane Winter.

Maybe I was wrong about Diane's playing with this woman's affection, Rita thought.

"But I'm dead to rights about who I'm looking for," she said out loud as she clicked her phone off.

Chapter 21

Rita was behind the wheel of her Jeep. She announced to her cell that she wanted to "call Laura Palomina."

Cannot find Serafina."

"Call Laura Palomina."

"Cannot find Laurel Palina."

"Oy," Rita groaned. She reached over and punched the number into the phone mounted on her dash. "Stupid . . . "

"What? Who is this?" Palomina's voice was rushed and angry. "I don't have time for this crap."

"Wait, wait," Rita begged. "It's Rita. I was trying to get my phone to call you and . . . never mind that. I need to have you look at something online."

"Can you just tell me?" Palomina asked. "I'm going to be here late tonight."

"Too complicated," Rita said. "I can come to your place or you can come out to mine. This is important. I think I've found something to take us to Diane."

"I'll come to yours." Palomina suddenly sounded tired. "And hope I'm not going to have bags under my eyes tomorrow."

♏

It would be another late night. Tomorrow she would gather Annie and they would tour Baltimore's Highlandtown neighborhood. Rita had made arrangements to stop and visit Charlene Zawaki's mother to query about her daughter and where she was.

Rita sighed as she trudged up her ancient farmhouse steps into her office. All the windows were open. The ceiling fan rotated in slow lazy circles. August was winding down though its heat still simmered in the night. Out there in the dark was a chorale of bush crickets with their three-pulse raspy song.

Rita cracked Annie's bedroom door. Snoring like a lumber mill at high noon buzzed from Annie's bed. The A/C was on low and her mother had yanked a summer spread up over her ears. Rita smiled and closed the door.

In her office, she pulled her hack-proof PC from its place on a bookshelf. She initiated the VPN Roswell had set up for her. Tonight she would be able to research ownership of the Whitlock foundation in the way Harry Potter used his cloak of invisibility. Her transmissions would be encrypted and they would travel thousands of miles and be passed on by obfuscated servers across a randomized path through any of sixty countries. Police software would not detect her. They would not see where she went or notice anything she might download.

The video conference app on her phone sounded. Roswell calling. She tapped a key and Roswell's face bloomed onto the screen.

"I'm checking in," Roswell said. Rita could see he had on his Red Bull T-shirt. He looked so fresh and bright that she immediately felt more tired than when she sat down. "I called the office this afternoon and Bev told me you had a real find on Diane."

"I have a name of someone Diane was seen with," Rita said. "My gut says that's the person who took her. Name's Charlene Zawaki. I have an address for her mother and I'm going to Highlandtown tomorrow to talk to her."

"My hood!" Roswell's face registered surprise. "And a woman? How did she get Diane to go with her?"

"This Charlene or 'CharleyZ' as she calls herself is no shrinking violet. She's a physical force to be reckoned with and, I imagine, pretty strong. I doubt she would have had to use a weapon to coerce Diane."

"I am so glad I could scrape up those old emails from Diane's account for you." Roswell gave a thumbs up. "Delicate question. Do you need me to scout this CharleyZ's email for info about where she might have taken Diane?"

Rita hesitated. Her head screamed "YES". Her better, more law-abiding persona shook its head. "Let's wait, Roswell. I am trying to walk a line that gets thinner with every passing day."

"Got it." Roswell nodded.

"How about this? If I get good information after visiting her mother tomorrow, I will move forward on that. If I don't, I'm going to call on you. Seem reasonable to you?"

"Absolutely," Roswell agreed. "And smart."

"Ok, then I'm going to spend this night rummaging through company ownership of Whitlock Foundation vendors. Kleptocracy uses shell companies and shelf companies to hide theft."

"Sounds like a long and tedious road," Roswell commented.

"Working on my first pot of coffee," Rita said.

"Good luck. Let me know what you need when you're done."

"Will do. Talk soon." Rita exited the video conference app and Roswell shrank into the home screen of her phone.

Rita turned back to her PC monitor. She heaved a breath of determination and started to type. Thank God this isn't a huge corporation, Rita said to herself. There were less than thirty vendors that Whitlock employed to perform everything from office cleaning to event planning to technology management and temp services.

Rita pulled up the website for the office cleaners first. L & M Commercial Cleaning's website popped into view with a slick stock photo. The photo banner presented three young people wearing company logo T-shirts, smiling in front of an ultra-modern office backdrop. She scanned the page. There was no "About Us" section.

Beneath the headline and the banner was a "Clients We Work With" with logos of five of the city's major corporations. They weren't the largest companies but the names would be immediately recognizable—trusted.

Rita scrolled down the page where the bulk of information was displayed in large individual frames with more stock photos that recalled the same workers portrayed in the banner. Each frame went into detail with links. One described the work the company would provide. Another was a copywriter's contribution of what to look for in a cleaning company. Following that was "Why L&M Commercial Cleaning." This section had another anonymous stock photograph with the same company T-shirts. The pictures were all purchased.

Rita decided, as she studied them, that the L&M logo had been photoshopped over the T-shirts. Not necessarily an indication of fraud. It wasn't unusual for companies with tight marketing budgets to have their webmaster use the same kind of art.

What did attract Rita's attention was the bullet point in "Why L&M Commercial Cleaning" that stated the company was a wholly-owned subsidiary of Greenmount Enterprises. There was no link so Rita would have to investigate that entity in a separate search. She scribbled a reminder note.

On through one hour after another, Rita clicked, scrolled and added to her notes. Her neck grew stiff and her eyes were watering from fatigue. She stood up to stretch and walked to the window for a change of scenery.

"You're up mighty late, girl." Annie stood in the doorway in her nightgown. "Do you know what time it is?"

"Unfortunately, I do, Mom." Rita walked over and gave her a hug. "Did I wake you?"

"No way. Never heard a thing. Had to go to the bathroom and saw your light on."

"Go on back to bed, Mom. I'm gonna be working for a while longer yet."

Annie squeezed Rita's hand and started for the bathroom.

"Mom, I asked Laura Palomina to come over and look at pictures of the woman I suspect of abducting Diane."

Annie stopped and turned slowly. She cast a suspicious eye but held her tongue.

"Nothing going on here, Mom," Rita promised as she held up her right hand. "Promise."

"It's not you I don't trust." Annie walked away.

♏

Rita leaned back in her desk chair. She'd been hunched over the keyboard for hours. She edged her head back further than normal to relieve the stiffness as she closed her eyes and squeezed the bridge of her nose. An engine rumble woke her within minutes. She stood slowly and went downstairs to the back door in the kitchen.

"Hey," Laura Palomina said with a tired smile.

"Hey back." Rita held the kitchen door open.

"I've been thinking about who this person could be since you mentioned it." Palomina brushed against Rita as she entered the house. "Can't imagine who this woman is."

"She's from Highlandtown. Name's Charlene Zawaki." Rita went to her coffee machine and started a new round.

"Highlandtown? Oh, my, God." Palomina shook her head. "Diane wouldn't be trying to bed somebody from there. This is either totally wrong or this woman is a crazy who's fabricated a fantasy."

"Coffee?" Rita asked. She had started to refute Palomina's statement, having observed Diane's careless attractions and seductions through the years. There were too many women who were first flattered and thrilled only to be discarded and ignored when the game lost its amusement.

"I have some herbal tea," Palomina replied. "Don't want to be amped up when I need to catch just a little sleep before I stagger into the morning news tomorrow."

It was then Rita noticed the gym bag.

"This shouldn't take long," Rita said. "Come up to my office and I'll show you the social media sites. See if it jogs your memory."

Palomina picked up the salmon-colored bag she'd brought and followed Rita upstairs. Rita pulled a chair behind her desk so that she and Palomina could view the monitor together. She explained how she had, by happenstance, found someone who knew Diane and had spotted her with this woman a few weeks before the abduction. She did not elaborate on the witness backstory. No need to rehash her past and her old attachments.

"I am going to say upfront; I don't recognize the name you gave me. Diane never mentioned a 'Charlene'. I would have remembered that," Palomina said.

"Exactly why I wanted you to look at the pictures." Rita

spun out into cyber space over the same secured and cloaked PC she'd been using for the vendor searches. "Ready?"

Palomina nodded.

Rita first went to Facebook. Charlene had no pictures of herself on her cover. It was a photo of Ladew Topiary Gardens, an historic estate and formal garden north of Baltimore and close to Diane's house.

"Ladew!" Palomina said with a grin. "Diane and I used to go for evening walks there in the summer. And we went to some of their music events."

There was no profile picture of Charlene. She had posted a shot of the previous winner of My Lady's Manor. Standing in the saddle, he hoisted his crop clearing the last fence, face fierce and triumphant.

"I remember this from last year." Palomina pointed at the picture. "So interesting. The proceeds from that race went to Ladew." She frowned. "This is starting to get strange."

Rita started scrolling through CharleyZ's news feed. One was a grainy news photo, copied and pasted. In that picture, Diane stood beaming and shaking hands with the governor of Maryland. Diane's pro bono work earned her that presentation. Charlene's posted comment was "That's my girl."

The next photo was a candid shot of Diane getting into her Mercedes. Then came another eerie shot of Diane at lunch with a client. Another photo was a back shot of Diane and her sister at the beach. Charlene had been stalking her prey for a very long time.

"This is sick," Palomina said when she and Rita had scrolled through post after post. "I'm surprised this nut didn't have a picture of us in bed."

Rita tapped into CharleyZ's Instagram. There they viewed a long distance but high-resolution shot of Diane and Laura Palomina. Another photo taken from behind captured its subjects who were holding hands and strolling along the Inner Harbor promenade. The caption read "Me and my girl. Groovin' on a Sunday afternoon."

Palomina gasped. "Do you think I'm in danger?"

Rita's first thought was you're really that narcissistic? "No, you're not the focus of this obsession."

"Yeah, but I'm in the way." Palomina turned to Rita.

"I believe this CharleyZ person is more interested in securing Diane for herself, as witness the abduction, than in doing you in to get to Diane. When somebody has this kind of delusion, they firmly see every word, every gesture of their 'loved one' as a true sign of their affection for them. It's a short hop from there to speculate that Charlene believed Diane was attempting to get out of the existing relationship to be with her."

Palomina shook her head.

"Seen enough?" Rita asked.

"More than enough," Palomina responded. "So what is it you want from me now? It's freaky that woman has been following Diane—and sometimes me incidentally—but I never noticed this Charlene person." She paused. "At least her face doesn't register with me."

"I was hoping you might have recognized her," Rita said. "It would be best if we had a witness to Charlene's being with Diane. Makes for a more effective case if we're not able to catch Charlene while she's holding Diane.

"And that would mean . . ." Rita stopped as the implication hit her.

"It would mean Charlene had killed Diane." Palomina spoke slowly. She swiveled to Rita. "Have you talked to the police about this?"

"No. I go to the police about this and they'll throw me right back in the prime suspect column. At this point, to both free Diane and keep myself from being thrown in jail, I need to the find the two of them together—alive."

"I want the story," Palomina stated.

Rita listened. Again Palomina reduced the kidnapping, the stalking and abduction of her partner, Diane's fear, and the threat to her life to a self-centered boost to her career.

"You can have it. All of it," Rita said. "If you need to get sleep, we're done here. I'm beat but I've got a little more PC time here." Rita closed her eyes and ran both hands through her hair.

"Different case?" Palomina stood and walked behind Rita. She slid her delicate hands onto Rita's shoulders and began to knead the tight, knotted muscle.

Rita relaxed into Palomina's hands; eyes still closed. "Different case," Rita confirmed for Palomina. The massage was slow but effective. Rita could feel her body tension lift and she leaned into it. She could easily fall asleep.

"Case I'd be interested in?" Palomina asked as she continued the bodywork. She moved her warm hands along Rita's neck, along her jawline and into her hair. Palomina ran her index finger on each hand on the edges of Rita's ears.

Palomina's question broke the mood for Rita. She braced herself. "Not really," Rita responded. "And even if it were, I'm bound to confidentiality."

Palomina moved from Rita's ears back to her scalp. This time Palomina grasped a handful of hair in each hand and gave a long slow tug. From there, she let her hands flow down the side of Rita's head onto her shoulders and directed them downward. Rita grabbed each hand.

"I've got work to do." Rita recovered herself and sat up straight. Palomina pulled back and paused.

"I can help you," she said.

"Not that kind of case," Rita said.

"What does that mean?" Palomina asked.

"It means no," Rita answered.

Chapter 22

"Are you up for a lunch with Mary Margaret today?" Rita poked her head into her outer office. Bev looked up from her PC monitor.

"Baby, I missed a day at the gym. I have got to get myself into shape for the Labor Day competition at Jimmy's."

"Can we go see you?" Annie stopped and considered. "Where is this 'Jimmy's'?"

"Rehoboth Beach, honey." Bev stood up. "I would love to have you come and see the show. Miz Annie, this girl gonna be 'servin' body' out there. You gonna love it!"

Rita sauntered over to sit with her mother. "Mom, had no idea you'd want to see a drag show."

"When our Bev is performing—you didn't think I'd be interested?" Annie sniffed. "You know I love Bev. But what body are you serving? You referring to some kinda group or organization?"

"Mama," Bev grinned. "Ima talkin' bout this body." Bev's hands swept out to her side as if presenting her presence and her finely hewn proportions. "Slay 'em is what I'm gonna do."

"Gorgeouser than I'll ever be, for sure," Rita nodded in agreement.

"You do ok in them tricked out tailored threads you wear. But you ain't dusted, baby girl."

"I have no idea what you're saying." Annie looked from Bev to Rita and back.

"Let's start over," Rita said. "Bev, you'll be at the gym. Mom, I asked Mary Margaret to lunch with us and am hoping that'll be alright with you."

Bev smoothed her blonde wig as she checked herself in her desk mirror. "Yep. A girl's gotta work on her fabulousness."

♏

Rita decided Annie could handle the Sip-N-Bite diner with its swarming throngs of hungry customers. Opened in 1948, the diner was an institution in this waterfront neighborhood on the southeast rim of Baltimore City. There, in the late 1700's, Irish merchant John O'Donnell developed a 1,900-acre plantation and named it after the Chinese city that was one of his most lucrative trading partners—Canton. While it was originally a community of shipyards and other working-class families, over time, it morphed into one of the trendiest areas of Baltimore. Today Rita knew she'd see stockbrokers and attorneys in Patagonia business casual vying for waitress attention with city workmen in steel-toed boots and safety vests, cops wolfing a quick lunch with their partners and retail clerks grabbing takeout.

When Rita and Annie entered the diner, lunch was at full tilt. Clientele bunched in the aisles. Every booth was occupied. A line of the now fed and anxious to return to work extended from the cashier station. Any music from the at-table mini jukeboxes drowned in the rumble of raised voices.

"Hang on," Rita said to Annie. "I see Mary Margaret." She tightened her grip on Annie's arm and elbowed her way through the masses.

"I had time so I got here early." Smooth stood and wrapped Annie in a hug.

"Is it always like this?" Annie asked as Rita let her slide into the banquette first. She seemed entranced by the crowd surge and ebb.

"Always," Smooth answered.

"I love this place," Rita said. "It's alive." She leaned back into the aging, once-red vinyl of the banquette. Permanent indentations deepened where prostitutes and politicians, office workers and construction crews had lingered over late-night coffee or sopped the last of their breakfast eggs with scraps of toast.

"Well, I'm sure this isn't just a friendly lunch." Smooth smiled a wry and knowing smile as she stared directly at Rita.

"Maybe," Rita did not look up but pretended to study the menu which she knew by heart and from which she ordered the same lunch every single time. Greek salad, extra pita, Coke.

"So let me have it," Smooth said when the waitress had taken their orders.

"What do we have?" Annie turned to Rita.

"We—and that would be me—discovered a smelly little scenario in the fraud frenzy Bunny dragged me into at the Gala," The waitress brought the drinks then and Rita guzzled a deep draught of her soda. "Fountain Coca Cola. Better than sex."

"Really?" Annie said. Rita ignored the comment as Annie reached over to test that assessment for herself.

"Ok," Smooth said with no reaction.

"No excitement. No curiosity?" Rita slapped both hands on the edge of the table and leaned toward Mary Margaret.

"I know you better than that. First, you toss a grenade to throw the audience off base and then you drop the real bombshell." The waitress appeared at the table and dealt out plates. She scurried back to the kitchen without asking if they required anything more.

"Crap." Rita leaned back in the banquette. "It's a tell."

"Umm." Smooth nodded with a big bite of BLT.

"There are three Whitlock vendors that are wholly-owned subsidiaries and those subs are, in turn, owned by a holding company." Rita stabbed her salad and waved a forkful of greens at Mary Margaret as she spoke.

"Tell me something sinister about that." Smooth took a sip of her iced tea. "'Cause I don't see anything shady in what you just said." She took a hunk out of her BLT.

"Wouldn't you be just the littlest bit suspicious if all those companies were from the same state—Wyoming?"

Smooth stopped chewing. She swallowed. "Well, well, well."

"Knew you'd say that," Rita smiled with her smug response.

"Wyoming?" Annie piped up. "Seems far-fetched for companies that far away to be doing business here."

"I'll tell you what makes it curiouser and curiouser," Rita said Her smile became a stern, stone smirk. "They all have the same street address."

"Whoa." Smooth put down her sandwich. "A shell game."

"My thought exactly," Rita agreed.

"A shell game? What does that mean?" Annie asked.

"It means Three-card Monte on a high stakes level." Rita dug back into her salad. Annie shook her head and returned to her lunch. "Embezzlement, Mom."

"You know, I thought Bunny was overreacting," Smooth said.

"I was doubtful too," Rita said. "Now I have this sudden urge to visit the Wild West. How do you think I'll look in a ten-gallon hat?" Rita paused as Mary Margaret started to speak. "Don't even say it."

♏

Cheyenne Regional Airport was a long, low-slung structure that, without recent upgrades and appointments, could easily have been mistaken for an industrial warehouse. Nonetheless, it was a foundational element of early American aviation. Constructed in the '20's, the airfield made a bid for national traffic with its inclusion as a hub with the inauguration of coast-to-coast air mail service.

Cheyenne bested Denver as it offered the best aerial route through the Rocky Mountains at a time when planes could not fly above 10,000 feet. In 1925, Congress awarded the Chicago-to-San Francisco route to Boeing Air Transport Company who chose Cheyenne as the location of its main overhaul facility. In 1927 Boeing Aircraft established its own carrier service which, when it merged with two other carriers, became what is now United Airlines.

The airport had two runways which Rita and Bev stared down on as they approached. A fierce Wyoming wind tossed the CRJ200 regional jet like the balsam gliders Rita had played with as a kid. She was no stranger to wild rides through all her years investigating in remote, often treacherous, terrain and at times behind the lines of battlefields. She reached over to Bev.

"Rough ride," Rita said.

"Honey, this is smooth as a baby's butt compared to being hauled by a C-5. You be strapped in 'cuz we all goin' down if the plane goes back to the taxpayers. You don't get up. You locked and loaded in that bus."

As Rita stepped off onto the portable airstairs, hot gusts tore through her hair. Dust and sand swirled around the departing passengers. Bev secured her wig with one hand and marched boldly down, her Dries Van Noten shirt flattening and billowing in the pulse of high winds.

"You know they test aircraft here because of wind velocities?" Rita asked over the hoarse swoosh of the blasted air. Both she and Bev turned their backs to the west streaming wind as they waited for carry-ons to be unloaded from the aircraft.

"What have you got in there?" Rita asked when she compared the size of her travel bag to hers.

"Change of clothes, baby." Bev smiled. "Girl gotta be prepared for any occasion."

"This was a hell of a long day," Rita said as they walked toward the terminal. "Let's make it an early night and we'll go to work in the morning. We can either take the last flight out of here in the afternoon or the first on the following morning depending on what we find."

"Gotcha, Genghis." Bev gave Rita a big grin that shone under her mirrored Maui Jim's.

"You think you're so cute," Rita smiled back as they reached the rental car counter.

"And ain't it the truth," said Bev.

Rita drove them out that evening to the Chop House. She wore jeans and a white polo with soft Italian loafers. Even in August, Cheyenne nights were cool and she had a denim jacket over her shirt. Bev wore a flowing Stella McCarthy matching outfit, white with hand-painted tropical bird accents. In deference to the locale, she had slipped on a pair of ankle-length vegan cowboy boots.

"You lookin' mighty butch tonight, girl," Bev said as she slid into the passenger seat of the rental car.

"And you are stylin' for sure," Rita returned.

"Mmm." Bev nodded. "You bring reinforcements with you?"

"I did." Rita pointed her thumb to the backseat where a handgun case rested.

"Anything on your mind that I need to know?

"A buzz at the back of my mind. Nothing specific."

Cheyenne's Chop House was sparsely populated this Tuesday night. The hostess smiled and showed them to a table. "Thought you might like the privacy," she said as she seated them just a little way from the main clutch of diners. "Your server will be right with you."

"She thinks we're together?" Rita asked as the woman departed.

"Now that is a hoot." Bev was already behind her menu, considering her choices.

Rita scanned the room quickly and took a few sidelong looks. No one seemed overly interested.

Dinner was quiet. Both Rita and Bev were tired from a day of early rising and more than eight hours of total travel time. Recessed lighting created a warm and relaxed ambiance while accent track fixtures softly highlighted paintings of the old west. Quiet piano music played just above recognition as background. Rita could feel herself relaxing.

"I could be wrong," Bev said as he pretended to focus on his steak as he sliced, "but one of the suits two tables over has kept an eye on us." He punctured his hunk of medium-well and lifted it to his lips.

Rita stiffened. "Are you sure?" She picked up her glass of water for a sip as her eyes went to the three men Bev had indicated.

"Pretty sure." Bev returned to her steak and cut another slice. "Familiar?"

Rita had seen them when she and Bev entered. Nothing registered then and nothing registered now. She noticed they were finishing as each had a brady snifter and the plates had been cleared except for coffee cups.

Rita signaled to their waiter. "Would you mind taking a picture of me and my friend? I'd like to text to envious friends." She handed her phone, camera app open to the young man. "We'll turnaround so we can get more of the restaurant in the picture if that's ok. Maybe two shots?" Immediately, she and Bev swiveled their chairs. Bev smiled and put an arm around Rita's shoulder. The photo would capture the man who had been so interested.

"Thanks." Rita took the cell phone from the waiter and took a quick look. The waiter's picture had a clear shot of the man two tables over.

"I think they leavin'," Bev said. She feigned more interest in her food.

"You're right. Here they come." Rita too pretended to be working on her plate but played it perfectly when she raised her water glass for a sip as the three men passed her table. None of them looked at Bev or Rita as they passed.

♏

Bev and Rita met in the High Plains Hotel dining room. In the late 1800s, Cheyenne was called "The Magic City of the Plains." When its first luxury hotel opened in 1911, owners took a bit of that moniker in naming their elegant lodgings.

The hotel was constructed with a center atrium above which was an open mezzanine for meeting rooms. Upon entering the Grand Lobby, guests are immersed in the grandeur of its original creamy marble tile which accents a collection of Native American and western art. The staircase leading from the lobby was a grand process of marble and steel. Today, in anticipation of an approaching salute to Labor Day, red, white and blue bunting draped the railing of the mezzanine. High Plains was an artful tribute to the old west where cattle kings and oilfield magnates and wealthy travelers converged and departed in their journeys.

"Happen to catch Matt Dillon when you came down for coffee this morning?" Bev asked Rita when they reached the ground floor. Today Bev wore no makeup. She had on jeans and a long-sleeved white shirt and navy merino sneakers. She was more "Charles Tyrell Wheatley" than "Beverly Hills" today.

"No, but kept expecting to hear the baby grand in the lobby plinking out saloon tunes," Rita said, stopped and added, "I want to get out of here on that three o'clock flight back to BWI. We can grab lunch at the airport."

"I'm ready to go," Bev said.

♍

The Fronter Corporation Services building was a short walk. Rita and Bev marched down the street to a three-story, unremarkable brick building. They stood in the entry for a moment to check the directory. Frontier was on the first floor. It was quiet in there and felt empty.

"Down here." Rita pointed to an office toward the back of the hallway where she could see a rear parking lot through the plate glass door.

They entered a small office. There was a high counter with no one behind it and another door slightly ajar from where they could hear a voice presumably speaking into a phone. When the voice stopped, Rita spoke up.

"Excuse me," she said. "Do I have the right office for Frontier Services?" There was a flutter of movement and a young woman emerged from behind the door. She wore a pair of black jeans, a white v-neck t-shirt that displayed a panorama of cleavage and Rita assumed she wore cowboy boots from the regular swoosh and clunk as the woman approached.

"How can I help you?"

"I'm trying to catch up with the principals of White and Wright," Rita said as she presented a card from the Whitlock Foundation that introduced Rita as their Director of Vendor Management.

The woman reached for the card with a wrist jangling with multiple sterling and turquoise bangles. She took her time. Rita thought to herself that the woman was trying to think of what she should do next.

"Are you police?" The woman looked up now.

"Well, no, I'm the new head of vendor management for the foundation listed on the card. I wanted to meet the folks who help us run the business and find out more about how they go about their jobs." Rita paused.

"Never had a call like this," the woman said. "What do you want to know. I'm the registered agent for the company. I'm the one who handles the mail for them. I answer inquiries, pay the taxes—that kind of thing."

Rita explained the role of vendor management and how it was her job to establish how the relationship would work, the policies and procedures, concerns that could arise on either side of the business arrangement.

"Have to tell you, the principals don't work out of this office," the woman advised.

"How do I reach them? I don't see any addresses and the phone numbers seem to be from way different area codes."

"Phone codes don't mean much anymore," the woman stated.

"How do I get an interview?" Rita asked. Bev turned from the counter and rested an elbow as he faced the glass office door.

"You contact me and I send it to the principals. When I get an answer, I'll get back to you. I need you to email me that request though." The woman glanced up suddenly as a man appeared at the door where Bev had been watching.

"Help you folks?" He walked behind the counter as if to bolster support for the young woman. Rita immediately saw he was one of the men she thought had been eyeing her and Bev at dinner.

"I was trying to see if we can get a sit-down with the management of White and Wright." Rita offered him another of the cards from Whitlock. "Sorry, but may I ask if you are associated with them?"

"I'm an agent for another group," the man said. Rita noticed the sidearm on his hip.

"So how do I find out who runs the company?" Rita asked. From the corner of her eye, she recognized that Bev edged closer to her and stood on alert.

"State of Wyoming requires an annual report. They'll be listed in there. Like this young lady told you, you send a request and she passes it on. You'll get a response when she has one." That advice did not seem a friendly offer.

"Got it," Rita said. "How do I get an annual report?"

The woman who was White and Wright's agent reached under the counter. "Last year's," she said as she placed two copies on the counter and pushed them toward Rita and Bev.

"Thanks for the help." Rita gathered the reports and started to leave.

"What happened to that young lady who was with you all last night?" the man asked with a shifty smile as he eyed Bev.

"Busy today," Rita said before Bev could respond. She noticed his hands were doubled into fists.

Later on the plane, with lunch bags on tray tables, Rita pulled one of the reports from her shoulder bag. She flipped to the Executive Compensation section where corporate management were listed. The CEO came first. Rita gave a sharp involuntary breath.

"This can't be right," she said and handed the report to Bev. The two looked at each other.

"Well, ain't this something!" Bev commented.

Chapter 23

"Marianne Whitlock?" Bunny's voice rose in alarm and fear. Leaning over her desk on her elbow, she raised her hand to her head as if trying to make it take in what she'd just read.

Rita had summoned her trusted investigation partners to her house the evening after she and Bev returned from Wyoming. She, Bev, Roswell, and Bunny were seated at the breakfast bar in Rita's kitchen. In front of each participant was the annual report of White and Wright, holder of three oddly conspicuous contract vendors to The Whitlock Foundation. White and Wright's CEO was listed as Marianne Whitlock.

"How . . ." Bunny started, shook her head and went silent.

"Not uncommon for companies like these to be formed. A company wants to jump into a business line and they don't have the required time in that business to start participating in bids. Or they want a fast track to corporate status with access to credit lines and investors."

"And every reason why they do it sounds scammy," Bunny commented.

"May sound like that, but these so-called 'shelf' companies aren't illegal in themselves. And Wyoming isn't the only state with these biz-friendly regulations on the books. Someone could just have easily done this via Delaware or Nevada incorporation." Rita responded.

Bev sat quietly and said nothing. Rita could visualize the ticking and clicking in Roswell's head as he listened. Bunny had dissolved into a silent dither on her side of the counter. Rita needed more. With every turn on this hunt, she felt she'd descended another rabbit hole.

"Now before we throw ourselves out a window, I proposed we take up the shovel. One more dig we have to make," she said.

Bunny snapped to attention. She leaned across the table. Rita could see Bunny wanted anything or anyone to be responsible except Marianne.

"All this said," Rita began, "this annual report proves absolutely nothing." Out of the corner of her eye, she saw Roswell nod. Bev perked up and Bunny hung her attention on Rita.

"What does that mean?" Bunny asked.

Roswell turned to her. "In my security gigs, I've had to track principals in this kind of situation before. Last one a guy was laundering money for a Mexican drug cartel with a convoluted loan scheme. My job was to trace the real actors and be able to diagram the entire flow of the money."

"It might not be Marianne? Really?" Bunny grasped at hope.

"I'm not ready to go there," Rita said. "But we'll have to find out who built this clever little house of cards." She turned to Roswell. "I'll be counting on you because none of us have those kinds of skills." She turned to Bunny. "And you'll have to keep your cool with Marianne and with Louise. No one who's outside this little band of truth-seekers should speak of this or react to any issues or questions about what's going on." She waved her hand to indicate the party.

"Got that?" Rita looked from one grim face to the other. In turn, each nodded without speaking.

♏

A silver-edged sliver of pink frosted the locust tree tops that bordered the farthest stretch of Rita's property. Mourning doves cooed their greeting to the day's first light and the scarred two-lane blacktop below Rita's driveway was empty, silent.

Rita lay oblivious in deep sleep. Her overhead fan turned lazy circles on a cool-for-August morning. And then it began.

Yowling at the back door. Sometimes shrill and even. Sometimes with a tremolo. Rita turned over without waking. The back door was beneath her bedroom window and even though she was a floor above, the sound was clear and unmistakable.

"Ugh," Rita reached for her phone and saw the time. More yowling. She staggered out of bed, yanked a T-shirt over her head and slipped commando into the shorts tossed on her comforter last night.

"Nice." She addressed the Great White Hunter who stalked around the trophy he had brought her. "Now there's some little chipmunk out there without a head. Aren't you ashamed of yourself?"

The cat looked up. He had ceased the yowling. Pleased with the attention he then slithered between her bare legs, smudging his cheeks against her skin to mark her as his own. She reached down to stroke him. He arched under the first touch but slapped at her with a claws-out paw when she tried a second time.

"You're such a people pleaser." Rita heaved the chipmunk head out into her vacant pasture and held the door for the cat.

Annie was sitting at the breakfast bar where Rita's cabal had gathered the night before. She had a mug of coffee and Double Stufs in front of her.

"Mom, let me fix you something worth eating." Rita slouched to the refrigerator and pulled out eggs.

"I have something worth eating, thank you." Annie sniffed.

"Well, I have to be in early today. Our dear person of interest has requested the pleasure of my company." Rita turned the dial on the stove and the burner glowed red. "I'm going to drop you off with Bev and I'll be back to the office before noon."

"Then what?" Annie asked.

"Then we're going to Highlandtown. I didn't get there before Wyoming as planned. I was thinking I could talk to this Charlene woman's mother and then have lunch at the Greek place you said you liked. Work for you?"

"Works for me." Annie popped open the Oreo and applied a quick twist of the wrist to her prey.

"Mom!" Rita was about to slide an over-easy egg onto a slice of toast.

Annie had thrown away the unfrosted biscuit portion of a disassembled cookie. Over time she'd developed an expertise in prying the sugar sandwich so that one cookie side would separate with all the prize frosting intact. Upon successful completion of the operation, Annie would eat that remaining sweet little slab of cookie.

"You eat 'em your way and I'll eat 'em mine!"

On the way into the office, the Jones Falls Expressway was a mad stream of people rushing to work, weaving through traffic, honking horns and cutting off other drivers. Rita dropped her mother off in front of her building where Bev waited to accompany the elevator-phobic Annie upstairs to the office.

Rita's head pulled its file drawer and riffed through any number of reasons Louise Mercilus requested a meeting this morning. Reason number one, Louise knew about the trip to Wyoming and this was a fact-finding expedition on her part to learn what Rita discovered. Reason number two, Louise knew nothing and was trolling for any scrap that Rita uncovered. Rita tossed that card out almost immediately. Louise Mercilus was not stupid and surely she made it her business to know the who and where of Rita's. Reason number three was more interesting. Louise would play the long game and either try to worm her way into Rita's confidence or come on to Rita with a sub rosa threat. Rita smiled to herself as she selected Door Number Three as the most probable.

"Good morning." Louise rose as Rita entered her office. "Bunny says you're a doughnut aficionado so I took the liberty of stopping by Blondie's on my way into work."

Rita was so pleased with herself. She could not help but smile as her imaginary three by five card of Reason Number Three popped into mind. Louise, believing she witnessed Rita's smile of approval and gullible acceptance of a peace offering, grinned back.

"And I have some great coffee," Louise said as she poured from the personal coffeemaker in her office. "Please, have a seat." Louise indicated the visitor chair beside her desk.

Rita took the hand thrown coffee mug from Louise. She declined the cream and sugar. Louise settled into her luxuriously sculpted office chair. She opened the doughnut box and displayed an assortment of six baked artworks swirled, filled and sandwiched with all manner of sugared accoutrements.

"These are spectacular," Rita said as she opted for a sunny open response. She tried to decide which of the proffered doughnut creations had the least sugar. At this hour of the morning, she wasn't certain her stomach would adapt to a sudden sugar bombing. Rita made her selection of a yeast raised pillow of a doughnut filled to overflow with lemon curd.

"I love the praline filled." Louise gleefully plucked a similar confection, fried and plumped.

"Mmm." Rita hoped she sounded like she was enjoying her treat. Inside her stomach kicked into nasty little signals of rebellion. I am not going to heave, Rita told herself.

"You know," Louise began, "I'm sorry we got off on the wrong foot. My fault. I'm very protective of this foundation—and Marianne. She's been so good to me. I want to help her succeed." She engaged Rita with her eyes.

"I understand." Rita took on Louise's stare. For a second, they sat locked in this contest of wills.

"I'd like to be able to help you." Louise looked away.

Rita had held her own. Curious, she thought, she looks away when she says she wants to help. A tell.

"I can give you good background on the vendors we have now. I can also give you some documentation on why we changed out who we did and why we selected the newer vendors that came on." Louise's doughnut was gone. She glanced at the open box with the remaining four doughnuts still fresh and exuding a come-hither whiff of bakery. She turned away and back to Rita.

"I'd like that," Rita said. The two bites she'd taken of her doughnut squatted like cannonballs in her gut. The sugar OD she'd ingested was making itself known. She was determined though, so she swigged coffee and that seemed to calm her stomach.

"And any help you need with the database and the system we use; I can sit with you and show you how things work." Louise paused. "I hope your trip the other day went well. I could have saved you some time if it was about any of our current providers."

Her first cast to snag information, Rita said to herself. She had never mentioned the trip to Louise nor to Marianne. Hell, not even to Bunny. Rita betrayed no surprise, and she wasn't going to ask how Louise came by the information. The larger question was how much did Louise know already about the results from that visit to Wyoming. She might have full knowledge and was testing Rita to see what she'd reveal. She might also just be casting in hopes of a strike.

"No problem," Rita said. "Thanks for the offer to help." She was not going to disclose any details.

"Got any more visits planned?" Louise asked. The temptation was too great and Louise scooped up a second praline filled doughnut. "Better have another before I scarf them up."

"Still working on my first," Rita said.

How Louise knew about her trip nagged her. She would not initiate more about the trip as she did not want to offer Louise an opening to ask more questions about it. For the next few minutes, they played catch with inane pleasantries, one to the other. Rita believed Louise was in the same position as herself, hoping for a sliver of information that could start a downhill roll to full revelation.

Rita took a deep breath and forged ahead. "Ever been there?" She watched Louise's face for any sign. Rita's question would reveal no information. Instead she hoped Louise would seize the bait and confirm she knew all.

"Never been west of the Mississippi." Louise laughed. "I'm an east coast girl." She sank her shiny white teeth into her second doughnut.

The response needed more validation, more substance. Rita's head scrambled for a word, a question, a comment. She blurted out, "What? You didn't want to be a cowgirl when you grew up?" She threw her head back for what she hoped sounded like an authentic laugh.

"Hey, closest I ever got to Cheyenne was watching Clint Walker on tv." Louise tossed the remaining hunk of pastry into her mouth. Even as the last morsel passed her lips, Louise froze. Only an instant, but Rita noticed.

Gotcha.

♏

Rita went back to her own office instead of searching through the temporary accommodations that Bunny had arranged for her in the Whitlock Foundation. Where the hell was the bug in that room, Rita asked herself. Or maybe it wasn't in the room. Her house, her personal office?

Only nine thirty in the morning and it was a sweat sopping ninety-one degrees in the city. Rita punched the buttons on the Jeep's AC controls. A blast of stale lukewarm air shot out of the vents. God, she hated navigating downtown Baltimore this early. Delivery trucks were double-parked. Knots of automobile-bound employees dammed up in the streets. Horns honked. Sometimes a truckful of unairconditioned laborers would start shouting in Spanish, throw up their arms and whistle piercing catcalls.

Rita leaned toward her cell mounted on the Jeep's dash. Roswell wasn't picking up. Did he have a gig or a meeting this morning? She couldn't remember. She swiveled her head from side to side looking for cops. One of the new white SUV cruisers bounced over a broken spot in Charles Street. Shift change, Rita said to herself. Not interested in an old dyke texting.

She tapped "CALL ME" to Roswell. Now a firetruck was roaring blocks behind her. She glanced in the mirror. Damn, right behind me. She ducked into an alley off Charles and took a side street to 33 Gay and her office.

Bev was handling monthly billing when Rita slouched in. Annie was ensconced on the waiting room love seat, coffee in hand. She was watching the morning news with Laura Palomina.

"Bev, come with me to the bathroom." Rita marched directly to the small powder room in the waiting area.

Bev looked up. She and Annie exchanged a look.

"Girl, you ain't switchin' teams, are ya?" Bev stood slowly, a furrow daring to crease her smooth and botoxed brow.

"Will you help me with this?" Rita's voice rose a decibel.

"I'm comin'. Damn." Bev hurried around her desk and squeezed into the office powder room beside Rita. Rita had water running at full blast in the sink. The second Bev closed the door behind her, Rita held a finger to her lips. Bev nodded.

Rita flushed the toilet as she reached up to whisper in Bev's ear. "Bug." Bev nodded again even as she involuntarily looked up to the ceiling light.

Rita pulled her cell out of a pocket and tapped a note: No talking anything about Whitlock until we find the bug! Bev nodded and leaned down as she now flushed the toilet.

She whispered, "Talk later?"

Rita nodded. She turned off the water in the sink. The toilet, having discharged its duty, was quiet again.

Annie stood outside the powder room. She jumped back just in time to miss Bev's brusque push on the door.

"Sorry, Mama," Bev said. She gave her a quick squeeze and went back to monthly billing behind her desk.

"What's up in there?" Annie demanded of Rita.

"Looking for a leak," Rita answered. "Maybe Bev'll have it found by the time we get back." From her desk, Bev looked up at Rita. She nodded.

$$\cdot\ \text{—}\ \textbf{Chapter 24}$$

Chapter 24

"There wasn't any leak in that bathroom." Annie buckled her seatbelt in Rita's Jeep.

"How do you know that?" Rita backed out of her parking space on the street and nudged into traffic.

"Because I do," Annie insisted. "You might as well tell me. I might blurt out something you don't want heard." She turned and stared at her daughter as if a withering glare could force her to tell all.

Rita sighed. "Don't do that. I hate when you stare me down." She gave her mother a quick glance and then focused back on her driving.

"So, what's it gonna be?" Annie demanded.

"It's a bug, Mom. I think our office is bugged." There was no hiding the irritation in Rita's voice.

"I need to know these things, sweetie." Annie settled back in her seat and released Rita from the grip of her stare.

"Don't call me 'sweetie'. You know I hate that." Rita took out her frustration by zipping into the curb lane within inches of clipping a landscape truck blasting Norteno tunes from the cab.

m

The very first residents of Baltimore's Highlandtown neighborhood were of German descent. It was they who, upon departure of Union troops in 1866, christened the area "Highland Town" because of its spectacular vantage point over the city. In following years, beginning in the early 1900's, this neighborhood saw a steady influx of Appalachian folk looking to find a better life working in the mills and factories of Baltimore. That prolific migration from Kentucky, Ohio, Virginia, and West Virginia became known as the Hillbilly Highway.

"Hollantown" as Highlandtown is pronounced in Baltimorese has always been a neighborhood of change driven by evolving economic currents and the desire of different ethnic populations to improve their lives and the lives of their children. Today that is evident in a new wave of Latino seekers.

"I don't think I've been to this part of Baltimore," Annie said. Her face was turned to the homes and cars and shops the Jeep passed.

"Been a long time, Mom." Rita said. "This was Dad's first foot beat when he became a cop."

"I didn't recognize it," Annie's voice drifted off.

Rita's GPS took her down Eastern Avenue. She pointed out the Patterson Theater housing the Creative Alliance. Inside were galleries, an updated theater, the Marquee Lounge and resident artist studios. This organic change into embracing the arts was a light year from the culture of industrial labor manifest in Highlandtown's original inhabitants.

"Roswell's mom has a studio in there," Rita said to her mother. Her phone GPS then piped up with instructions to make a right within 0.2 miles.

Back in the day, everyone called them "row houses," now in real estate ads, these narrow, two-story brick dwellings were often referred to as townhomes. When first built, cheap "salmon" brick was the façade of choice for these side-by-side houses for blue collar workers. This brick had been so porous, residents painted it in the style of the up-scale buildings of the day; houses became a soft blue or a dove grey. It kept the home's façade from crumbling and introduced a minor note of individuality.

Rita glanced at her phone screen and its GPS app. She was close to the address on East Pratt. She ticked off the numbers until she idled in front of Charlene Zawaki's listed address.

The front was grey, spare and unadorned with any personalization, unlike the houses with which it stood shoulder to shoulder. The window frames were smudged here and there with mold and their once white surface was greyed and dotted with curls of peeling paint.

"Mom," Rita said, "do you want to go in with me or do you want to wait out here? My two cents is that you come in with me. Gonna get hot out here."

Rita and Annie stood in front of a tired front door. There was an unrepaired gouge at the bottom where a boot or a hand truck might have struck its surface. The door, like the windows, bore aging, ravaged paint. The doorbell did not function.

Rita knocked. She could hear the muffled sound of a television. She waited a minute and knocked again. She heard no stirrings from inside. Third time's a charm, she said hopefully to herself.

The door of an adjoining row house opened. A woman about Annie's age walked boldly out on the stoop. She was work camp thin with the creepiest arms and face Rita had ever seen. She reminded Rita of some spidery alien life form. The old girl wore a "You Can't Fix Stupid" t-shirt, too-big pull-on pants and a pair of neon yellow Crocs.

"Likely passed out on the couch," said the woman. "You ain't the cops are ye?"

"No," Rita jumped in before Annie could say anything. "Bringing my mom to meet an old friend." Annie kept her silence.

"Didn't know Magda had any friends." The woman cackled. "Lemme give youse a hand there." She came down off her stoop which was separated from the Zawaki's by a wrought iron railing.

"Last kid kinda did her in," the old woman said. "Took up drinkin' after Stan died."

Rita and Annie backed to the first step so that the woman could have free range at the Zawaki front door.

"Magda, get off the damn couch and get out here," the woman yelled, all the while pounding the door with her fist. "Get up." She turned and gave Rita and Annie a wink.

"I'll get her sorry ass outta there for ya."

Other doors opened on the street. Window shades fluttered as snoopers flocked to the commotion.

"Dammit," the neighbor muttered to herself. She proceeded to launch another round.

"Magda, get out here." More door pounding. "Think I heard somethin'." The woman rested her ear against the door. "All yers, ladies." She backed away and motioned for Rita to take position in front.

Slowly a sliver of an opening appeared. Television sounds grew louder. A puffy, bloodshot eye in a heavily lined face peered out at Rita.

"What?" The voice behind the door was throaty with a smoker's rasp.

"Mrs. Zawaki, I'm Rita Mars. We spoke a day ago about meeting. We were going to talk about Charlene?"

It took a pronounced pause for that intelligence to formulate in Magda Zawaki's head. She nodded and opened the door.

Her neighbor turned to go back into her own house. "Fer god's sake, Magda, turn down that damned tv. I can hear every single price they guess."

"Sorry," Magda said so low her neighbor would never have heard her. "Sorry," she said again to Rita and Annie.

Rita stepped inside and was immediately in the Zawaki living room. From this entrance, she had a clear shot all the way to the back door. This cheap variation of a "shotgun" layout was one room wide, no hallways; residents moved through room after room. Rita guessed there was a stairway somewhere in the middle that led to bedrooms on the second floor.

"Been sittin' in the kitchen. Cooler there in the mornin's." Maga's legs protruded from a formless dress. Her legs and feet were swollen to deformity with edema. She had a new oversized band aid that barely covered an angry purple bruise. She shuffled toward the back of the house in slippers whose fuzziness was beat down to a matted nap.

"Hope you don't mind. I had mentioned that I might be bringing someone. This is my mom, Annie," Rita said as Magda tossed a casual gesture for seating at the small kitchen table.

"Kids," Magda shook her head as she went to her ancient, stained Mr. Coffee. "They'll drive you crazy. And Charlene was my last. Came way too late in life. Surprise, my Stan said, and he was happy 'bout it." She turned down the volume on the small tv sitting on the counter then reached into a cupboard for coffee cups.

"Mrs. Zawaki, you don't have to fix anything for us. I appreciate it. Just have a few questions and you can get back to your day."

"My day," Magda sniffed. "My day is a lotta nothin' but pain in my legs and waiting til it's time to go to bed." She abandoned the coffee maker and joined Rita and Annie at the table.

"Whatcha wanna know about Charlene?"

Rita had decided not to start with discussing the fact that Charlene was holding Diane Winter hostage. She would determine from what came out of the conversation whether or not Charlene's mother knew where she was.

"Do you happen to know where she is at this moment?" Rita asked.

"I never know where that girl is. She'll come home and shut herself in her room. Won't come out all night." Magda shifted in her seat. "Next mornin' she'll be up and gone to work. Never says nothin' to me. Never tells me nothin'. So only thing I know is, right now, she should be at work."

"I'm afraid Charlene seems to have quit her job. I was hoping . . ." Rita began.

"That's another thing she does. Takes a job. Stays a month or so then she up and quits. Ain't no way to make a livin' if you ask me. What's she gonna do when I die? Ain't enough left of this house or any insurance money from Stan's passin' to keep her goin'." Magda made a few tsk sounds as she shook her head. From there she lapsed into an introspective silence.

"Mrs. Zawaki, you must know your daughter has gone missing." Rita threw out her implied question and let it hang in the air. An implied question begged for an answer. Rita looked to Magda Zawaki and used the power of silence as pressure to squeeze Charlene's mother into a response.

For a long while Magda held her head down, avoiding Rita's gaze. She gripped the arms of her chair and raised the heel of one foot. Her slippered toe began a quicktime tapping. Still Rita watched, letting the tension grow.

"She in trouble?" Magda asked.

"Not the worst kind," Rita said and added, "yet."

Tears streamed down Magda's face. "She don't mean nothin'. She wouldn't never hurt nobody."

Rita's voice was soothing. "I understand that. What I don't want to have happen is police getting involved. They won't understand and it concerns me they may hurt Charlene."

Magda nodded. The tears poured a little faster. "I don't know where she is exactly," she said, fighting back a sob. But the dam burst. With a body shudder, she blurted out, "I know some places she could go if she wanted to hide. I don't know which one she's at."

"I understand." Rita reached forward and placed a comforting hand on Magda's arm. "I give you my word that if I find her first, I promise no harm to her. Can you live with that?"

Magda sucked in a sharp breath and nodded. "I got no choice here. I'm afraid of her with the police. You promise you won't shoot her?"

"I promise," Rita said. "And I understand how painful this has to be for you."

♏

Sundown. The fiery sun of August streaked the winding Choptank River with dazzling splashes of orange. Inside the Delmarva Shore Motel, a wheezing HVAC unit whispered a stream of stale, lukewarm air. Diane sat at a scarred desk and peered outside at the pool.

It was almost dinnertime for families and mothers were wrangling children out of the water. In a few minutes, the pool was empty. The water was still and there were no shrieks or out-loud laughs.

"I want to swim," Diane said without turning around. Her captor was engrossed in *Pretty Woman* with Richard Gere and Julia Roberts. CharleyZ did not respond.

Diane rose from her seat and pulled out the travel bag packed for her by Charlene. She hoped there would be her old tank suit at least. A tiny smile rippled across her lips when she found it. She went into the bathroom.

"Hey, what's with the bathing suit?" Charlene paused her movie. She eyed Diane.

"I'm going to swim. I'm going stir crazy being stuck in this place." Diane had a thin, worn bath towel over her shoulder.

"You ain't goin' without me." Charlene stood up. "I didn't bring no suit."

"I need to move." Diane assertively opened the door. Charlene followed.

As soon as Diane dropped her towel on the deeper end of the pool, she slid into the water like an otter. It was her element. She was a strong swimmer and with minimal strokes she was at the opposite end. Diane felt Charlene's hungry eyes on her as she glided through the water. With renewed strength in the pull and draw of her crawl stroke, she flipped into a fluid turn that barely ruffled the surface. Still, she couldn't shake the notion of Charlene as predator and herself as prey.

Back and forth, again and again until Diane hauled herself out of the water. She tilted her head and hopped on one foot to expel a trickle that she had taken in one ear.

"You looked good doin' that," Charlene said. She lifted a corner of the towel to draw it around Diane's shoulders.

"Years of swim team," Diane squeezed her wet hair with the towel.

"I took swimmin' once," Charlene offered.

"Mmm," Diane said.

"Patterson Park rec center," Charline continued. "Almost finished, but I got into a thing with some black girls. I was gonna show 'em who's boss, but my mom made me quit." Charlene looked down then. "Never went back."

"I see," Diane turned her back on Charlene and headed to the motel room.

In the room, Diane pulled a hoodie over her head. Charline stuck an arm out to stop Diane before she could lower the sweatshirt.

"Not yet," Charlene said. It was almost a plea. "I—I want to see you. Never seen anybody I know who could move like you do in the water. I coulda never got that good." Her voice trailed off with a shadow of sadness.

Diane turned to her. "Yes, you could, Charlene. Takes sticktoitiveness." A drop of water from Diane's hair plopped down onto her chest just above the bodice of her swimsuit. It took a slow trickle into her cleavage.

Charlene's eyes followed that slow downward plunge. She lowered her head until she was eye to eye with Diane. She closed her eyes and lightly touched one of Diane's arms.

In this intimate proximity, Diane could smell the mix of unwashed clothes and toothpaste. Charlene's lips brushed hers, unable to fulfill an intended kiss as Diane turned her head and pulled away with a step backward. Charlene's light touch on her arm tightened into a pinching vise. Diane tried to pull away.

Without warning, Charlene's broad, open palm swung a roundhouse blow. The slap resounded in Diane's ears. It stung and she could hear a crack that snapped her head in a trajectory toward her shoulder. Tears sprang instantly to her eyes. She wondered if this had dislocated her jaw.

Diane fought for control of her emotions. She was determined not to show fear. She brought her hand up to cradle the landing spot of the slap. It was hot.

Charlene recoiled. "You," she accused Diane, "you're a liar. You're hateful and mean. You pretend yer bein' nice to somebody and then you cut 'em off at the knees to hurt their feelin's. I don't know why I didn't see this before. "

"I don't do that." Diane began to cry. She sank down on the edge of the bed behind her.

"You were never worth the risk. Never. And I was too dumb to see it," Charlene yelled.

• ——— ❧ ——— •

Chapter 25

Magda Zawaki gave Rita three locations as possibilities for Charlene's hiding place. The first was that she might be holed up with a friend. Charlene had had a brief relationship with a woman who also lived in Highlandtown. Magda had also suggested that Charlene could be anywhere and living out of her camper truck. Rita had shuddered at the possibility. The thought of scouring the highways for a chance spotting made her crazy—and she was not going to the police as she had promised Charlene's mother. Finally, Magda told Rita that Charlene might be hiding near her older brother's hunting trailer on Maryland's Eastern Shore, a more rural part of the state and the area where that surprising video of the altercation with the prison road gang had taken place.

Rita propped her feet on her desk, notepad on her lap, and began to organize a timeline with an overlay of logic. Yes, the hunting trailer appeared to offer the most credible situation. After all, Diane and Charlene had been seen there. Still, with the attention that commotion stirred, Charlene might have moved very far away from that area.

There was no way out of it; Rita would have to check out each of Magda's suggestions.

♏

"Your next clients are here." Bev tapped a chat to Rita who was behind closed doors in her office. "Not your usuals. Four—three men and a woman. Lookin' all unfriendly and shit."

"Send 'em." Rita typed back.

The gang of four entered her office. Rita stood and smiled. She came around her desk and introduced herself. She offered her hand. Not one of the visitors moved to return the handshake. They stood like an enforcing wall in a row facing her.

"Ok, please take a seat." Rita had moved four chairs around the front of her desk.

"We'll stand." The first man in line spoke. He held out a business card: Joshua Pillot, Christian Merchants Association.

"Suit yourself." Rita studied the individuals who had taken a position between her and the door. The men were in suits, two wore black, the third a deep charcoal. Shiny shoes, new, no scuffs. The woman wore a black and white knit skirt suit. Her heels were low, and she carried no purse. None of them smiled. None of them fidgeted. The delegation from the grim reaper, Rita said to herself.

"We're here because your recent inquiries are causing us to lose business." The lead man in the line spoke again. "We're being maligned. We want it to stop." Rita thought it curious that she did not see one nod of a head in concurrence. The backups were silent and stone-faced.

"And why do you think I am the person causing you financial problems?" Rita sat up.

"We've heard it informally."

"You verified it?" Rita asked.

"We don't have to. We know this to be true." The man's voice was harsher.

"I see. You believe any innuendo that you want to be true."

"That's not what I said." Harshness devolved into an underlying snarl.

"You come to me with accusations. You can't verify the basis of that accusation, but you wish me to act on it?" Rita gripped the speaker with her eyes.

"We want you to stop." The speaker emphasized his point with a finger stabbing in Rita's direction.

"The rest of your group have not identified yourselves. I have an appointment listed in my schedule as representatives of Whitlock Foundation vendors. If you want me to work with you, I need a shred of accurate information regarding who you are or represent as well as the actions I am taking that seem to your group to be unlawful or unfair," Rita stated.

"I think you know very well," the group's spokesman said in rebuttal. "You have my card. You can check with any background check service. I represent Baltimore's Christian Merchants Association. We are part of a national organization dedicated to freedom to do business based on our Christian principles."

Rita stood up and walked around to face the foursome who stood between her and the office door. "And yet you refuse to tell me where you obtained information that I, personally, was coming after your business—or why I would."

Rita marched around the visitors and opened her office door. Pointedly, she held it wide. "I think we're done here." She stood waiting for the exit of the four. She could see anger rising in the spokesman's face. His features tightened, lips drew thin, eyes streaming malice at her.

"You haven't heard final words from us," Joshua Pillot said.

"A threat? Really?" Rita said. "What happened to 'turn the other cheek?'"

Pillot was the last to exit. He paused inches from Rita's face. "'For the weapons of our warfare are not of the flesh but have divine power to destroy stronghold','" he said.

"Ah, Corinthians," Rita said with a grim tone. "Though I see you as more deserving of admonitions from Jeremiah— 'Do not listen to the words of the prophets who prophesy to you, filling you with vain hopes. They speak visions of their own minds, not from the mouth of the Lord.'"

As soon as the outer door closed, Rita was at Bev's desk. "That was a fun lot."

"Yeah, remind of cops in my hood when I was a kid," Bev said. "Just weren't wearin' the blue. What'd they say?"

Rita glanced at her mother watching the news on the waiting room television. Annie seemed focused on the tv and unaware of the Bev-Rita conversation.

"Came here to try and get me to back off Louise Mercilus. They wouldn't come out and speak her name, but their reference was undeniable." Rita settled on the edge of Bev's desk.

"Who the hell were they?" Bev asked.

"Said they were members of the Baltimore Christian Merchant Association. Never heard of 'em. I'm gonna do some research on that group."

Bev tapped on her computer keys. Rita slid off the desk and walked around to view a website with Bev.

"Spiritual warfare," Rita read out loud. "What does that mean?"

"Means they think you're both creations of the devil. You need to be hunted down and eradicated." Annie turned from the television she had been watching to address Bev and Rita.

"Well, I see your hearing hasn't missed a step," Rita said.

Annie returned her attention to *The View* where Whoopi Goldberg was pontificating. Annie ignored Rita's comment and came back with, "My daddy would tell me 'Sometimes it's time to lay low and peep high.'"

"I'm not laying low." Rita put her hands on her hips.

"Didn't think that for a minute." Annie leaned back in her seat and took a sip of coffee.

♏

The next morning, Rita left Annie with Bev when she headed out to Lou Ann Kosek's apartment in Highlandtown. Annie seemed to have lost her energy after a few days straight in the heat, waiting for Rita's interviews to end. Rita thought she saw a sigh of relief escape her mother when she told Annie that it would be better to have a leisurely lunch with Bev who would then take her shopping at the Galleria.

Rita zigged and zagged through morning rush hour stragglers. The radio, uncharacteristically, was off. The A/C was on. The silence was an opening for thoughts about the previous day's visit from the Christian Merchants Association. Who were those people? She needed to confirm membership.

Rita considered the visit. Surely actual Christian Merchant Association types would consider a request before a threat. But if they were, in fact, from the organization why come at me without a weapon plan? The threat of a lawsuit? A loss of PI license? So deeply vague on whom they represented. Which can only mean . . . the car in front halted abruptly.

"Shit." Rita's reflexes kicked in. The shrieking of slammed brakes pierced the Jeep's interior. She tapped the bumper of the Chevy Malibu ahead. Rita grabbed her registration and insurance card and slid out of the driver's seat.

Rita instinctively looked beyond the car she'd hit to see what caused the sudden need to halt. The street was clear. She glanced at the parked cars. No one had pulled out without looking.

A man emerged from the Malibu. Rita had noticed a heavy-duty Ford pickup behind her when she was driving. She glanced back and saw the truck pulled within inches of her rear bumper. That driver sat unmoving behind mirrored shades. He made no move to get out of the truck, but he did not back up for Rita either.

Within seconds the Malibu driver was in front of her. She reached toward the Jeep to grab her phone but the driver of the car slammed her arm in the door. The impingement threw Rita off balance. She buckled with the pain but refused to cry out.

"You don't listen real good, do you?" The driver continued to press on the door. It pinched Rita's shoulder and she flinched.

Rita said nothing but she was able to see the first three numbers on the Malibu's back tag. She turned to see what she could on the truck. The last three digits.

"I'm talking to you." The Malibu driver gave a jolt to Rita's shoulder. She winced and turned back to him but said nothing. She stuck her free hand into her back pocket and touched the keys that long ago she'd programmed.

"See how easy it is to reach you?" The driver stepped forward so that his face was inches from Rita's. Still she said nothing. In the distance was the wail of a siren.

"Back off of your snooping, bitch." Rita's aggressor spit his words at her. Saliva drops spattered on her cheek. She kept a watchful eye on the hand movements of the man ranting at her, but she as well glanced into her side mirror to monitor whether the truck driver behind was going to get out and join his fellow thug. The siren grew louder and suddenly a patrol car careened around the corner of Bank Street.

The sudden appearance of the police caught Rita's attacker off guard. He took a step backward. The truck blocking Rita's

Jeep roared as the driver backed up and sped off. The guy holding her pinned to her vehicle with the driver side door, turned on his heel and burned rubber in the opposite direction. Rita watched him make a right a few blocks up.

"Ma'am, are you the 911 caller?" The cop who'd been driving the patrol car asked. Rita assumed he'd been on the force for a while. He adjusted his Sam Browne belt under an ample belly. He gripped the butt of his Glock-17 as he approached Rita.

She lowered her freed arm and massaged her shoulder. "Ma'am?" The cop stopped walking, uncertain of the dynamics of the situation before him.

"Sorry, officer. Two men had me immobile between a Malibu and a Ford 150. The guy in front jumped out and smashed my door against my right arm so I couldn't get away."

The cop's partner was on the other side of the car. He peered in to ensure there would be no surprises from the Jeep's interior. He nodded the "all clear" to the policeman in front of Rita.

"Did you get any plate ids?" The lead officer continued his wariness. Rita shook her head. "Are you armed?"

"Me?" Rita was surprised by the question. "No, I was on my way to an interview." At this point, she sank down on the running board of the Jeep.

"Ma'am, I need you to stand up where I can see you," the cop said, but Rita noticed he had dropped his quick-draw stance.

Rita explained the confrontation as she remembered it. The cop noted the descriptions of the vehicles and drivers involved. He then explained there wasn't much he and his partner could do without further information to go on. Rita thanked both policemen for their prompt response and promised to contact them if she remembered anything that could be more significant. When the patrol glided away, residents started opening doors, pulling back curtains. Passersby gawked but no one came forward or offered assistance.

Rita climbed back into the Jeep. She tapped the phone mounted on her dash.

"What's up?" Bev cheerily answered the phone.

"I poked the bear," Rita said. "Keep up the happy talk on your end but I need you to keep an eye on my mother. Do not let her out of your sight."

"Sure thing, shortnin' bread," Bev responded. "Can you tell me a little more about the party?"

"When I get back into the office, ok? I'm on my way to interview a girlfriend of this CharleyZ woman." Rita surveyed 360 degrees through the Jeep windows.

"Well, that's special," Bev said. Rita could picture her grinning as she lied through her teeth.

"Yeah—and not in a good way." Rita started the Jeep. "Keep her safe, Bev."

m

The Highland View apartments rose from the heart of Highlandtown, replacing the warehouse of a long-gone Baltimore retailer. It rose above community rooftops, a new and shining structure of whitewashed brick as part of a concerted revitalization effort that managed to survive the fits and starts of bureaucracy and commercial partnerships.

"Miz Lorta," Rita said when the door to CharleyZ's friend's apartment opened, "thanks for agreeing to see me today. I won't take long."

The woman opened the door wider and Rita entered. "I'm not sure I can help you," Ceci Lorta said as she led the way to her living room. "Can I get you an iced tea?" The woman was taller than Rita. She was Hispanic with beautiful black hair which she'd pulled into a French twist. She had a plain face but piercing eyes and a full sensuous mouth.

Rita declined and the two women sat, Ceci on the end of a new sofa, Rita on a club chair closely perpendicular.

"I haven't even seen Charlene in more than a year," Ceci said.

Rita went on without acknowledgement. "I understand from her mother that she lived with you for a while. You were partners?"

Ceci laughed. "We were not partners. Charlene was trying to get herself together and go to school—like I did. I'm a paralegal now but when she moved in, I was getting my degree at the University of Baltimore. She said she wanted to do that too."

"But . . ." Rita said.

"Charlene could never stick to anything. Not sure if it was because she was born so late in Magda's life, but Charlene would try something new, a sport or a job—anything. She'd be all in for a while, and when she didn't zoom up the ladder or get a raise or the activity wasn't panning out as she'd dreamed, she'd up and leave. Just go."

"Not a good game plan."

Ceci sighed. "Charlene never planned. She never thought beyond the next few days or weeks."

"She told some folks she was getting a law degree at UB," Rita said.

"Not that I ever knew. I know for a fact she never took the LSAT."

"But she lived here?" Rita asked.

"I'd been looking for a roommate to share expenses. Charlene asked if she could move in. I said ok. For about six months, she made her share of the rent and then she quit the job she had and moved back in with her mother." Ceci glanced at her watch.

"A woman was abducted from the building where Charlene was working as security and garage attendant." Rita saw the look on Ceci's face morph from tired to distressed.

"That doesn't sound like Charlene. Too much planning involved in that." Ceci shifted to the edge of the sofa cushion. "And I never thought of her as criminal. She was a follower, not a leader, not somebody who'd think up that kind of thing by herself."

"Nonetheless, she was spotted with the woman she allegedly abducted halfway down Route 50 toward the beach."

Ceci was quiet and Rita could sense her trying to understand this uncharacteristic behavior. Rita spoke. "Is she capable of violence? Have you ever seen her get out of control."

"She'd get frustrated and throw stuff. Hurting someone? No way." Ceci glanced again at her watch.

"Last question, I promise," Rita said. "Did you and she ever visit any places across the Bay Bridge. Did she ever mention any places over there? I promised her mother I would do everything in my power to find her first. Magda was afraid the police would hurt her, and they might if she tried to stand up against them. The woman she has with her is my ex-partner and I don't want her hurt either."

Ceci paused and nodded. "Did your ex maybe suggest or talk about something like running away together? Charlene could easily have misunderstood."

"Don't know," Rita answered. "What I need help with is places she might run to for hiding. Any places you can think of like that?"

"We went down to the ocean a lot. She loved the boardwalk. But if she's scared and hiding, I don't think that'd be the place." Ceci stopped talking.

"I'm not going to hurt her, but I've got to be the one to find her first."

"I get that. Just trying to think." Ceci looked at Rita. "Her brother had a trailer near Cambridge, near Blackwater refuge. You know where that is?"

"I do," Rita said.

"I remember very clearly after the 9/11 attacks in New York she said she'd drive down there with her camper and hide out. Said she could say there a long time with provisions and nobody would want to cross that marsh to get to her."

"Does she have any weapons?" Rita asked.

"Old .22 handgun. Bought if off some street kid. Never saw her shoot it." Ceci now looked pointedly at her watch. "I'm sorry but I'm going out to dinner tonight and I have to get ready." She stood. "I don't know how much I've helped you."

"First direct answers I've gotten about her. You've been a great help," Rita said. As she entered the elevator to get back to the street, she thought to herself, twenty-eight thousand acres of wetlands and wide-open fields with brackish sinkholes that could swallow a body with one wrong step. How do I ever?

• ━━◦⊙◦━━ •

Chapter 26

"Do you think I was followed?" Bunny Blyth-Cramer said in a hushed voice. She was the first to arrive for Rita's hastily called meeting. They were convening at Rita's house in the late afternoon. Roswell had a gig so he would be joining by Zoom from his current project.

"Did you leave from Marianne's or the Foundation office?" Rita asked.

"Marianne's," Bunny responded. "Told her I needed to emergency babysit for my granddaughter. Louise was still in the downtown office." She paused. "I think."

"We are where we are," Rita said. "We have to play it as it lays." She finished setting up chairs for Bunny, Bev and Mary Margaret and flipped her video equipment toward the chairs so that Roswell could join.

It was an atypical late August day. The thunderstorm from the previous night had freshened the air and swept away the humidity. A soft breeze played with the curtains and a dappling of sunlight scattered across Rita's home office carpet. Annie was taking her afternoon nap. The last physical attendee, Mary

Margaret Smooth, steered her old Camry onto the blacktop behind Rita's house just as Roswell popped into view on Rita's pc monitor.

When everyone was assembled, Rita began, "Thanks for getting here on short notice. I'm going to get right to it." She gave a rundown on her experiences with the Baltimore Christian Merchants as well as the "swoop and squat" maneuver where she'd so recently been pinned down on a city street by unknowns.

"Oh God," Bunny said. "I never dreamed we'd be getting into violence. Never in a million years."

"I'm thinking you've found a way into Mercilus' criminal enterprise, and her accomplices are coming out to close the hole." Mary Margaret sat up straighter. "Are you taking this to Marianne Whitlock or the police?"

"Thought about it," Rita said.

Before Rita could elaborate, Bunny piped up. "If you go public, it will kill the Foundation. People will get skittish and take their money to another charitable cause." She shook her head and looked from Rita to Mary Margaret.

"That's an accurate assessment," Rita said. "And making it public would expose the Foundation, as well as Marianne, to defamation lawsuits. Taking the offense with a move like a defamation claim is one of the most used embezzler tactics. A news story about impropriety, with or without the name of the suspect, buys the suspect time and delays the fraud investigation. Great ploy for the bad guys."

The small group fell silent as they considered what Rita had just told them. At last, Roswell spoke from the pc monitor, "So we need to speed up and find that smoking gun pretty quick."

"That is our dilemma," Rita agreed.

"What is it you need? What's the smoking gun?" Mary Margaret directed the question at Rita.

Rita hesitated but responded, "Usually you bring in a forensic team and they perform analysis after analysis until they find the 'telling' mismatch of figures that completes the link. This can take weeks, months or even years." She paced as she spoke.

"So, we've done all this work for nothing?" Bunny asked.

"No, the work we've completed touched a nerve or the bums would never have tried to scare us off. However, we're basically blind in a swirl of numbers and transactions so we haven't been able to make the connection." Rita stopped to face her disheartened audience.

"Bunny, do you know the accounting systems well enough to help Roswell run the exception reporting for Whitlock Foundation revenue and expense elements?"

"It's been a long time since I ran reports for Marianne. I . . . I might be rusty," Bunny said. "Should we explain our situation to the accounting consultant we contract and get him to help us?"

"We don't know who in the organization we can trust." Rita's face betrayed her concern. "You haven't shared what we suspect about Louise, have you?"

"Oh, no," Bunny responded quickly. "No one."

Rita considered her suspicion about the bugging of her office at the Foundation offices. She had not had time to plan how to go about it. A just-in-time announcement and surprise sweep was no way to keep Mercilus believing she had everyone fooled. That scenario could only lead to Louise fleeing with no chance of Whitlock Foundation recouping monies taken. And the fallout for the charity would be not only loss but the resulting news cycle that would feature Whitlock's "absconding" executive director.

It was true that Louise believed Rita was on to her in the intuitive way investigators smell deceit. Louise also believed, in Rita's mind, that there was at this point no evidence. Louise was right about the lack of evidence. This forced Rita to move quickly with swift, precise action and no room for sloppy mistakes.

Rita studied Bunny for a moment. "If you have shared with anybody, please tell me. I need to know if we have other employees involved in this theft. We don't want to get attacked when we're not prepared." Rita held Bunny with her eyes.

Bunny replied with a definitive, "No. I spoke to no one about this."

"Good," Rita said and turned to the pc screen. "Roswell, I want to run our reporting first just with Bunny's guidance. If we find nothing, I'd like you to explore whether there is a forensic accountant you've worked with—and trust—who might be familiar with the software Whitlock uses and who might be able to help us spot telltale transactions."

"I will make the list and send it to you. You'll be able to do due diligence on them before we might need them," Roswell replied.

"Good deal. And this goes for all of us. We don't want to put any discussion, offhand remarks or people into the mix that we aren't completely sure of. Got it?" Rita looked from person to person. Each nodded in agreement. "And be careful in whose company you speak, even to where you can be overheard by someone who's involved. Does that make sense?"

"This sounds so cloak and dagger," Bunny said. "Should we be afraid of physical danger?"

Rita stopped. Typically, embezzlers were not killers. Usually upon discovery, they caved. But Louise was different. She did not think for a moment that Louise was siphoning funds from Whitlock totally for herself. The visit from the Baltimore Christian Merchants and threats from the staged fender bender convinced Rita Louise was part of some larger malevolence.

"In my experience, embezzlers aren't killers. When was the last time you read a headline about a fraudster shooting his way out of the bank he stole from?" Rita asked. "This is accounting crime, not the wild west." Bunny's slight rise of her eyebrows and nodding head demonstrated her acceptance.

"I'm not a one-person team here," Rita said. "Smooth," she said to Mary Margaret, "any thoughts?"

Mary Margaret homed in on Rita's cue about non-violence. "I don't know all the details," Smooth replied, "but I'm with Rita about keeping mum unless it's to one of our small group. I also agree we should be wary of our surroundings when we're discussing something about this case with someone we trust."

Rita turned to the pc monitor. "Roswell, you've been tapped before to work cases like this. Any thoughts?"

Roswell cleared his throat. "I work mostly data theft, but I have had a few projects where I've worked with a forensic accountant before. Never seen violence from anyone we tracked and eventually was charged and prosecuted. My issue is going to be how savvy this Mercilus woman's team is. I want to be in stealth mode til it's too late for the thieves to realize."

"Got it," Rita said. "And I have a task for you, so if we could chat off video conference after this meeting?"

"No worries," Roswell agreed.

Rita turned to Bev last. She winked at her assistant as the others looked toward Bev. "I need you make sure nothing goes off the rails."

"With apologies to Cap'n Mary Margaret." Bev made a gesture like the tip of a hat. "I be keepin' it smooth, baby."

♏

Rita adjourned the meeting. Bunny was gone. Bev and Mary Margaret waited outside in rockers on Rita's front porch. Mary Margaret had taken a beer from Rita's fridge. Bev had a diet lemonade and chatted to Smooth about an upcoming drag event she planned to join on Labor Day. Annie was still snuggled in her nap.

As she waited for Roswell to call back, she revisited the guidance she'd laid down to her tiny band of investigators. She was most concerned about Bunny. She'd never worked with Rita on a case before, and even with assurances, Bunny had been the one person most shaken about the threat of violence. Would she step up or collapse in the shadow of an unsettled attitude in the face of danger?

Roswell buzzed her phone. "Hey, it's me. What do you need?"

"Thanks for the help," Rita said first. "You did that bug search at my house, my office at home and the office I have at Whitlock Foundation. Nonetheless, Mercilus had knowledge of my visit to Wyoming and I want to know how."

"I can do another sweep of your office," Roswell offered.

"Too narrow," Rita said. "I want you to sweep everything all over again. The tricky part will involve the Foundation offices. We need a pretext and some subterfuge. Have you ever done anything like that?"

"Not really," Roswell said. "In my work like that, the client usually has me going through his facilities at night. It isn't broadcast to the employees, but it isn't secret squirrel either."

"Hmm, let me think a minute about how." Rita could stick to sweeping for bugs in her office alone, like last time. Too much was left unexplored if she did that. She could also conjure a cover story and some kind of fake authority id. And if Roswell decided to punt, how long would it take to find a replacement.

"Run something by you?" Rita asked at last.

"Go," Roswell responded.

"How about you, as building maintenance, check for a leak or an electrical problem? I'll have a badge made for you with a fake name. You'll have your tools for finding eavesdrop setups. I will get Bunny to send out an email about the visit from building management. What I'd count on you most for, besides finding audio snoops, is social engineering."

In this case, Roswell would use his skills to convince Foundation employees, particularly Louise Mercilus, that he was indeed from the building's maintenance staff. Additionally, he would have to be credible to Mercilus. He had to know building management staff names and duties, maybe some little stories about one or two of them, maybe stories about the building itself. If the trick failed, Mercilus could freak and skip and the entire investigation would evaporate.

"I am very, very good," Roswell said.

"I'm not going to ask how you've decided that," Rita responded but inside her head she drew a sigh of relief. "I'll get you an id and the regular box of tools and a uniform," Rita added.

"Great." Roswell said and then continued. "Can I ask a question about that staged car accident? How did you get the police there? Exactly to your location?" Roswell asked.

Rita laughed. "Hey, dude, I know you've seen the 'I've fallen and can't get up' ads on tv. Got a variation of that I carry everywhere. It's a very tiny wifi and mobile enabled GPS. Activated signal goes to a central monitoring station and appropriate action is taken immediately."

"I guessed right that you had a panic button. Very cool," Roswell said.

"Cool indeed," Rita said as she nodded in agreement.

♏

August heat returned to bloom with a stifling vengeance. The very air swaddled like a hot wet blanket. Rita's breathing was labored as she forged her way along on her morning run. Even the usual heat sheltering shade offered on the tree-lined running trail seemed oppressive. At mile three, Rita's head urged her to stop. But Rita rejected the idea. It is a five-mile day, she said to herself.

When her course was complete, Rita bent forward onto the hood of the Jeep. Her singlet and running shorts were soaked through. She reached into the vehicle and extracted an icy Gatorade from its cooler. She gulped half the bottle. It came back up almost instantly.

"Crap." Rita heaved the thirst redeeming drink. It wasn't uncommon in this kind of weather. She marveled that she continued to repeat this same behavior with its same response every time. Yes, I am insane, she said to herself as she picked up the bottle and sipped more slowly to counter the thirst and the heat.

The heat this morning run mirrored the cases she was enmeshed in each waking moment. True, she was moving forward. But she felt hamstrung. The embezzlement demanded a needle-in-the-haystack event and she fretted that it would drag on and on without that blind chance moment of discovery.

And Diane was still out there. For Rita, this situation was intolerable. She felt she was failing. Am I too old for this work? Am I not doing something I would have acted on earlier in my career, when my head was younger? At that moment a just-washed SUV pulled in near Rita's Jeep. She immediately jumped to alert mode. But it was another woman she'd seen and sometimes ran with on this trail. They exchanged waves and the other runner jogged off.

At her house, Annie stood in the kitchen by the coffee maker. Rita's clothing had dried in the Jeep's AC, but her hair was flattened to her head and her face still red from heat and exertion. She had early signals of dehydration. Body-dragging fatigue. Low level brain fog. The systemic narrowing of every capillary in her head made her feel like she was wearing a too-tight cap squeezing pain across her scalp.

"Honey, you're gonna have heat stroke running in this weather." Annie took a dish towel, wetted it and added ice. "Here, why don't you lay down on the sofa for a minute and let yourself recover."

"I have a lot to do today," Rita said but she took the cold, wet dish towel.

"Won't get it done in your condition." Annie perched on one of the breakfast counter chairs. She had a coffee cup in one hand. With her other hand, she slid a Double Stuf off the plate of cookies in front of her.

"Yeah, I know." Rita kept her eyes on her mother, waiting.

"What?" Annie asked. "You're waiting for more?"

"Waiting for you to tell me I'm too old for what I'm taking on," Rita said. "Go on, let's get it over with."

"You'll never hear those words from me," Annie said. "One thing I understand from living forty years with your father. 'Quit' wasn't a concept in his universe." Annie paused. "And for me to introduce it to you, as his daughter, the truest replica of his mindset and his ways, would just be a plain ole waste of my breath."

Chapter 27

"You know I could have been at the beach working on my tan and looking for companionship," Mary Margaret said. After much begging, cajoling and wheedling, Rita had finally gotten Smooth to agree to using her time off to travel to the Eastern Shore area of Maryland to check out the possibility that Charlene Zawaki was holding Diane in her brother's hunting trailer. Annie would go with Smooth.

Rita believed the unknowns who had accosted her would not suspect Annie would be in her downtown office with Bev. She would be free to help Roswell set up the ruse of his identity as a building maintenance worker and subsequently sweep the Whitlock Foundation offices for listening devices.

"Smooth, you told me yourself you've given up on that tanning thing. Wasn't it you bitching about crows' feet and furrows and . . ." Rita recounted, but Smooth cut her off.

"Enough," Mary Margaret groaned. "Geez. Yes, I don't sit out and toast my skin anymore. But I need downtime. Switching from human traffickers to embezzlers is not down time, for pete's sake."

Rita wanted the least exposure for her mother in difficult-to-secure venues like city streets. The surprise attack in Highlandtown still burned strong in her memory. She trusted Bev with her life, her mother's life, but even she had limitations in wide open spaces. Nonetheless with Annie and Bev stowed securely in the office, Rita felt free enough to meet with Mary Margaret alone.

Rita sighed. "I understand that, Smooth, I do. And I'm sorry. You and I haven't had the chance to weekend down at the ocean. We haven't had a one-on-one lunch in weeks. The Diane case combined with the Whitlock fraud make it so much harder for us to get together. I'm not only looking for Diane, but I've got your buddy, Billy Bolton, poised to pounce on anything he thinks he can charge me with. Now I have some crazies jumping me in broad daylight without a clue at this point as to who they are."

Their lunch was over at the Sip N Bite. Rita picked at a pile of leftover potato chips. As she spoke, Smooth's face softened. She shook her head and leaned back in the banquette. The diner had quieted from full body contact to the clamor of dishes and flatware into busboy tubs.

"I know. I know," Smooth said. "I'm sorry about nagging you. I miss you. I miss hanging out. And I'm actually looking forward to taking your mom with me tomorrow. She's always been my second mother, especially now that mine is gone."

Rita stretched her hand across the table. "My sister will be returning in a week and Mom will be going back home with her. And I'm scared, Smooth. That faked accident gave me a reminder of how easy it is for people to have a false sense of security. I was too complacent and bang, bad shit could have happened."

Smooth took Rita's hand. "I get that," Smooth agreed. "And I will be watching out for her tomorrow. I'll also be checking my car undercarriage for trackers and keeping an eye out for anybody following us."

"I know you will." Rita smiled. "And I want to give you a panic button that signals my security service like I used the other day on the two goons who attacked me." Rita drew a credit card sized silicone disc from her slacks pocket. "Remember how it works." Rita advised. She gave Smooth an overview of what situation each of the three buttons were to be used for.

"Give this to your mom?" Smooth asked.

"I want you to hold on to it. I'm not sure I want her to know the danger, and I don't know if she'll remember in an emergency. But I do want access to something an attacker isn't expecting to be used to get help," Rita explained.

"Got it," Smooth said as she withdrew her hand from Rita's grasp and slid the small silicone device into her uniform breast pocket.

As Smooth did so, the Sip N Bite's proprietor, Nick, approached the table. "You two getting married? I see you holding hands here at the table and I think 'hey, maybe wedding reception for me to cater'," he teased in a heavy Greek accent.

Rita laughed. "She's too good for me, Nick. She'd be marrying beneath her station."

♏

Captain Mary Margaret Smooth rolled up to Rita's house. She'd been to the car wash for a quick spritz to shake the road dust, dump her collection of old paper trash and vacuum the floor mats. She took one last inspection of the front seat passenger area. All clean. On the back floor, she verified she had the leather envelope with photos of Diane Winter and Charlene Zawaki.

That envelope also had a clear picture of the camper pickup. It was taken the day of the road crew dust up. On her phone, Smooth had a downloaded copy of the news video of that event. She leaned down and patted her ankle to confirm the Beretta Pico .38.

"Hey, Miss Annie, we are going to have a great time today." Mary Margaret wrapped her arms around Rita's mother.

"I haven't been down to that part of the world in so many years," Annie said as she and Mary Margaret released from their hug. "Rita's dad and I used to take a week every summer and spend it in Ocean City. Sarah and Rita loved it. We walked on the beach and spent bunches of money on games for the cheapest prizes you could imagine. And . . . I'm going on here." Annie's face flushed with excitement. She grinned at Smooth.

"Don't you worry about it." Mary Margaret had her own thoughts about Ocean City where she and Rita as teenagers would drive down for the day and meet friends. They would deepen their tans on the beach during daylight, then stay half the night bopping to house music in a boardwalk dancehall. They always factored in the price of that fun would be lectures and tales of parental anguish about their safety and how late it was for them to be out in the big, bad world. Smooth loved these memories and smiled to herself.

On the way to the destination, Mary Margaret and Rita had zeroed in on, Annie and Smooth exchanged shared stories of neighbors. They had no disagreement as to whom they liked best in the community. Old Mrs. Hastings was the first choice of both. She made chocolate chip cookies in the winter and offered them warm and gooey to kids on the block when there were snow days. In summer, it was homemade lemonade.

As for their street's biggest bastard, Mary Margaret nominated a bully three years older than Rita and her. Whenever he saw them together, he would yell "queer" as loud as he could and follow them for a while crying out his accusation. While Annie agreed that was truly bad, she knew that her old next-door neighbor, a middle-aged divorced schoolteacher, was still in prison for child sexual assault. Time passed without notice as the two continued their "best" and "worst" game about people from the past.

"Are we getting close?" Annie asked after a stretch when the game had petered out and both grew quiet. "I'm getting hungry."

"We are where we're headed," Mary Margaret announced. "Let's grab some lunch." She swung into the parking lot of a seafood restaurant.

"The Chesapeake House," Annie exclaimed. "This is wonderful. Broiled crabcakes. This is such a treat. Another place I haven't been to in years."

"Thought you might like it." Mary Margaret wheeled into a just-vacated spot close to the entrance.

The waitress seated them next to the panoramic window that showcased the harbor and the marina just outside their table. It was a picture-perfect view of cruisers and sailboats and fishing craft with flying bridges. The brilliant sun on the water gave the vista a glossy photo aspect, cheery and bright.

They decided to split dessert. The lunch crowd was gone. Across the room the barman was restocking and prepping mixers for the evening's happy hour and dinner customers.

"I know there's no such thing as a free lunch." Annie impaled the last fragment of key lime pie and popped it into her mouth. "What are we doing for my daughter here?"

"No fooling you." Mary Margaret took a sip of her cooling coffee.

"Nope. I know her like I know myself." Annie picked up her own coffee cup. She held it poised at her lips and closed her eyes as if she were tapping into clairvoyance. "This is close to the place where that news video of Diane Winter and her kidnapper was filmed."

"Yes." Smooth nodded.

"And I believe you have specific places you want to visit to ask if they've seen Diane recently. You might also have a better picture of the kidnapper. You'll ask about her." Annie paused and opened her eyes. "How'd I do?"

Mary Margaret could not help but grin. She scribbled her name on the lunch check. "Maybe Rita inherited her detective skills from you and not from her dad. You nailed it."

"Oh, I picked all this up from him," Annie said. "Rita was the perfect student though. She may have butted heads with her father, but she took in everything he knew, everything he did."

"That's why they butted heads," Mary Margaret theorized.

"Exactly," said Annie.

♏

Now's the tedious part of this gig, Smooth thought to herself. Canvassing. More like fishing when you have no idea where the fish are. She remembered her patrol years of knocking on door after door. Some people never respond. Some are afraid. And some make shit up. Like the postman though, you keep on keeping on through lies, shrugs or fantasies and never stay your appointed round. That one sterling nugget could be out there, waiting to be found.

Smooth shook off her memory of those tedious scavenger hunts. "You ready for an hour or two of shopping for suspects?"

"Shopping?" Annie repeated. "Never heard it called that." She slid into Smooth's car.

"I call it that." Mary Margaret laughed. "Shopping sounds like more fun than 'canvassing'."

"I see," Annie said. "So what's the game plan here?"

"Rita and I reviewed the business map on this area. We're going to visit a few low-end motels, a grocery store and as many gas stations and convenience stores as we have time. I'll show 'em my pics and maybe have a hit. Before that though, we check out a hunting trailer the suspect's brother owns in this area."

"Got it." Annie sighed. "Shouldn't have eaten so much. Made me sleepy. But I'm fine. Need me to help ask questions?"

"Maybe." Smooth set her GPS and rolled out of the parking lot. She headed for the trailer that Charlene's brother kept for himself and his hunting buddies.

Smooth made a turn off the main east-west route of U.S. 50 onto Church Creek Road. She'd never traveled off Route 50 before to explore the tiny rural towns which dotted the area. These were towns like Crapo (with a long a) and Bucktown and Toddville where she was headed now. Smooth thought of old Twilight Zone episodes where someone takes a wrong turn and ends up in an alternate dimension. That is how she felt as she exited a four-lane thoroughfare into a foreign universe.

Here on these narrow, two-lane backroads that only locals and hunters knew, it was empty. Ten minutes in and they'd seen no sign of human habitation. No Mickey D's, no bustling gas stations, no people out and about. Just road and leafy walls of towering white oak, alder and ash. Good spot for a horror movie, Smooth thought.

"Peaceful, isn't it?" Annie said.

"Mmm," Smooth nodded. Peaceful like a grave is how Smooth considered it.

A pheasant flushed from a thicket and its wings almost touched the windshield before it lofted. Annie jumped in her seat. Mary Margaret's heart pounded in her throat, but she kept steady hands on the wheel.

Smooth wound down Toddville Road. Ahead she spotted a turnoff. At that moment, her GPS piped up to announce close proximity to her destination. She turned into a rutted dirt path wide enough for only one car. She took a deep breath. This route was a perfect setup for an ambush.

Poison ivy vines and sapling branches squeaked as they scraped against the body of her sedan. Mercifully, it had not rained, so while the ride was slow and bumpy, Smooth wasn't concerned about getting stuck.

"You doing ok over there?" Smooth asked Annie.

"Little claustrophobic," Annie confessed.

"You're locked in and there is a 455 rocket under the hood." Smooth reached over and patted Annie's hand.

The forest seemed to thin a little and instantly Mary Margaret was almost on top of the clearing where an old moss and rust stained double wide rested on its travel wheels. Leaves and a few errant branches littered the roof. Smooth braked and reached for binoculars from her glove box. The first place she surveyed was the ground leading to the trailer door. No tire tracks. "Can you still drive?" Smooth asked Annie as she looped her binocular neck strap over her head.

"I can probably hit the gas and go straight," Annie responded. "Are we in trouble?"

"Doesn't look like anybody's in that trailer," Smooth said. "But I need you to get out safely should there be unexpected company. My GIS info shows a fire trail big enough for a service vehicle just about half a mile straight ahead. To get back to Route 50, you'd turn right at that crossing and it'll take you straight to 50. Can you remember that?"

Annie nodded. Smooth drew the Beretta from her ankle holster. She had her service Glock in the trunk. For a moment, she considered whether someone like Charlene might have a street weapon like an AR-15, a MAC-10 or even a modified Glock "switch" which turned the weapon from handgun to machine gun. She stuck with her Beretta and counted on her marksmanship.

"Lock the doors," Smooth whispered to Annie as she eased out of the car, closing the door as quietly as possible. She heard the thunk of the locks snapping into place.

There was an eerie silence that enveloped Smooth as she crept from tree to tree. A warbler trilled now and then to pierce the quiet. Smooth caught a glimpse of movement from the corner of her eye. She flattened against a broad trunked pine and watched the area where the rustle came from. Nothing.

Smooth was now within about sixty yards of the trailer's front door. She noticed a spider web with dewy sparkles that spanned from the top of the door to the trailer's roof overhang. Does this mean a long period of no visitors or did a spider spin it overnight?

That rustle from the corner of her eye appeared again. Smooth slid around the pine she hid behind. With her binoculars she focused on the bushing undergrowth from where that movement originated. A squirrel leaped suddenly from the shrubby forest floor onto an oak and skittered upward.

To Mary Margaret, her transit of a full circle around the trailer took forever. But when she was finished and certain no one was inside, Smooth stepped boldly to the door. She peered inside.

The interior was gutted to essentials. There were bare iron bunk beds, no bed linens. Other than those, there was only a cheap tattered sofa at the end of the trailer. There were no dishes, no trash, just clean and spare in the structure's tiny galley area. Smooth then went from window to window. Nothing. Charlene Zawaki was not here.

Smooth turned her back on the trailer and returned to her car where Annie was in the driver's seat. Upon seeing Smooth approaching the car, unhurried and calm, Annie leaned her head back and breathed a sigh of relief.

"No car chases today." Smooth opened the door for Annie who hopped out.

"Thank the Lord for that." Annie went around to the passenger side and got in.

With the trailer eliminated for now, Mary Margaret could move on to the list of places where she would show the pictures and ask for sightings. At the Ocean Highway Inn, the manager said he'd never seen Diane or Charlene, but he did ask if there was a reward. At the grocery store, the manager allowed her to query cashiers and department managers but no one recognized the pair. At Walmart, Smooth didn't get complete access to employees but she did perform her "show and tell" for a number of cashiers.

"Not getting any good feedback," Mary Margaret said to Annie. "We've been here a long time and I want to be across the bridge before rush hour. I'm going to stop for gas and then we're headed home."

"Sounds great to me," Annie agreed.

Smooth pulled into a station on the west-bound side of Route 50. It was busy and she had to wait for an available pump. She started the gas flow and tapped on Annie's window.

"I'm getting us some water—or whatever you'd like—and then we'll be outta here. Anything besides water? Anything to eat on the way back?" Mary Margaret asked.

"If they have any little packages of Oreos . . ." Annie said.

Smooth disappeared inside the station's convenience store. Annie sat back in her seat and watched the ebb and flow of vehicles gassing up. One lane over a pickup with a camper pulled in. A tall, heavy-set woman in jeans and a T-shirt got out and started the pump.

Something about her face. Annie picked up the folder Smooth had left on the driver's seat and opened to the photos of Diane and Charlene.

"It's her," Annie said out loud to herself. She swiveled to look through the glass front of the gas station store. Mary

Margaret was checking out. Should she get out of the car and go inside to let Smooth know? Should she honk the horn to alert Smooth? What should she do?

The woman pumping gas put the handle back in place. Stop her; Annie was frantic. The woman in the pickup waited for the truck in front of her to move. Annie saw that Mary Margaret was looking her way as she approached. She began to gesture "come here" wildly. When she saw Smooth notice her, Annie started jabbing the air to point at the pickup truck with the suspected Charlene.

Smooth rushed to her car and practically threw her bag of bottles of water and cookies at Annie. The pickup rolled behind the departing truck that had been blocking it.

"Keep an eye," Smooth commanded.

"She's turning right onto 50," Annie announced.

Smooth edged out of the pump islands. The pickup had a clear shot to turn right. For Smooth though, a mammoth gasoline tanker pulled in front of her as it prepared to deliver gasoline to the station. Ahead both Annie and Mary Margaret could see the pickup disappearing into traffic headed east.

"Damn." Mary Margaret slapped her steering wheel.

In and out, enduring angry honks, near misses and uncooperative traffic lights. Smooth and Annie craned their necks to try and see around the flood of vehicles that signaled rush hour. They scoured the highway for any glimpse.

"We lost her." Mary Margaret shook her head.

Chapter 28

A goodly number of residents in the smaller quieter hamlets of Maryland's Eastern Shore opted for a federal paycheck as the only local jobs were generally low paying retail or owner run trades. Every day these seekers of better compensation would drive almost two hours each way to the Washington, DC area to their job. Some hardy souls drove it alone and many more carpooled to share the tedious drive. Nonetheless, the East-West route from Maryland's Route 50 was slammed with bumper-to-bumper traffic for early morning and mid-afternoon rush hour. Locals bitched but lived with the madness.

Charlene chomped a piece of bubble gum as she touched the gas, hit the brakes, over and over. Diane leaned her head wistfully on the passenger door window. She couldn't jump out. Charlene had the child locks activated. For good measure, she used handcuffs to secure Diane's left hand to the seat belt lock.

Rush hour here would start the same way every day. It followed like the formation of a Category 5 hurricane. First a trickle of additional cars approached traffic lights at the same late afternoon hour. This trickle would accelerate to a torrent, morphing to flash flood and gushing to crescendo with the roadways awash in an impassable tide of commuters across the William Preston Lane, Jr. bridge. Horns honked; drivers zoomed through red lights as the tide of vehicles inched down the lanes. Plenty of near misses and screeching tires.

"I don't know how anybody does this every damned day," Charlene said.

Diane said nothing.

"Makes me crazy."

Diane closed her eyes and willed Charlene to shut up. It hadn't worked so far. Diane had given up on the advice she offered about waiting til after rush hour. Charlene said it would be harder to spot her truck if there was a lot of traffic.

I am never getting out of this, Diane said to herself. A tear pooled in the corner of her closed eyes but she let it be. Charlene turned the radio up on a country music station she'd found. Kenny Chesney sang "Nowhere to Go, Nowhere to Be." The song deepened Diane's despair.

Diane felt the twist of anxiety that so lately intensified her sense of futility. In her mind's eye, she saw herself thrashing in the truck, screaming as loud as she could. She never went there though. That one silencing slug Charlene delivered before was deterrent enough.

Finally a tiny road ahead offered access to a new place to hide. The Bay Day Motel, "We Cater to Hunters and Fishermen", loomed ahead. It was a six-unit building which had not seen freshening for years. Every door faced a busy Route 50 with the swoosh of cars and frequent blasts of eighteen-wheeler air horns twenty-four hours a day. At night, Diane thought she would go crazy from the sound. She suspected Charlene wanted to move frequently to avoid recognition.

Charlene parked the truck around the back of the building so it wouldn't be seen. She went to the passenger side, extruded Diane from the handcuffs and locked her meaty paw around Diane's arm to prevent escape. Diane half stumbled and was half dragged along to the end unit that Charlene had rented. Charlene went back to the truck and brought in her cooler.

"I'm gonna order pizza for dinner," Charlene announced.

"We had pizza last night," Diane said in a flat and expressionless tone.

"Different kind tonight." Charlene turned the key in the door and poked Diane's back to get her inside.

The room was dark. Curtains had been drawn all day to ward off the heat of the sun. Near the door was a cooler. Charlene pushed Diane toward her own bed and reached into the cooler for a beer.

Charlene belted down the first beer and extracted a second. Diane had not seen this behavior before. She clicked the remote by her bed and the tv displayed a surprisingly sharp picture of the early evening news. On the screen, Laura Palomina sat in the primary anchor chair.

"On the local front, police still have not been able to find local investment fund advisor Diane Winter." Diane watched as her last annual report photo crowded the screen. With a side eye, she looked to see if Charlene reacted. Charlene headed back to the cooler for beer number three.

"Yer famous." Charlene chuckled. She belted down the third can and went to sit on her bed.

Diane did not respond. She wanted to yell at the television, "I'm here. Come find me." The police were nowhere according to Laura. That, she believed was accurate, Laura would not hesitate to snoop and pry or bribe anyone who had inside information. Diane had never counted on the police.

Rita was a different story. Was she so hurt, so angry that she didn't give a damn about finding her? Maybe she hadn't understood the cryptic clue she'd left. Maybe Rita had found a new lover. Maybe . . . Stop, you're working yourself into a bad head state, Diane said to herself. I need to think clearly.

Charlene got off her bed and went back to the cooler. Beer number four came out. She wobbled to the bed, stubbing her toe in the process. She cursed a stream but sat on her bed to watch the television. She was fixated with a blank beer bombed stare.

"I'm fucked," Charlene said out loud. She never looked away from the tv screen.

Diane said nothing. She'd seen her mother fall into these drunken states. Her heart sped up and her palms dampened. She cast a sidelong glance at her captor in the next bed.

Diane fell into her childhood defense mode. This defense prompted her to make herself as small as possible and to refrain from initiation of conversation or response to drunken comments.

That state enveloped her without bidding every time she faced a material threat. Involuntarily, her lips parted as she panted silently.

"I'm completely fucked," Charlene shouted and threw beer four at the motel room door. The can's pop top sprang. Beer ran down the door and the can settled at the bottom where it disgorged its content.

Charlene launched herself from the bed and began to pace. "Fuck," she muttered under her breath and strode back and forth.

Diane froze. Every muscle seized. I have to stay still, she said to herself. If I'm quiet, I'll be alright. Still, she kept focused on Charlene. She was all Diane could see as her surroundings blurred and the only thing in her field of vision, sharp and clear, became Charlene's rageful pacing body. Diane knew that sign like she knew the warning signs from her childhood.

"Got to get out of this," Charlene said as she passed the tv, pivoted and marched back to the door. She paused. She did not pick up the smashed beer can. Diane frantically tried to calculate the next move as Charlene touched the dent made by her furious salvo.

"Waddayou lookin' at?" Charlene snarled in Diane's direction.

Diane lowered her eyes and did not reply. She pinned herself tighter to her bed. She bent her head but not so much that she couldn't still have Charlene in her sight.

Charlene took a step back and opened the cooler. She popped the top on another beer and drained it in one long gulp.

Beer leaked from the corner of her mouth as she took it in. Finished, she swiped her mouth with a sleeve.

Tremors from tight muscles and fear rippled through Diane's body. How many would it take to put Charlene to sleep? Diane could not remember how many cans were still in the cooler. She prayed the alcohol would overtake Charlene and knock her out. That was her mother's modus operandi, but Charlene was so much larger than her mother. Diane had no way to gage if this could save her tonight.

Charlene pulled a cell phone from her T-shirt breast pocket. She put it against her ear and waited. Diane started to mute the tv but decided that could shoot Charlene into another beer-fueled rant.

"Ma," Charlene said at last. "I gotta get out of here." She walked to the room's only window to improve cell service.

Diane strained to hear. Charlene's mother must have asked where she was.

"I ain't sayin'," Charlene said in a too loud voice. "No, and I ain't stayin' on the phone long. Cops probably listenin' in right now." At that thought, Charlene put an index finger to the only window's curtain and slid it aside. Satisfied the SWAT team wasn't at the door, she let the curtain fall back into place.

"Ma, listen to me," Charlene said. And then again, "Listen to me. Have the cops been to see you?"

Diane perked up. She held her breath and hoped Charlene's response would give her a clue that the police were closing in. She kept her head down to seem disinterested.

"Who?" Charlene asked. "Oh, yeah, that one. Snoopin' bitch. No cops though?'

Diane took a deep breath. Cops are clueless, but that snoopin' bitch had to be Rita. Please be Rita. Diane closed her eyes and repeated that desperate wish. She's coming to get me. She's coming to get me. Right or wrong, Diane clung to the thought like a rope to the drowning.

"Look, just answer the phone even if it ain't my phone number. Been usin' those throwaway phones you buy at the grocery store." Charlene's mother must have interrupted. "Ma, ain't nobody hurt and nobody gonna get hurt. I gotta go now."

Diane had never seen more than one phone on Charlene. She wondered where the others were stashed after her comment about having more than one burner. Did she have more and could Diane find them and call for help?

♏

For this night, Rita asked Bev to keep Annie at her place in the city. Annie had protested. Why couldn't she sleep in her own bed at Rita's? Rita countered with justifications about the projection of a very long night and Annie's waking frequently when she knew others were up and about. The harangue was brief when, frustrated, Rita asked her mother for this one favor.

"Somethings afoot," Annie challenged Rita.

Rita held her ground and stifled her tells. "Mom, please do this as a favor. Please."

"You can't fool me, girlie. You know I'll find out," Annie said.

"Of that, I have no doubt," Rita responded with a sigh. She wrapped her arms around her mother, kissed her cheek and left to join Bunny and Roswell at her place when her office hours were over.

Roswell had already let himself in at Rita's house. "Bunny's in the bathroom," he said. "I have several reporting functions running." He glanced at his watch. "I started as soon as Bunny got here and gave me access."

At that moment, Rita's cell phone rang. "Magda, have you heard something?"

"This ain't going to be much help, but Charlene called me just a little bit ago," Magda said.

"Did she say where she was?" Rita asked.

Bunny entered the room and, sensing the seriousness of the phone call, came closer to Rita and Roswell. Her face furrowed into a frown as she listened. Rita pointed at her desk and made a gesture as if writing. Bunny grabbed an open notebook which was already scribbled with notes and a pen. She held onto both as she waited to record information.

"What was the number she called from?" Rita repeated each number slowly for Bunny.

Rita spoke again. "Did she say anything that could be a hint at where she is?" Rita listened to Magda's response.

"Did she say anything about how things are going. Anybody hurt? Is Diane still with her?" Rita asked. "You did a good thing, Magda. I made you that promise about keeping Charlene safe. It still stands."

Magda started to cry. Rita could not make out the words through the sobbing.

"Please listen, Magda. I'm not asking you to lie to police. I'm asking that you don't volunteer. Do you understand what I mean by that?" Rita asked quietly.

"Yes, exactly. Don't phone them after we hang up and report Charlene called you. Can you do that? Are you ok with it?" Rita gave a thumbs up to Roswell and Bunny when Magda replied that she would follow that instruction.

"Magda, I know you're scared for Charlene, and I know how much pressure and fear this puts on you. I need one more thing, a promise from you, Magda." Rita paused. "If Charlene calls again—on the same or even a different phone number—please text me with the info as soon as you hang up. Can you do that?" Rita said.

With the call over, Rita turned to Roswell and Bunny. After a quick recap, she advised she was submitting a formal ping request for Charlene's call to Magda asking for a location. Once the form was completed, she would view Roswell and Bunny's reports for exceptions.

"Will you get a response tonight?" Bunny asked.

"Nope," Rita answered. "If I'm lucky it'll be two days. If not, it can be as long as a week which is why I asked Magda to report any further calls." She did not mention that her request for triangulation on Charlene's phone could set off a new round of fury from Billy Bolton.

Roswell had moved to one of the three laptops he'd set up to run different reports on Whitlock's accounting software. One of the laptops popped a message that the report was complete.

"Finished the first one." Roswell tapped a few keys and a report appeared on the screen. Bunny and Rita huddled around him as he opened the results. "You guys let every single employee have access to your money systems—all of them? No secure organization does that."

Bunny piped up. "We have such a small management team, Marianne decided we should have cross-training and access. What's wrong with that? She trusted all of us."

"But all of you aren't trustworthy, are you?" Roswell asked. "No wonder we're here looking for a thief. You made it so damned easy."

The second machine came to a rolling stop. Another finished report presented itself. Accounts Receivable exception reporting revealed a surprising number of cash payments.

"This doesn't seem like the usual method of donation. Cash? No way. Donors want documentation for tax purposes," Rita observed.

"I had no idea," Bunny said.

"Looks like lapping to me," Roswell theorized as he scrolled page after page. "And look who's been recoding that cash. One Louise Mercilus."

"What's lapping?" Bunny asked.

Roswell explained that lapping was one of the most common methods for committing financial fraud. An employee creates false invoices, disbursing funds to an account under their control. The employee may write checks to himself and record them as payments to one of the company's vendors. In a donor situation, a donor may submit a check. The thief deposits it in one of their own accounts, takes a portion in cash that is then recorded as the donation.

The most worrisome of this scheme for the thief is that it requires daily management of the situation. Invariably, the examination of vacation and personal time reveal that only one person has never taken a day off and that person usually turns out to be the thief. The lack of segregation of duties provides clear passage to the thief as one person alone manages the end-to-end process.

"Roswell, take a look at the PTO records and tell us who is our dedicated employee who never takes time off?" Rita smirked.

"Only one," Roswell said as the third laptop was now showing results. "Louise Mercilus hasn't taken a day since she got here more than a year ago."

Chapter 29

All of the late summer sun passed into another realm. No streaks of fiery oranges lingered. A slice of crescent moon hung in a star flung velvet sky. The Great White Hunter stood at the kitchen door when Rita slipped down to make more coffee. He never meowed to go out; he would stand at the door switching his tail to signal his desire to hunt.

"Quit with the baby bunnies, dude," Rita admonished him as she barely had time to crack the screen door before he slithered through and disappeared in the direction of the woods.

"Like he listens to me," Rita said to herself. She glanced at the stove's clock. It was a little after nine. Her cell phone trilled. Crap.

"Hey, you're not holding out on my story, are you?" Laura Palomina asked, almost as a joke.

"Never," Rita promised her. Not asking about your partner first? Rita said to herself.

"I'm finishing up the Volunteer Awards Dinner for Hopkins Hospital. I'm going to drop over. I'm only five minutes away at Hunt Valley Inn. See you in a few." Laura clicked off before she could hear Rita say she had company.

"Damn," Rita said. She texted that message, but Laura responded that she wouldn't mind. Reporter tactics. Rita had wielded them herself. She wasn't going to stop Palomina.

Rita's head rifled through ways to get rid of Laura and her keen news story senses. The minute she saw Roswell and Bunny in her house with three laptops spinning like laundromat washers, Palomina would morph into all the worst a reporter could be. Rita would have to endure constant calls and emails and personal unexpected visits. She would have to choose every word, every phrase and every action with deliberate consideration of its possible meaning. It made her tired to think of it.

Folks," Rita said when she returned to her home office, "Laura Palomina is on the way here. I did not invite her. She's the partner of Diane Winter. I'm pretty sure she wants to know what I'm doing on that case. The problem is that if she comes up here and sees you two, she's going to go into high alert, thinking there's another story in the works."

"Not that Palomina woman." Bunny sniffed.

"Yes, that Palomina woman," Rita confirmed.

"Do we need to leave? Bunny and I can pick up and go to my place to continue," Roswell offered.

"We can't run and hide every time this woman is going to show up," Rita said. "You two stay here with the process. I'm going to keep her downstairs and give her the runaround to get her out. Before she gets here though, I'd like you to park over at the Mondieu house next door so she won't see your cars."

"She's such an attention hound," Bunny said. "She tried to be in every big donor picture at the Gala. I shoulda had a cattle prod."

Twenty minutes later, a splash of gravel signaled the arrival of Palomina's Porsche. Rita advised Bunny and Roswell not to speak or walk around. It was a hundred-year-old farmhouse and though refreshed to a more modern semblance, floor joists were as cranky and creaky as its age. Rita put her fingers to her lips as she exited the office.

Palomina was at the kitchen door. Having been at a formal dinner, she wore a simple black sheath with spaghetti straps and a cleavage promoting neckline. She had never taken off her FM heels. Palomina was resplendent and flaunted the look and attitude. This is not going to be easy, Rita's head recoiled with the anticipated effort required.

As soon as Palomina entered, Rita turned away into the kitchen. "No hug?" Palomina feigned rejection.

Rita turned and Laura Palomina was in her face. "Been a while since we last talked." She pressed her body against Rita as she enveloped her in her arms.

Rita was surprised by her body's reaction. She breathed in Palomina's heady perfume and felt a rush of electric response, not a jolt but a full-on flow where every synapse fired at once. The exhilaration lit her head and melted her resistance. Her knees threatened to buckle. Rita pulled back but Palomina had her securely in her grasp.

"Hostage taking?" Rita managed to say.

"You're not that naive," Palomina stated. "Or are you?" Even as she spoke, Palomina brought her red lips to Rita and finding no objection, she smothered Rita's lips with a smoldering kiss that left her breathless.

Palomina's perfume and scent of her after-dinner Courvoisier were like opiates. Her lipstick was waxy and warm and inviting. Rita leaned into the kiss. What the hell are you doing, Rita's head shouted at her.

A late-night breeze slammed a door upstairs. In an instant, Rita shot out of her trance. She blinked. Palomina's face betrayed her surprise at Rita's passionate response. Rita released herself from the reporter's seductive embrace, annoyed at herself and yanking her emotional armor back in place.

"Well, well," Palomina said. "Little thaw in the Ice Queen?"

"Get over yourself." Rita pulled from Palomina's grasp.

"Thought you might need help." Palomina slipped out of her heels.

"You have new information about Diane?" Rita asked. "Put your shoes back on. I have work to do."

"You're playing hard to get." Palomina was still within reach of Rita, and she rippled her long fingers through Rita's hair.

Rita seized Palomina's hand. "I'm working."

"Ok. Ok. God, you're difficult. All work, no fun. No wonder . . ." Palomina stopped.

A silence dropped like a theatre curtain after a stage accident. Palomina lowered her eyes from Rita's face. Rita pursed her lips as she stifled a surge of tears that threatened to storm her face and betray her vulnerability.

"I'm sorry," Palomina said quietly. She made no move toward Rita. "I really am."

"I don't know if I believe that," Rita responded. The tears roiled just beneath the surface, but she took a deep breath to stuff them down.

"Understood." Palomina slid her toes back into the torture chamber of her six-inch heels. "Can't say I didn't try. Can't say I won't try again."

Rita stood her ground. She watched Palomina's investigation of the counter and coffee pot behind her. A flicker of understanding crossed Palomina's recently experienced lips. Without turning, Rita recognized immediately that she'd seen the extra cups. To acknowledge was to affirm; Rita refused to look back.

"You have company. It's not a new love interest." Palomina studied Rita's face. "Something you're working on."

Rita stood silent and steeled herself against the betrayal of any reaction. Palomina waited and hoped for a tell. It never appeared.

"I'll be around." Palomina walked to the kitchen door and touched the handle. She turned. "If I learn anything, I will not keep it from you."

"Thanks," Rita said. Deciding high drama was over, she came to the door beside Palomina.

"I want you to find Diane. I'm not as heartless as you might think." Palomina paused. "She and I were already on our way out of the relationship but no one deserves to be taken."

This was unexpected news to Rita. She did not return the volley. She held herself in poker mode, showing her opponent nothing.

Palomina turned to Rita before she departed. "That cop Bolton has been bugging me about you. I'm telling him nothing—but be careful. The guy's a snake."

"Thanks for the warning," Rita said. She finished pouring coffee and heard the roar of the engine and the splash of gravel as Laura Palomina sped off. She dumped cookies on a plate, balanced the coffee and headed back upstairs to her office.

"Breadcrumbs?" Bunny was saying to Roswell with a quizzical grimace. Before he could respond, Rita entered the room.

"Yeah," Roswell answered. "Think of it this way, like a physical crime scene. Cops'll dust for prints, look for stuff dropped by the intruder, even shoe prints."

Rita hurriedly set down her tray. She scooted over to stand behind him. The screen was awash in what was gibberish to her. Roswell had frozen a black background with white letters and symbols.

"What's all this mean?" Rita pointed at the screen and letters.

"Hacker's using JavaScript," Roswell said. "But that's not as important as the instructions I see here. There's also info in the logs."

"You said breadcrumbs." Rita reminded him.

"What we're looking at right here—right now—are the fingerprints and the inevitable shards of evidence that get left behind in the hackers' wake."

"This makes sense to you?" Bunny asked.

"Absolutely." Roswell nodded.

Bunny and Rita watched as Roswell's fingers flew over keys. The laptop monitor refreshed at fast-forward pace. Roswell would scan a screen and start typing. Another screen, another round of input with his fingers racing as if acting on their own.

"Whoever did this, they've been using Mrs. Whitlock's id to access the database," Roswell said as his hands skittered across the keyboard.

"Please tell me it isn't Marianne who's the thief." Bunny was mesmerized by the constant burst of new screens.

Neither Roswell nor Rita spoke. Roswell's focus was the hunt. Rita had never believed Marianne Whitlock was the thief. Naïve and too trusting had been her failures. She had opened the door to the wolf, but she was not the predator.

"Logs tell me the IP address and her login info doesn't match." Roswell stopped for a moment. "They used a VPN. Routing through multiple servers to try and hide where they came from."

"Who was using her credentials?" Rita asked.

"What I have seen tonight are two things: an unknown and potentially a thief has accessed the Whitlock Foundation monies via the ACH. This is a too common event for non-profits." Roswell's fingers jumped into action again.

"What does that mean?" Bunny asked with a face that blanched with fear.

"I'll take this, Roswell. Keeping digging." Rita pulled a chair up to Bunny's. "The Automated Clearing House network, the ACH, is the central clearing facility for all Electronic Fund Transfer, or EFT, transactions in the U.S. Thieves need only two pieces of information to pull off ACH fraud: a checking account number and a bank routing number. Hackers usually come by that information via a phishing email that allows criminals to install a malicious app to reveal and steal bank account passwords. I'm guessing this is how Marianne's account was compromised."

"And there are no debit blocks, alerts or filters in this system," Roswell threw over his shoulder. "It's a piggy bank waiting to be smashed."

"Oh, God," Bunny put down her coffee cup. "Are we dead or can we do something?"

"I'm pretty sure I can follow the VPN routes to get to the thief," Roswell said. For the next twenty minutes, he clocked through the back end of the Foundation's non-profit management software.

Both Bunny and Rita turned their attention to watching Roswell rip through screen after screen. As he worked, he slipped in ear buds and phoned someone to whom he spoke in a low voice. Rita heard the words "routing table."

"I'm putting in a Traceroute command," Roswell said.

"What does that do?" Bunny asked.

Roswell did not respond but continued to hammer his keyboard. Rita watched as he invoked the command and waited for a response. He then sent the command again.

"How long will it take?" Bunny asked as a tossup to either Rita or Roswell.

Rita shrugged. "Can take a while, depending on how many hops or router locations they use to befuddle investigators."

Bunny reached for the cookies. Rita sipped her coffee. Roswell plugged doggedly onward without speaking. Finally he stopped and seemed to be listening to someone.

"Howard Partners," Roswell announced. "At least in this hack, the guy was working out of an old warehouse renovated for office rentals. Down on Cross Street."

Bunny's jaw dropped. "You're sure? "

"I'm telling you where the intrusions into your system came from. Doesn't mean they actually have an office there or that the hacker is still there." Roswell thanked the person on the other end of his conversation and swiveled his chair to Bunny and Rita.

"I've got some more work to do on this, but at this point, I can say with confidence, there are transaction records being tampered with." Roswell sat back in his seat.

"Can you tell me how?" Rita asked.

"Simplest terms? A donation comes in and immediately is altered. Part goes into the Whitlock Foundation account and part goes into another holding account where that portion is then divvied among a mix of accounts identified by code as vendors or charitable groups. I need to work with Bunny to verify these downstream recipients. I suspect they are not actually part of Whitlock's vetted vendors and charities."

Bunny shook her head in disbelief. Rita nodded. She had seen so many of these slick financial scams. She thought back to Cheyenne and the man who had such interest in her and Bev when they visited the "offices" of White and Wright. That whole shell company scenario smelled even more after Roswell's discovery. I need to connect the dots; Rita's head told her.

"What do we do next?" Bunny turned to Rita. Roswell continued to tunnel through the invisible pathways of the web.

"Roswell needs to dig deeper. Once he has a clearer picture, account names and their contacts, we'll sit down with you and determine who's real and who's a scam. I'll be investigating who the principals are in the companies that appear to be facades only. When we have this last piece, I'll complete a report for you on what I found. No mention of Roswell, but there'll be enough to contact authorities and bring in a forensic accountant. Since the internet makes this a RICO case, I'll bring in the FBI. They will arrest the people involved."

Bunny listened as Rita recounted the steps involved. When Rita finished, Bunny still said nothing. She rested her elbows on Rita's desk with her chin in clasped hands. Rita waited for her unasked question.

"I'm thinking about the Foundation," Bunny said.

"And . . ." Rita responded.

"Can we keep this out of the papers? Keep it away from Laura Palomina?" Bunny asked. "I don't want to blow up all the work Marianne's done to make this organization go."

"Depends," Rita answered. "When the FBI see the report, all they're going to know is that we 'suspect' fraud. No way in hell can I reveal Roswell's work. At the moment they're here, the situation will be their case. There's precedent for a low-key collar but it all depends on who's the special agent in charge. "

"That isn't reassuring." Bunny tapped a perfectly shaped thumbnail against her teeth after she spoke.

"I'll be with you and we'll have a prep session before you meet with them. I suggest you have a session with you, me and your general counsel too before the FBI charges in. We want our side to be logical, calm and aimed at reputational preservation. If the agent balks, we take it up with his or her boss." Rita paused. "It'll be easier than it sounds."

"I have to trust you on this," Bunny said. "I don't have options."

"In this world there are people who make things happen," Rita said, "People who watch things happen and people who wonder what happened. Louise Mercilus is going to be a member of that last group."

Chapter 30

The night's work had been tedious and long, finishing just after the devil's hour of 3 AM. Roswell's skills sent the investigation on a luge run through a galaxy of numbers and characters undecipherable to the uninitiated. From this seeming morass of gibberish, he'd managed to compile clean, clear evidentiary reports. Even Bunny understood them.

A well-versed hacker thief, like a clever cat burglar, had tiptoed into the software machinery and keyed instructions to make Whitlock Foundation's financial management system bow to another's will. Circumstance and a marked trail through cyberspace pointed to Louise Mercilus as that thief.

Rita's eyes were scratchy. The long stretches of screen time had taken their toll. She decided she would wait on a morning run. She texted Bev that she would be late into the office. She would be there just before lunch. There were calls to make about the findings of the night before. She knew exactly who to bring in on the sophisticated scam Roswell uncovered. She'd worked with the Baltimore field office so many times over the years, she had the card of the special agent who handled RICO cases.

After coffee, she went upstairs to take a shower. Maybe she'd feel less depleted if she let cool water rush over her body. She set up her iPad with a national news station and took off her clothes. Just before she stepped into the welcome catharsis of clean, her cell pealed its Stevie Nicks "Stand Back" ringtone.

"Be careful today," Roswell said. "After I went back to my place last night, I decided to wander deeper in that rabbit hole we found. Rita, the trail leads to some scary places. Names like The Aryan Church and Patriots for American Justice came up and those are just two of the groups I saw. These are guys on the FBI domestic terror watch list. And I found where a lot of the diverted check money is going to members of these groups."

Rita froze; she felt a shiver of excitement and the hair on her neck stood up. "So that's it. Funding the hate with money stolen from the liberals. Too cool for school." Rita's head wandered off with this scenario. "Roswell, you're brilliant."

"Just doing what you asked me," he responded.

"Hey, I think somebody's coming up my drive. Probably lost," Rita said, "I don't recognize them. Listen, I have to get to my office before noon. I'll call you as soon as I'm able. Keep searching. I love you."

"Watch your back," Roswell said and clicked off.

"Crap." Rita had tiptoed to the bathroom window and lowered her top-down shades to peek out. A man in jeans and a pair of high-top tactical desert boots stepped out of a vehicle. This guy seemed familiar. She hurried back to her bedroom and threw on shorts, a sweatshirt and her flip flops. She eyed her father's Glock which nestled in a leather shoulder holster suspended from a clothes hook on the back of her bedroom door.

A firm but unhurried knock sounded on her back door. Rita slipped the weapon from its home and walked downstairs. The Glock rested in her shooting hand though it lay against her thigh quiet and out of sight from the visitor at her door.

The knocking was louder and more rapid. Rita had the gun but no phone. She'd left it in her bedroom. Damn, she said to herself, what was I thinking? She hesitated, go back upstairs or . . .

"Mars, I know you're in there," a male voice announced. "I'd hate to break up your pretty back door."

No doubt now. Rita sprinted back upstairs for her phone as she heard glass break. Where was the phone? She dialed Bev's cell and threw it into her night table drawer under all the junk in there.

"Isn't this cozy?" The sickening comment came from her doorway. "Nice view of the valley out the front. Security view of your back pastures. Hand over the gun." He gestured at her weapon with his own, a Desert Eagle.

For an instant, Rita considered firing a round but it took more than one shot from a Glock to fell a suspect like him. Conversely the cannon that the intruder pointed at her would drop her like a flushed pheasant.

Rita turned to face the threat and surrendered her gun. "You're the guy in the Malibu." The street scene of the swoop-and-squat accident on Bank Street popped into her head. Rita's head spun as it searched for some way to get away. She showed her intruder only calm with a confidence and bravado she prayed she could maintain. She wasn't going to give this guy the satisfaction of fear.

"Well, aren't you clever," the man said as he began to inspect her room, probably for her phone and more weapons.

"What is it you want exactly?" Rita pivoted to watch him scan the perimeter of the bedroom, searching, inspecting, dumping drawers and opening her jewelry box. She caught a strong scent of cigarette smoke. Happened every time she got into a very tight spot.

Transfixed, she lost her sense of the room. She could see her father in his long-sleeved black uniform. His patrol hat dipped low so the visor touched the official issue aviator shades. He'd just come from his second administrative hearing. Another anger management rip.

Rita and her mother waited for him outside police headquarters. They held hands with expectant eyes that begged to know the outcome. Neither would speak first; to do so would seal her father's lips. He hated talking about his troubles.

"No one saves us but ourselves," Rita's father said. He started for the car and pointed a finger at her. "Remember it."

"I asked you where your phone is." The man with the gun grabbed her arm and shook her. Rita's head returned to the situation at hand. The intruder's grip was strong, squeezing her upper arm like a hungry python. Rita had sized him up as ex-military. He was fit, biceps straining against his white polo shirt. No logo.

"I don't know. I put it down somewhere," Rita responded.

"Lying, bitch." She was unprepared for the swift backhand across her left temple. She reeled. The blow showered stars in her field of vision. She rocked backward but kept her feet. She felt as though she were underwater and struggling to swim to the light. Her bedroom had been aglow with bright morning sun and now it was murky fluttering with waves of clarity followed by intense shadow. Stand up, she said to herself. Stay here. The effort was gripping.

"Let's take a tour and find that phone for you," the man spit at her. "Don't want you inviting somebody to break up our little party."

Rita heard the words as she tried to keep her balance and stop the spinning the backhand launched in her skull. She feared if she moved she would topple. She stood as still as she could and gathered her will to act. Stand up. Find an exit. Find a weapon. Because no one saves us but ourselves.

"Let's look in the kitchen. Move!" The man gave her a rough shove and Rita almost buckled with the shock. She tried to throw off her confusion with quick shakes of her head. She held onto the stair railings on either side of the steps. She'd had them put in for her mother years ago.

A glimmer of clarity. Rita searched the kitchen for something to use as a weapon. The Desert Eagle was no small threat to neutralize. Even with body armor, a chest shot could crush your sternum. She glanced at her knife block, but it was too far away and the guy with a semi-automatic would be too quick. Get him to talk while I'm searching for an opportunity. Talking and that keen interest in her phone might be enough distraction.

"Why are you even here?" Rita scanned the counter. The coffeemaker was on. It would be hot. Too far away to grab and douse her attacker.

"You're breaking up our fundraiser." The man laughed as he yanked open cabinets and drawers with his gun hand while keeping a biting grip on Rita's arm.

"Your fundraiser?" Rita made herself sound woozier than she felt.

"Don't play stupid." The guy spread a pile of mail across the counter to check for Rita's smartphone. "I know you've been poking in your little foundation's money records and found our stash. You and that geek you hired. You think we don't know what's next?"

"What's next?" Rita repeated.

"I said stop playing dumb or I'll shoot you right here." He spun Rita around so that she was facing him at such a close range that his weapon poked her ribs. "You think you've stopped us. No way. We're taking our country back and all the little do-gooder liberal charities are gonna help us. You know, like Robin Hood."

How many other charitable organizations are infected with this blood-sucking blight? How big is this scheme? Who is behind it, Rita wondered.

"And Louise," Rita said, "she's your inside person?"

"Louise is a soldier. She can't add one and one." The man punched her gut with the gun barrel and knocked the wind out of Rita. "Takes a man to run something like this." He gestured toward the last column of drawers.

"So why are you . . ." Before Rita could finish, her next-door neighbor, Loretta Mondieu, appeared in her doorway.

"Yoo Hoo," Loretta trilled. Loretta's erratic dementia decisions often sent her to Rita's back door looking for Uncle Hodge.

"Get rid of her," the man hissed. He stood behind Rita with the muzzle of his weapon pushed hard into her backbone.

"Oh, my," Loretta tsked. "Your glass is broken. I hope no little bird flew into it." Lorretta stepped inside. "Rita, dear, I didn't know you had company."

The man behind her stepped forward, the gun now out of Rita's back as he moved to deal with Loretta. My chance, Rita's head shouted. Quick. Find it. Something, anything. She grabbed the handle of her glass blender jar on the counter.

"Lady, you need . . ." Before he could finish, he turned back to Rita whose move he had sensed.

With a summoning of strength, Rita swung the heavy glass container like she was ripping a home run. As her father had taught her, she delivered a true and punishing uppercut. The Desert Eagle roared, its payload striking the refrigerator. For a moment, the man stood, though his eyes told Rita he was out. He crumpled like a surrender towel.

"Oh, my," Loretta said. "This may not be the best day to visit. I'll just toddle back over to my house."

"Loretta, I need your help," Rita gasped with a last breathless effort. Before she could instruct Loretta on what she needed, Bev's white escalade fishtailed to a gravel spewing stop outside the kitchen window. Rita let her body rest against the breakfast bar as she sank to the floor.

"Can I get you some water, dear?" Loretta asked.

Bev threw open the remains of the door with a .45 in hand, trigger hand extended in deadly force mode. "You ok?" she asked Rita.

Rita nodded.

"He dead?" Bev lowered her weapon when Rita shook her head "no". "Keep an eye case he wakes up." She handed the gun to Rita.

"I think I'll just go home now." Loretta waved and was gone.

Bev went to the Escalade's front passenger door to help Annie exit. "Your mama been worried sick, girl. What the fuck's goin' on here?" Hardly taking a breath, she apologized with a hint of tremble in her voice. "Traffic was horrible. I woulda been here sooner."

Annie knelt in front of Rita. "You've got a nasty bruise." She touched the angry purple patch on her daughter's face. "Let me get ice."

Rita retched and vomited.

"We'll get you to the hospital." Annie ignored the puddle in front of Rita and, on her knees, gathered Rita into her arms and held her. "You are gonna be alright."

The unconscious assailant stirred and groaned. Bev reached down and took back her .45.

"He's one of the guys who threatened me in the fake accident. He admitted to the theft of money from Whitlock. Said Louise wasn't a key figure." Rita looked up at Bev as she spoke. "Will you call the FBI field office for me and get somebody out here. I don't want to hold this guy, and I'm not calling the crazy-ass Baltimore police."

Rita's head throbbed with a crushing head-squeeze of an ache that amped up with every movement. She was so tired. She wanted to lie where she was on the kitchen floor and never move again until that pain was gone.

"No, no, no," Annie said. "Let's walk."

Rita wanted to cry. She knew her mother was right. The backhand across her temple concussed her. She had to stay awake.

Bev stood over the prone body of Rita's attacker. She held both her own .45 and the Desert Eagle. While Annie pulled Rita to her feet, Bev rested the assailant's gun on the counter and used her cell to call the local FBI field office.

♏

In a fever dream, Rita stood with her father, Robert Mars. Sometimes they were in an out-of-focus jungle and sometimes they stood in her father's makeshift shooting range on the farm where he'd taught his daughter to shoot. He adjusted her arm. Rita could see he was speaking though she could hear no words.

She, however, knew he would take her through transitions from upright to kneeling to prone.

"When the enemy is upon you," he said in every training, "it's a chess move on a roller coaster. Be ready. Be right."

A transparent Diane Winter wavered in and out. No Charlene. The figure of Diane stuck out an arm as a plea. Rita raised an arm to help. She heard herself groan. A hand from above grasped hers.

"Who are you fighting?" Rita's mother asked. "It's ok. We're here with you. Be still. Rest."

Rita opened her eyes and for a split second did not recognize her own bedroom. The ceiling fan turned in a half-hearted circle. Watching the motion revived the nausea she experienced earlier when she'd first been slugged by the gunman. She replayed that event in her head.

"That guy . . ." Rita said weakly. Her caretakers, Annie and Mary Margaret Smooth were by her bed. Annie sitting close. Smooth standing, arms folded with a face drawn tight-lipped in a mixed expression of fury and fear.

"FBI has been here. They took him," Smooth said. "They're picking up Louise, and Roswell has names from his discovery of the Whitlock system hack. They asked you contact them for a full debrief when you're feeling better."

"Hey, baby, me and your girl, Smooth, stayin' here tonight," Bev added. "I don't believe there's only one person behind what's happened. Never know if somebody else comin' along for one more try."

Rita nodded and with that came another round of nausea. I have to get back out there, Rita said to herself. I have to finish what I started.

Chapter 31

Rita lay in twilight sleep. At times, she was certain she was awake, though she did understand that Robert Mars was not standing at the end of her bed. Yet he was so vivid that she reached for him. He stood frozen in time in the holographic projection of her injured brain.

When her father's image faded, she closed her eyes. In a heartbeat, she returned to the previous morning's assault. The man in blue jeans with a massive pistol, the muzzle pressed against her spine. One nervous moment and she would never have walked again—if she survived. Sweat beaded at her temples though the night was cool. Only by opening her eyes could she make that apparition disappear.

How to rid herself of these phantoms? Rita rose from her bed. She went to her bathroom window that overlooked the parking pad in the back of her house. A perfect crescent moon lay on a sky field of black with clear twinkling stars scattered around it. She splashed cold water on her face. For the moment, her head returned to the present.

The concussion had sapped her strength.

For a long while, she stood at her window, watching night pass. In the distance, she heard the bark of a hunting fox. The Great White Hunter was out there somewhere stalking, waiting for his moment. Rita did not want to think about the passage of time.

In her most unguarded moments, her brain opened its theatre of the past. Violence had been a visitor in her childhood. Blundered chances, miscalculated decisions and roads not taken. Failure was the recurring theme in these haunting vignettes. Anguish overtook her like a towering wave. She tried to flee. Her body responded by twisting her heart and every human fiber with crippling pain. She could hear herself screaming for help. She stood gasping for breath. No one saves us but ourselves. In this moment, she believed herself incapable and she was afraid.

Her cell phone rang. Rita pounced on it as she glanced at the clock whose illuminated numerals lined up 2:17 AM. At first eager, then reluctant. The fear lingered. Rita pushed back and picked up her smartphone. Magda Zawaki was calling.

"Magda, are you ok?" Rita's words tumbled out.

"I'm ok," Magda replied. Her words were still slurred from being yanked from sleep. "I . . . I got a call from Charlene. She's scared and that makes me scared."

Rita's head seized the moment. Self-doubt evaporated. She ramped into action mode, her head riffing through a deck of scenarios that could play out.

"What did she say?" Rita plugged her ear bud in so that she could dress as she talked.

"She wants to come home," Magda answered. "She wouldn't tell me more than that. I asked how that other lady was. She said she was ok. Charlene's afraid to go to jail so just 'cause she says she wants to come home don't mean she'll give herself up to police."

"I get that," Rita responded. Somewhere within her limited imagination, Charlene thought there was a way to come home, send Diane on her way and the whole business would be over and forgotten. "You know that can't be all that happens though. Right, Magda?" Rita heard a stifled sob and a loud sniff.

"I didn't say that to her." Magda's words broke with a burst of crying. "I don't know how that would ever happen. I didn't say that to her. I was afraid she would run further away." She was trying to speak and outrun the sobbing. She blew her nose without turning away from her phone.

"Yeah, she might do that," Rita agreed. She was fully dressed now in old jeans and beat up sneakers. She pulled a front zipped hoodie over a paint splattered t-shirt. "How long ago was it Charlene called?"

"I called you the minute I hung up." Magda had gathered herself. Her speech was slower, easier to understand.

"Do you know where she is?" Rita asked. When Magda did not respond, Rita prompted her, "Magda?"

Rita let the pressure of silence weigh on Charlene's mother. "If you don't tell me, I'll have to call it in to the police unit that tracks suspect calls. The night manager will report this immediately to the detective leading the investigation. At that point, it's out of my hands. The detective will mobilize his team and head out after your daughter." Rita could hear Magda's sharp intake of breath on the other end of the call.

"I don't know. I don't know," Magda blurted with a fresh round of crying. Her voice pitch rose with her fear. "I swear. I know she's someplace near that wildlife place. I'm thinking she's at the trailer her brother uses for huntin'."

"You mean in Blackwater?" Rita said.

"Mmhmm," was the only sound Magda could make. More stifled sobs this time with hiccups.

Magda confirmed that Rita was correct. Rita offered to take Magda with her, but she declined. Rita glanced at her watch. She had to get on the road. When Magda declined, Rita asked for the number that came up on her cell when Charlene called. Rita entered it into her own phone. She promised Magda she would stay in touch and might phone her during the hunt for any other calls or information from Charlene. She extracted a promise that Magda would phone her if she got new calls from her daughter.

Rita tiptoed into her guest room where Mary Margaret was sleeping. She was in deep slumber, but her body lay as if she'd been flung onto the bed. Both arms were above her head and both knees were bent as if she'd fallen asleep while running. The room had a dim night light, and Rita could see Smooth's wallet and keys on the night table. She swiped the keys.

"I'm taking your car," Rita whispered in her ear.

Mary Margaret did not respond.

Rita prepped a workout bag with extra clothing, an extreme lumen flashlight, tools and handcuffs, water and a can of mosquito repellent. It would be muddy, bug-swarmed and smelling of sulfurous swamp gases. She strapped her shoulder holster into place and threw extra magazines into her bag. Just in case.

♏

It had been a long time since Rita had driven Smooth's reconditioned Charger. She'd driven the speed limit toward the destination Magda had given her. At this hour, police in this part of Maryland were bored but alert. Thank God Smooth had installed a muffler that muted the roar of a gas-powered beast that could outrun any cop car.

Almost two hours after she began her drive, GPS guided Rita toward the 28,000 acres of Blackwater Wildlife Refuge. No radio music, she had to be alert for a siren or lights. And she didn't want to broadcast her arrival. She maneuvered the same narrow one-lane through the forest that Smooth and Annie had traveled just a few days before.

As she neared Charlene's hideout in her brother's hunting trailer, she decided the muscular hum of Smooth's Dodge might wake its inhabitants. She lowered the car's beams to fog lights only and drifted so that she could see the trailer from the driver's seat.

Once out of the car, she fitted her shoulder holster snug around her body. She checked the pistol for ammo and patted a second magazine into her jeans. Satisfied she was prepared; Rita followed the same reconnaissance as Smooth. Only one door. Interior dark with no sign of movement. Sunrise was a few ticks away.

Rita wanted to try the trailer door, but was concerned it might wake Charlene. She needed surprise. One more glance at her watch. The sky was already lightening into that soft, satin blue that heralds the coming of the sun. A noise behind her sent her flat against the broad trunk of a Blackjack Oak. She held her breath until she saw a foraging raccoon waddle from under a wild rhododendron. She exhaled and turned back to the trailer. She waited.

Mosquitos swarmed Rita's face. She'd remembered to cover up with a long-sleeved sweatshirt and jeans. She dreamed of coffee though the morning promised to come in hot. As she sat, she formulated scenarios and numbered them. Thinking still made her battered head hurt, but she needed to think ahead, especially in her impaired condition.

Once she had considered how the initial encounter could take place—and her response—Rita crouched and edged her way toward Charlene's truck. She slid needle nose pliers out of her jeans' back pocket. She squatted behind the vehicle and inserted the slim jaws into the valve stem of the driver's side rear tire. Within seconds the valve core was out and air swooshed out in a rush. Rita retreated to her hiding place. She waited.

Now a white-hot halo of sunlight edged the tallest treetops and the world promised to deliver another day. Rita listened to waking bird song, but she kept her eyes focused on the trailer door. A light muted by paper shades snapped on. Rita stood up.

Out of the trailer came Charlene and, with her right hand, she gripped Diane's arm. Rita scanned Charlene quickly. She had a hunting knife wedged in her belt, no sheath. No guns.

Rita's projected scenario two popped into her head. She had that strategy memorized.

"Charlene," Rita called as if she were hailing a friend.

Charlene froze. Diane gasped Rita's name.

"You get back and get outta here," Charlene challenged. She yanked Diane in front of her as a shield.

"Your mom sent me, Charlene," Rita said in the most even voice she could project. She took a step forward.

"Yer lyin'," Charlene's voice rose within a breath of hysteria. "Yer a cop. Now get back and let me get in my truck and leave or I'll have to do somethin' I don't want to."

Rita had assumed this bravado response. She was not about to let Charlene barricade herself and Diane in close quarters.

"I know you're scared," Rita said. "I would be too."

Charlene stepped sideways toward her truck and dragged Diane with her. Rita knew her options would be to stop Charlene with her voice or step into the space between Charlene's perceived getaway vehicle. She could not afford to accept chance.

"Charlene, my name is Rita Mars. You may know me from my newspaper writing. I'm not a cop." Rita walked confidently into the open space between the trailer and the truck.

"Lyin', bitch." Charlene had yet to draw the knife. She wrapped Diane's neck in an unpressured chokehold.

"I'm here to help get you home," Rita said as a sweat bead rolled from her temple. "I want you to understand that. Why don't you phone your mother to confirm it?"

"I ain't lettin' go of my ticket outta here."

"Charlene, what can I do to reassure you?" Rita shuffled a step forward. As she did, Charlene tightened her grip on Diane. Diane was wide-eyed with tears rolling freely.

"Don't let her kill me," Diane pleaded. "She'll do it."

"Charlene, you aren't a killer—are you? You've never killed anyone before, have you?" Rita asked in neutral tones.

"I ain't killed nobody," Charlene yelled. "But I will."

"Charlene, if you haven't by now, you don't want to start. I want to get you out of here safely and killing somebody isn't your best bet for that." Rita watched Charlene's face as she took in what she'd heard.

"I want to get in the truck and I want you to let me drive away." Charlene made a move toward Rita and her getaway.

Diane stumbled and Charlene yanked her upright.

"Listen to me, Charlene. If I do that, the cops will be on you. I won't be able to stop them. And if you harm your captive—if you even threaten to harm Diane—the cops might shoot you down. Do you understand, Charlene?"

Rita's question stopped Charlene's edging toward her truck. Rita heard an emphatic "Fuck." Diane pleaded with her eyes. She had the haggard look of exhaustion and her clothes were wrinkled as though she'd slept in them since she'd been taken. Her hair had not seen a comb.

"I'm telling you, Charlene. I'm here because your mom asked me to look out for you. I promised her I would not shoot and I'd get you safely back to Baltimore. I made that promise and I want to keep it."

Rita could see Charlene's eyes casting about as if searching for a way to assess the truth of Rita's words.

"I don't wanna go to jail," Charlene said.

Rita told her in straightforward terms that she could not promise that. She explained that at this point, there were many options she, Charlene, could take to help herself. If she let Diane go now, without harm, without an armed police response, she could buy herself leniency.

"I won't prosecute." Diane half turned to Charlene as she spoke.

"I know that's a damned lie," Charlene spit back at her. "I see how you look at me." She tightened her grip on Diane's neck.

The sun was high enough now to shower light beams between the trees like signs of hope and redemption. Charlene fidgeted. She pulled the hunting knife from her belt. Diane's eyes were wild with fear.

"Charlene, you don't want to do that," Rita said. "You need to make it out of here and you need for the law to see how compassionately you've acted in this situation."

But Charlene grew antsy. She pulled Diane with her as she got closer to Rita and the truck she saw as her salvation.

"Diane, you think you're so smart." Rita pivoted to a different approach. The concussion symptoms signaled a rise in their intensity.

"Don't talk to her." Charlene's voice rose. She pressed the upturned knife blade against Diane's throat.

"Diane, I want to think about the damned Jabberwock you left me. You do remember the Jabberwock?"

Diane raised her head. She recognized the reference.

"Stop this shit," Charlene yelled and with her sudden yelp, the tip of the knife traced a thin bloody line below Diane's jaw.

Rita nodded.

With that, Diane sank her teeth into Charlene's knife hand with the ferocity of a mad dog and clenched like her life depended on it. Charlene screamed and tried to disengage. In the struggle, Charlene lost her balance and slid to the ground on her side.

Rita rushed the two with gun drawn. She stood over the fallen Charlene who had lost her grip on Diane. Rita's eyes never left the big woman at her feet. She deftly twirled handcuffs from her sweatshirt pocket and snapped Charlene's wrists behind her back into the steel cuffs. Charlene lay sobbing on the ground, curled in a fetal position.

Diane threw herself into Rita's arms. But the excitement and the heat and the sudden strike left Rita drained, and as she gazed skyward, the forest canopy spun like a fast-rolling carnival ride.

"I knew you would find me," Diane said and hugged Rita in so fierce an embrace, she thought she might pass out.

"Let go," Rita said. "I'm afraid I'll pass out." As if on cue, she heard police sirens in the distance. She leaned on Diane. "Just keep me upright til the cops get here." Rita kept the Glock aimed at Charlene, but her fight was gone.

"I'm sorry I hurt you," Diane said. She held Rita a little more loosely but did not let go.

For a moment, Rita wanted to fold into Diane's arms like that one summer night. The memory arose of a night with a soft breeze floating the sheers from the window like dancing spirits. Rita gave her trust to Diane in the way true believers embrace their faith. She found peace with herself and breathed with the rhythm of the woman beside her. She had wanted to capture that moment and make it stay. And just as that night could not be collected or saved, the memory evaporated like a snowflake in the sun.

Diane rested her head on Rita's. "'Jabberwocky' with those 'jaws that bite' was so perfect. I got it immediately. It was an amazing ploy."

"I'm texting your partner," Rita said. "Her story is here for the taking."

"It's not just a story," Diane objected and touched Rita's face. "You saved my life."

Rita turned from the touch. "I did what I thought was right." She struggled to stand as two police cars blasted up the forest road behind Smooth's rocket. "And now I am closing that door behind me."

Local cops rushed to the two, and in the business of policing, Rita and Diane were separated.

Chapter 32

In her dream, Rita ran on her favorite trail. It was morning with a cooling breeze. In this dream, her feet barely touched the path. She sailed. She smelled the rich scent of earth dampened by dew. Her knees pumped without complaining. And there was—music?

Rita sat up in her own bed. It was almost twenty-four hours since she'd played her hand with Charlene Zawaki. She remembered so little after the police arrived. She picked up her cell.

"You got your story," Rita said.

"And so I did. I owe you." Laura Palomina laughed. "Called to thank you."

"I didn't start a ledger," Rita said.

"How about lunch this weekend? It's the least I can do."

"I have plans," Rita said.

"I'm not going to stop trying," Palomina teased.

"Sure you will. It'll be a game. It'll be amusing for a while, but then someone else will come along and I will be old news and a waste of time." Rita rolled out of bed.

"Maybe," Palomina agreed, "but you can't blame a girl for trying."

Rita took care on the steps down to her kitchen. She remained suspicious of her strength and balance. Gathered around her breakfast area were Smooth and her mother.

"Honey, should you be up and about?" Annie came to inspect her daughter. "Pupils aren't dilated. That's a good sign. I was so worried about you."

Mary Margaret stood and gave Rita a quick hug. "Mighty fine negotiation. Diane told me about the Jabberwocky trick."

"I was afraid she wouldn't remember. I was lucky." Rita wandered to the coffeemaker.

"I'd say the embezzlement scheme you uncovered was not a matter of luck. That is some catch," Smooth said.

"What did the FBI have to say?" Rita poured her coffee and joined Smooth and Annie at the breakfast counter.

"Cozy little ring of far-right guys," Smooth explained. "They used their religious connections to gain trust and access to Whitlock, and the FBI thinks this is a pattern they're using to steal from other organizations like Whitlock. They were going to commandeer liberals' money to bolster white nationalism and destabilize liberal institutions."

"My hat's off to Roswell on that. I just asked him to look where I thought it made sense." Rita took a long, slow sip of coffee. "And we should keep his name out of it. What about Louise?"

"FBI didn't pick her up in time. She got away," Mary Margaret said.

"The thug that slugged me called her a soldier," Rita said. "The guy said she was a nobody in the organization." Rita took another hit of coffee. "I don't believe that for a minute. In a little while, she'll be another right-hand performer in another naïve do-good non-profit. Maybe someone will spot her scam and maybe they won't, but she'll be out there trying to run the table."

A car rolled onto Rita's back parking pad. Her sister's husband was behind the wheel. He waited as Sara popped from the passenger seat.

"I got Miss Annie all packed," Smooth said.

"I'm gonna miss you, Mary Margaret." Annie gave her a lingering hug. "And you, my girl. I'm proud of you." She embraced her daughter and held her until Sara walked in. "And be careful out there in the wicked world."

"Ready to go?" Sara breezed through the kitchen door. "Holy crap. The entire right side of your face is a bruise." She reached to touch Rita's face, but Rita gently brushed off her attempt. "What the heck happened?"

Rita picked up her mother's suitcase. "I got voted captain of the debate team." Sara shook her head but did not continue with questions.

"Love you like the rock of ages, Mom," Rita said as she slid her mother's bag into Sara's truck.

"Have fun?" Sara asked.

"You can't imagine how fun it was." Annie winked at Rita. Smooth looked away to keep from laughing. "I can't wait to see what happens next year."

Enjoy an excerpt from . . .

DRIVEN
A Rita Mars Thriller

By Valerie Webster

⸻ ❦ ⸻

Chapter 1

"Rita Mars, this is a voice from your past."

"Who the hell is this?" Rita demanded.

It was eleven o'clock, and the dreary end of a long day. A miserable October rain tapped on the office windows. Through the water washed glass, Baltimore's Mitchell Court House next door was a smear of grey and black.

"I first met you devouring Hershey bars in the newsroom at midnight." The man was gleeful.

"That narrows it down."

Great clue. Hell, she'd been a reporter for seventeen years before she started the agency. Rita cradled her chin. The police department snitch who gave up the narcs ripping off drug dealers? The accountant with the guilty conscience who squealed on the HUD housing contracts?

"We were a pair and then again we were not."

"Look, pal, I don't know—"

"I was the snow king and you were the fire breather."

Rita started to hang up, but there was something eerily familiar about that line.

"You never know when you've had your last chance," the man said.

"Bobby Ellis." Instinctively, Rita touched the worn chrome Zippo in her pocket that bore those very words. Chills ran along her arms and the hair bristled at her neck.

"Bingo," Ellis said.

"God, I'm so glad to hear from you. Where are you? When can I see you?"

"Sunday."

"Halloween?"

"The Overlook Inn in Harper's Ferry. Breakfast at ten. I'll have a lot to tell you. A story for above the fold. "

Rita scribbled his instructions on a blank notepad. "Tell me now." Above the fold on a newspaper's front page was reserved for big time news.

"Just be here."

Rita thought he was hanging up.

"By the way—ever think you'd see me alive again?" Ellis asked softly.

"No," Rita said. "I never thought I would."

Chapter 2

Rita Mars sang along with the Shirelles. She glanced at the Jeep's speedometer and then at the rearview mirror to check for approaching troopers.

The West Virginia countryside blazed with yellow and scarlet. Sunlight sprinkled the rock-strewn pastures with brilliance and made the car's white hood shimmer like a snowfield. Even the black and white Holsteins seemed brighter than usual as they ripped up the last shreds of yellowed pasture grass.

Though it was late October, Rita had the top down on the Jeep. It was good to ride on this open road alone with the sun and wind. She couldn't really be forty-five this year. She ran thirty miles a week and could still get into jeans the size she'd worn in college. Rita peered over the top of her Raybans and took another look in the mirror. Ok, so her dark hair was shot through with silver.

She smiled. It made her look more interesting. After all, how many older women had she fallen madly in love with in her younger years?

Rita flipped the radio off and concentrated on her meeting with Bobby Ellis. She hadn't seen him in forever. Yes, she had thought he might be dead. A superior journalist, he'd thrown it all away with a coke habit that he paid for with a career and a marriage. No one had seen or heard of him now for more than two years.

After he disappeared, a malaise had set. Rita abandoned investigative reporting and spent her time working on a detective's license. She was going to right wrongs instead of writing about wrongs as she described her abrupt life change.

She sighed. She wanted to return to the happier thoughts that had so recently danced in her head.

A red truck with a rainbow sticker on the front bumper appeared in the oncoming lane. Rita's smile came back and she waved as they raced past each other.

"We're everywhere. We're everywhere," she hummed to herself.

She returned to her former mood of excited anticipation. She was seeing Bobby again.

They had been reporters together on the *Washington Star*. More like brother and sister than co-workers, they had fought over editorial recognition, wept on each other's shoulders, and held each other's hand during their respective long, dark nights of the soul.

Rita tried sweet talk at first when his habit began to devour him. Then she got tough. They fought bitterly. In the end, he surrendered everything to the white powder.

She'd been as angry with herself as with him. She couldn't make him stop. Like a flashback, the feelings were the same when she thought about her childhood. She hadn't been able to stop the runaway train her father rode either. Alcohol carried him far and fast. In the end, he stuck his police revolver into his mouth and killed his pain.

Bad memories again. Rita shook her head and switched the radio back on.

"There she was, just a walkin' down the street . . ." Rita sang along at the top of her lungs and pushed the accelerator just a little farther with her docksider.

Five miles and three oldies but goodies later, she slowed as the road narrowed to the twisting mountainside lanes that led to Harper's Ferry. Down the sheer embankment on the passenger side, she could see canoes below on this rocky segment of the Potomac. She took a deep breath. The cobwebs of leftover memory cleared. It was a gorgeous day. At the top of a steep winding hill, Rita spied the flag pole that stood in the center of the Overlook Inn's circular drive. Old Glory ruffled its red stripes in a soft October breeze that seemed more spring than autumn.

The parking areas along the drive were jammed with American made pickups and SUVs. Lots of military bumper stickers and window decals. Families just out of church hopped out of cars and headed for the Inn's dining room and Sunday brunch buffet.

As she reached the crest, she had to slam on the brakes. The drive was blocked by two Harper's Ferry sheriff's cars, a West

Virginia trooper vehicle—blue gumball lights twirling—an ambulance from nearby Ransom, a fire truck, and a dented beige Crown Vic with county plates.

Guests and townies milled around the west annex. A tall, grim-faced sheriff's deputy held them at bay.

"What the heck is this?" Rita jumped out of the Jeep.

Inside the interior of the Overlook lobby was cool and dark. The desk clerk was a woman with long red nails and a plunging neckline to her sundress. Her blue eye shadow made her look like an alien. Oblivious to Rita, she leaned across the far end of the registration counter to stare out the front door toward the commotion outside. Rita pulled off her Raybans.

"What happened?" Rita asked.

"Man killed hisself." The woman continued to lean and stare over the counter.

The taste of metal rose in Rita's throat. "Killed himself?"

"Room 107. Maid found him." The clerk's sense of duty returned and she walked toward the center of the counter where Rita stood. "Can I help you with something?"

Rita felt icy from the inside out. She dug her hand into her pocket to touch that Zippo talisman she always carried.

"I came here to meet someone." The words jumbled in her mouth.

"Name?" The clerk absently flipped the registration book behind the counter.

Rita said nothing.

The clerk looked up then and said once more. "Name?"

"Bobby Ellis," Rita whispered.

The two women stared at one another.

Ignoring the angry comments as she elbowed her way, Rita plunged through the people gawking around the Overlook's west annex.

"Lady, you can't go back there." The tall sheriff's deputy in charge of crowd control barred her way with his nightstick.

"I came here to meet him." Rita pushed at the deputy's stick. He towered over her slim, five-foot frame and easily brushed her back.

"Meet who?" He kept the nightstick between them.

"Bobby Ellis. The man in room 107." Rita pushed harder this time.

"I said you can't go back there. Police business." The deputy almost knocked her off her feet.

"I have a right. He's my friend." Rita grabbed the stick this time.

The deputy yanked the stick, pulling her toward him and he leaned his face inches from hers. She could smell the nasty scent of Skoal on his breath.

"You are not goin' anywhere if I say so." He twisted the stick, Rita still hanging on. She let go when her hands ached from the tension.

Tears and rage streamed across her face. Her hands clenched into fists as she raised them once more to do whatever damage she could. Motion behind the deputy on the path to the rooms at the back of the annex stopped her.

"Coming through." A med tech in navy pants and a starched uniform shirt guided the front end of a stainless gurney behind the deputy. On the gurney was a black vinyl body bag.

"Bobby." Rita lunged forward as the deputy stepped aside to make way.

But the deputy was quick. He snatched at the back of her denim shirt, catching her so that the banded collar cut into her throat. Rita gasped.

"Lamar!" A booming command came from behind.

The deputy let go and Rita tumbled against the tech.

"I'm sorry," the tech said. "Nothing we could do when we found him."

Another big paw touched her arm. It was gentler this time. This was the giant who pulled Lamar's chain, a giant with a sheriff's badge and sweet, sad eyes.

"I know this is hard, miss. But I'd like you to come down to the hospital with us and help with a positive ID. Then I'll help you any way I can."

The sheriff put an arm around her shoulder. "I'll walk with you and we'll get him into the ambulance. Is that all right with you?"

Rita nodded.

Her knees were like water, but she walked. Crying, stumbling, held now and then by the giant. She kept one hand on the gurney, the other frantically worked the worn engraving on the lighter in her pocket.

About the Author

VALERIE WEBSTER spent a career developing law enforcement applications for surveillance, security and forensics. She's worked on the southern border, on the aftermath of 9/11 and tracked cyber crooks. As a writer, she honed her skills through the Mystery Writers of America Mentoring Program and Sisters in Crime. Her debut work, *Driven: A Rita Mars Thriller* is a Colorado Independent Publishing Association (CIPA) award winner. Valerie makes her home near Boulder, CO. Learn more about Valerie and her work at valeriewebster.com.

More Mysteries

Rita Mars Will Return! Be among the first to hear about Rita's next case at valeriewebster.com.